ORACLE

FIRE ISLAND

C.W. Trisef

Trisef Book LLC

How to contact the author
Website – OracleSeries.com
Email – trisefbook@gmail.com

Oracle – Fire Island
C.W. Trisef

Other titles by C.W. Trisef
Oracle – Sunken Earth (Book 1 in the Oracle Series)
Oracle – River of Ore (Book 3 in the Oracle Series)
Oracle – Solar Wind (Book 4 in the Oracle Series)
Oracle – Mutant Wood (Book 5 in the Oracle Series)

Written by – C.W. Trisef
Cover designed by – Giuseppe Lipari
Text designed by – Sheryl Mehary
Back cover photography: "The Intihuatana Stone" by Kaitlyn Rose Tierney, and "The Navel of the World Rock" by Jae Rossman. Used with permission.

CHAPTER 0

JUNE 19

It was nearly nightfall when a tall figure strode across the back lawn of the mansion house. There was visible stress in his step—worry in his walk—as he moved swiftly despite the bulky load in his arms. He was carrying a trunk, old-looking and odd-shaped, as if it had once been a chest containing buried treasure. The dirt lodged in its intricate outer designs besmeared the fellow's collared shirt, which he didn't seem to mind since his entire outfit appeared soiled from consecutive days' use.

The man's long shadow, as well as his unkempt hair and unshaven face, was almost indiscernible as twilight fell on the large property. The recent moisture from a brief but drenching rainfall was now rising as steam from the warm earth like a hotplate, enshrouding the landscape in thick mist. His heavy footsteps squished in the soggy grass, saturating his dress shoes, while strands of Spanish moss tickled his unflinching face as he passed under the skeletal branches of mighty oaks.

The gentleman's destination was a rickety old shed, sitting in the middle of the deep and murky marshland that dominated the backyard acreage. Almost entirely hidden by overgrown shrubbery, the shed seemed solely accessible by boat, and even then only if it could withstand the carnivorous wildlife. As he neared the bank of the swamp, the man purposely stepped on the tail of a fake skunk, which concealed a button that triggered an elevated walkway to rise from the boggy waters like bumper guards at a bowling alley. His march unabated, the man's sloshing turned to clogging as he left the lawn and boarded the bridge, with hungry croc-odiles hoping for a misstep.

At last, the man arrived at the dilapidated establish-ment—an oft-neglected shack full of never-used tools, rusted and encrusted by the humid, salty air ever-blowing in from the Atlantic Ocean next-door. He stepped on a false bullfrog near the half-hinged door, prompting the bridge to collapse, before slipping inside. He set the chest down on the planked floor, then straightened his aching back. His disheveled hair brushed the ceiling so perfectly that it was obvious the place had been made for him. As if he had done it countless times, his hand found a lever on the wall, which he promptly pulled.

The shed's floor began to lower, quickly descending into the earth. The elevator plummeted several stories, its only cargo being the man and his trunk. It stopped upon reaching a set of double doors, which shot open. The man picked up the chest and walked across the threshold into a room that was, in every way, the opposite of the shack from whence he came. Cables and cords, screens and phones, antennae and computers—all the latest and greatest tools, amassed as part of an extensive surveillance and communications system.

Setting the trunk nearby, the man sat down in the only chair and depressed a large, blinking button directly in front of him. Immediately, the startling image of an aged man appeared on the edgeless glass screen, which filled the wall on the other side of the room like in a movie theater.

"Stone!" the ancient man growled. "You're late!"

"A thousand apologies, Lord Lye," Stone sorrowed, "but be it known that I have not so much as slept a wink since you released us from Coy's yacht just yesterday."

"Did you dispose of Quirk?" Lye asked abruptly, showing no compassion for Stone's grueling labors.

"Yes, my lord," answered Stone without remorse. "He was thrown overboard long before we returned to the mainland."

"And what is Bubba's present location?" Lye pressed.

"He's on his way back to Fire Island, per your instructions, my lord," Stone informed. "He left just hours ago."

"Excellent," Lye hissed. "Now, what of the trunk? Did you relocate it like I asked?"

"Of course, my lord," said Stone submissively. "I retrieved it from my office on my way here, and I have it with me now in the Keep. As soon as we conclude, I will give it to Charlotte to archive."

"Has she found the cleats?" Lye questioned with sudden vehemence. "Has Charlotte found a second pair?"

"Unfortunately, she has not," Stone regretfully informed. "I have instructed her to search the Keep until a second pair is found."

"Very well," Lye grumbled with displeasure. "At least we have the key in our possession. Did you find a secure holding place for the key?"

Stone made no reply. His mind was drawing a blank. His heart began to pound.

"The key, Stone," Lye interrogated urgently. "Where is the key?"

"I—I don't have a...have a...," Stone stuttered. "A key, sir?"

"YOU LOST IT?!"

"I don't remember you giving me—"

"HOW COULD YOU LOSE IT?"

"I'm sorry," Stone pled for his life, "but I—"

"FIND IT!" Lye roared with fury. "I MUST HAVE THAT KEY!"

"It shall be done, my lord," Stone vowed, "but, may I ask, to what key are you referring?"

"The key I gave you on the yacht, you fool," Lye howled, "right before I melted the lock and released you."

Suddenly remembering, Stone said with a shaky voice, "Yes, my lord, I remember now. It seems, amid all the excitement of your unexpected arrival and the flurry of instructions you gave me"—Stone braced for harsh punishment—"it seems I mistook the key as belonging to the lock of our cell, and, consequently, I left it on the yacht."

Lye said nothing for a moment. Then, in quiet tones, he resumed, "I am greatly disappointed in you, Stone. I thought I could trust you with this most important responsibility, but you have failed."

"I will do everything in my power to find the key, my lord," Stone pledged.

"No, no," Lye dismissed. "You've proven it's too essential to delegate. I will recover the key on my own, even if I have to infiltrate Coy Manor in the process." Then, as if pleased with his own words, "Yes: infiltrate Coy Manor; I think I'll do that. I've been meaning to make such a visit."

"As you wish."

"Now that Quirk is out of the way," Lye continued with renewed vigor, "I will be sending you another acquaintance of mine before the start of the new school year. She is a very able woman; you might learn a thing or two from her." Stone looked down in shame. "I suspect you will put her to good use at that deplorable school of yours."

"It shall be done, my lord," Stone promised.

"I need you and her to take good care of Ret and his friends," Lye directed. "Keep them alive, keep them safe—all of them."

"Including the mother?" Stone cringed.

"For now," Lye advised. "I need them; I need Ret."

"But, sir," Stone disagreed, "I thought you—"

"Do you have scars on *your* hands, Stone?!" Lye bellowed. "Can *you* open the Oracle? Can *you* collect the elements? Hmm? Can you?!" Stone cowered in silence, worried that his master might somehow reach through cyberspace and strangle him. "I *need* him, Stone, and I need him *alive*."

"Forgive me, my lord," Stone quivered. "I was under the impression you wanted to kill Ret, sir."

Lye lowered his guttural voice and said, with a menacing smile, "I don't want to kill him—yet."

CHAPTER 1

HOT TOPICS

Never had such extreme heat been known to plague Tybee Island. Summer had only just begun, and already the coastal community was breaking records thanks to the triple-digit temperatures, with the humidity not far behind. The whole town languished under the searing conditions and the unpleasant realization that the hot season was only heating up.

This was the state of things when the Coopers and the Coys returned to their homes after their adventures in Sunken Earth. As if someone had flipped the preheat switch upon their departure, the island was baking by the time they came back. Day after day, the relentless sun appeared in the east and burned its path across a cloudless sky. Flowers withered, leaves wilted, and people wanted nothing more than a front seat by the air-conditioner.

Unless, of course, it was broken, as the Coopers unfortunately discovered soon after walking through the front door of their modest home.

"Good grief," Ana had moaned upon entering the house's stifling heat, "will somebody crank up the AC?" One of her least favorite things to do was sweat—or "glisten," as she had corrected Ret.

But, on account of the family's unfortunate finances, the all-important air-conditioning remained unfixed. Ever since Jaret's presumed death (though Pauline still referred to it as his "disappearance"), the Coopers' income had been reduced to a mere pittance called a pension from the U.S. Coast Guard. Thus, there was no room in the family pocketbook for expenditures that were not saved for well in advance.

And so, as the windows went up, Ret went down to the beach, thoroughly convinced that the coolest place to be was at the water's edge. Now that he had mastered his control over everything earthen, Ret was finding all sorts of practical applications for his newfound powers. For example, rather than burn his bare feet on the beach's sand, which the sun's hot rays had transformed into a cast-iron griddle, Ret pushed away the top inch of sand with his mind before each of his footsteps, exposing a cooler layer beneath that was much more comfortable to the touch. Further applying this principle, Ret carved a sort of dugout into the sandbar near his favorite nook on the beach. The sandy roof, which he held up at will, shaded him underneath as he sat a few feet below the level of the ground in his cool bunker. He even dug a few trenches that led from the ocean to his hollow so that when the waves rushed upon the shore, several channels of cool seawater not only flooded the floor but also dripped through a series of holes in the roof. It was his favorite place to beat the heat.

But although Ret had found a way to lighten the burden of the weather, the sad tale of Sunken Earth still weighed heavily on his heart. Hardly typical, the past year had been quite an eventful one, filled with emotion. Along with his sister, Ana, and her best friend, Paige Coy, Ret passed his first year of high school with flying colors, rising to the top of his class in every regard. Despite his lack of close friends, he was very well-known for an underclassman, mostly on account of his unusual physical features: his pale-white skin; bright blue eyes; radiant yellow hair; and, of course, the scars on the palms of his hands, which he tried to keep concealed at all times. Ret was well-liked by all, but just as many seemed to keep their distance from him, except for two bothersome characters: Principal Lester W. Stone and his "geography" teacher, Mr. Ronald Quirk. From the onset, they had made it clear (perhaps accidentally, to Stone's dismay) that they knew, needed, and would be watching Ret very closely, for, as it turned out, they were working for the evil Lord Lye, an age-old nemesis with sorcerer-like powers and unheard of longevity.

Yet Ret himself was but half the object of his enemies' dastardly designs. The boy meant nothing to them without the ball—the Oracle, an ancient sphere capable of unlimited power when filled with Mother Nature's six pure elements. Fortunately, the once lost-at-sea Oracle was in the possession of none other than Mr. Benjamin Coy, and together the Coys and Coopers uncovered the meaning of the first of Ret's illuminated scars: the hook and triangle.

Into the Atlantic Ocean's Devil's Triangle it led them, to one of our planet's unexplained mysteries: a road of submerged stones, lying on the ocean floor near the island of Bimini in the Bahamas. With the help of Ret as a descendent from the rightful family line, the road turned out to be a secret passageway to the lost city of Sunken Earth, a vast civilization completely enclosed under the Atlantic.

But Lye had beaten them to it. With his powers of mind and cane, he ruined Sunken Earth's system of peace and equality and made himself king, seizing control of the hidden society's life-sustaining earth. With the help of his newfound friend and ally, Lionel Zarbock, Ret summitted the great mountain, where he met the first of the Guardians of the Elements. One of the eight ancient Fathers, the Guardian of the earth element taught Ret of his unique position as one with the scars, capable of restoring the six elements to the Oracle and curing the world. And, in spite of Lye's best efforts to stop them, Ret procured the first element and escaped Sunken Earth with his life.

But, oh, at what terrible cost! The Guardian; the Coys' butler, Ivan; the people's princess, Alana; and the thousands upon millions of citizens of Sunken Earth—all dead. Every single one a casualty of Ret's doing. Blood spilt at *his* hand! Life drowned at *his* discovery! Surely there had to have been another way to get the earth element, Ret mourned, one with less death and destruction. Ret tried to convince himself that this whole Oracle business was his purpose in life—his destiny to fulfill—but the stunning gravity of it all cast a dark cloud of doubt in his mind. Was there no other way? Then perhaps it would be better for everyone if he just forgot all about the Oracle—buried it deep in the earth where no one would ever find it (he could do that, you know)—leave it alone, pretend it never happened, and try to live a normal life.

No, that wouldn't help. Ret had started something; he had set something in motion. He could feel it. That, and the news was abuzz, overflowing with stories that would never allow him to push the subject completely out of his mind. Take, for instance, the story on the front page of today's *Tybee Times:*

WORLD PUZZLED BY ATLANTIC'S MASS GENOCIDE

LONDON—Ever since scores of dead bodies started washing up on Caribbean shores three days ago (and more appear every hour), everyone from Australia to Algeria has been wondering one thing: what in the world happened?

The facts are few but certain. As of yesterday at 11:59 PM (GMT), a total of 113,892 corpses have been collected, mostly from the shores of the Islands of the Bahamas but also along the eastern coasts of Cuba, Haiti, and the Dominican Republic. Ranging from the aged to the infantile, these lifeless castaways have also drifted as far south as Jamaica and as far north as Virginia, USA.

Suddenly, Ret looked up from reading the newspaper to see who had called out his name from across the beach.

"Ret Cooper!" yelled Ana, sounding a bit distressed as she hurriedly hopped toward him. "If you don't teach me that vanishing sand trick, *you'll* be the one who pops the blisters on my scorched feet!" Ret obliged, waving his hand to unveil a welcome path in the hot sand.

"That's better," Ana grinned.

"Listen to this," Ret said to her as she joined him in the hollow. He resumed reading the article.

According to the World Health Organization (WHO), none of the bodies has been identified. "We're in a profound stupor," said WHO representative Michelle Dubois. "Our DNA tests have not found a single match among world archives." When asked if WHO would appeal to the public for identification purposes, Dubois said, "We have no intention of doing so because the bodies are too waterlogged and decomposed, rendering any attempt at visual recognition futile. Besides, due to the overwhelming volume of specimens, they are being disposed of almost immediately."

Autopsies performed by WHO yield no evidence linking the genocide to any sort of pandemic virus or sickness. This has led scientists to believe that the victims drowned as a result of last week's catastrophic seismic activity. According to the U.S. Geological Survey (USGS), a magnitude 18.3 earthquake occurred, with its epicenter somewhere between Miami, Florida, USA; Bermuda, UK; and San Juan, Puerto Rico, USA. Other experts from around the globe have their own hypotheses, however. Geologists at the European-Mediterranean Seismological Centre (EMSC) confirm the 18.3 magnitude but disagree with the USGS in categorizing it as an earthquake.

"We feel it would be a misnomer to classify last week's seismic activity as an earthquake due to the indefinite location of its epicenter as well as its arbitrary reading on the Richter Scale," the EMSC said in a statement. "We do not see a sufficient number of common earthquake characteristics to classify it as such."

"Whatever it was, it was colossal," said Roger Reedley, a spokesman from the World Data Center for Seismology in Denver, Colorado, USA. "The largest earthquake ever recorded was the 9.5-magnitude quake in Valdivia, Chile, in 1960. Last week's activity registered an unfathomable 18.3. That's not just two-times the size of the Valdivia quake; that's not how the Richter Scale works. To give you an idea, a 9.0 quake releases 1,000 times more energy than a 7.0 quake. Yeah, and we're talking 18.3 here. I don't have a calculator with a big enough screen to throw exact figures at you, but this mega-quake released as much energy as an explosion of hundreds of teratons of TNT. That's hundreds of trillions of tons of TNT. Mind boggling, isn't it?"

Supporting the claim made by the EMSC, there were remarkably no tsunamis in connection with this seismic phenomenon, although just about every coastal nation issued tsunami warnings. Typically, beach waters will recede just prior to the arrival of tsunami waves. While many countries reported receding tides, no giant waves ever appeared, and water levels still haven't returned to their previous heights. The U.S. National Oceanic and Atmospheric Administration (NOAA) reports that the sea level along all American shores has dropped more than one foot (0.3 meters).

"Satellite imagery suggests a great disturbance in the waters of the Western Atlantic and Caribbean," the NOAA's National Hurricane Center said. "The water appears to be swirling, as if rushing to fill some vacant space."

Jin Lee of the Japan Meteorological Agency agrees with this observation. He says a very large swath of what was thought to be the seafloor suddenly gave way to a massive empty space immediately below it. "In a very real sense," says Lee, "there was a giant air bubble trapped under the earth's crust, and something was triggered that popped it."

The Russian Federal Space Agency claims the incident was not an earthquake at all but instead the impact of a meteorite from outer space. They assert this as a more logical explanation for the profound magnitude, absence of tsunamis, and sudden presence of a crater on the seafloor.

But the U.S. National Aeronautics and Space Administration (NASA) balks at this proposal. "A massive sinkhole may have appeared at the bottom of the ocean overnight," said NASA engineer Vincent DeGraw, "but we're pretty sure we would have noticed a meteorite the size of Texas hurtling towards us."

"Well this is the most confusing article I've ever heard," Ana said, rolling her eyes at all of the acronyms, statistics, and theories presented in the paper.

"Hold on," Ret urged, "there's more."

"Oh, hooray."

Despite the wide array of opinions, it may be quite some time before hands-on research can be conducted. The western Atlantic Ocean and Caribbean Sea are closed to all naval and air transportation until further notice, including rescue crews and research teams. Even the Bahamas have been evacuated in anticipation of aftershocks.

Recent events have been of particular interest to scientists at the International Atomic Energy Agency (IAEA).

"Hey, that's where Lionel works!" Ret pointed out with excitement.

"Is that right?" Ana asked, trying to sound interested.

Shortly after the incident, the United Nations (UN) approached the IAEA and asked for a status update on all of the nuclear reactors around the globe. Dr. Lionel Zarbock, the IAEA's leading physicist, was chosen to deliver the oral report at the emergency UN council held just 48 hours after the Atlantic tremor. He told world leaders, "After thorough investigation, the IAEA is pleased to report that all of the world's nuclear operations are secure following the quake that shook the world. However, based on global positioning data of reactors in and around the mid Atlantic region, my colleagues and I have reason to believe that the recent implosion in the ocean may have disrupted the regular movement of the earth's tectonic plates."

Despite Zarbock's warning, however, the UN classified the issue as not immediately threatening and voted to examine it in the near future once more pressing issues have been addressed.

"What?" Ret said in disbelief. "How could they just dismiss Lionel like that?"

"He's a physics nerd, not a plate guy...or whatever they're called," Ana suggested.

"Yeah, but still." Ret refocused on the final words of the front-page story.

As the death toll rises daily, people around the world demand answers. Earthquake, meteorite, tectonic bubble—what really caused such a tragedy? The world may never know.

"Well, *I* know," Ana asserted, "and I don't have any degree or work for some fancy agency. We *all* know what *really* happened."

"Do you think we should tell someone?" Ret wondered.

"No way, Jose!" she counseled. "Don't you remember the last hour of our trip back here on the yacht? When Mr. Coy lectured us on not telling a soul about what happened?"

"Yeah," Ret recalled, "and it doesn't sound like Lionel has told anyone what *actually* happened either."

"Besides," continued Ana, "it would probably do more harm than good. Mom just got back from talking to the school board."

"Why'd she do that?"

"You know Mom," Ana explained with a sigh. "Ever since we got home, she's been thinking of ways to get Principal Stone fired—expose his 'real' side. She hates the guy; you'd think he strapped her to the front of a speedboat or something." Ana grinned. "She even said she'd rather home school us than send us back to any institution under *his* leadership. But I told her *I'd* rather go to school under the threat of death every day than suffer through home schooling."

Ret shot her a glare as if to say, "Are you for real, girl?"

"Priorities, Ret," she sighed, flinging her brown hair over her shoulder. "Priorities."

"So how'd it go?" Ret inquired, curious as to the outcome of Pauline's visit with the school board.

"Not so hot, from the little she told me," said Ana. "She gave them all the dirt on Stone—how he planned the raid on our home, then tricked her, kidnapped her, and held her hostage. But when they asked for proof—even just a reason why Stone would do such awful things—Mom was speechless."

"She didn't say anything?" Ret said in awe.

"What would *you* have said?" Ana rebutted. "That her adopted son has enchanted scars on his hands that led us to an underwater road where we swam into the bowels of the earth and found a lost city that killed itself in a war over a clod of magic dirt?" She paused to take a breath. "Yeah, right. Next stop: loony farm."

"Well it's true, isn't it?" Ret persisted.

"Of course it is, Ret," Ana confirmed, "but that doesn't mean it's believable. Sometimes truth is harder to believe than fiction, and people don't seem to like it as much as the fake stuff. Why do you think reality TV is so popular?"

Ret wasn't following. His and Ana's opposing perspectives on life were clashing yet again. "So what's Pauline's next move?" he inquired, trying to redirect the conversation. "Tell the police?"

"No, I think she's done trying to sack Stone. When the board dismissed her, she said she wouldn't leave until they told her why they wouldn't even investigate her claims. So they said things like she's still loopy from

Jaret being gone, or she's bitter from some romantic interest with Stone, or she's just coming up with old wives' tales to pass the time. Someone even asked if she had been drinking. Can you believe that? Pauline Cooper—drunk! Since when did the honorable name of Cooper go down the tubes in this town?" Ana's face showed her frustration.

"Sounds to me like the school board is full of Stone loyalists," Ret observed.

"Anyway, as soon as the board started questioning Mom's mental stability, she got all fired up—you know, huffy. They had to call in security to escort her out." Then, with slight pain in her face, Ana said, "She's not taking it very well."

Ret also ached for poor Pauline. There was nothing she wanted more than the happiness, success, and protection of her children. Yet, the more she tried to secure their safety, the more it appeared she contributed to their danger. It seemed an odd thing to Ret that a person's efforts at fulfilling some personal desire could have the opposite effect—that so much pulling toward was actually pushing away; that a step forward was actually one backward. If that were the case, Ret reasoned, then the solution would be simple: just turn around.

"Hey, is that a picture of Quirk?" asked Ana, pointing to a photograph on the back of the newspaper.

Ret turned the paper over and started to read the small paragraph under their former teacher's portrait.

TYBEE SAYS GOODBYE TO ONE OF ITS OWN

TYBEE ISLAND—The Island has been fortunate so far, as none of the casualties from the recent tragedy in our Atlantic Ocean has been a Tybee native. But our luck has run out with the death of Ronald Quirk.

"Mr. Quirk is *dead?*" Ana blurted out incredulously.

Very little is known about Quirk. It has taken his passing for the community to learn just how mysterious a man he was. As Tybee High School's World Geography teacher last year, the Times turned to Principal Lester W. Stone for his comments on this member of his staff.

"Ronald was a fine man who will surely be missed," said Stone. When we asked questions pertaining to Quirk's background, education, and family, Stone declined to answer, admitting he was too emotional and would discuss the matter at a later date.

"Stone was 'too emotional'?" Ana repeated in

disgust. "That doesn't sound like Stone at all, that big ninny. What a liar."

Stone did not say who would replace Quirk when classes resume this fall. Given the lack of knowledge concerning any relatives, the school board held a brief memorial yesterday in front of the school. No one attended.

"Ouch," Ana cringed with a chuckle.

"Yeah, that hurts," Ret agreed.

"Like I always say, you can tell a lot about a person by how many people come to their funeral."

"When have you said *that?*" Ret challenged her with a playful smile. Ana stuck her tongue out at Ret.

Having finished the short obituary, Ret put down the newspaper. For several seconds, he stared at the picture of Mr. Quirk. It was the same one that was in the yearbook, and it captured the essence of Ronald Quirk to a tee: his glasses sat slanted on his crooked nose, with salt and pepper curls dangling at random from his head. The student body was stunned to find an actual picture of Mr. Quirk in the yearbook, fully expecting him never to give his consent to be photographed. But it seemed the flash of the camera provoked one of his eye spasms because, in the end, the Quirk that was captured had his entire left eye shut, left lip peaked, and left nostril flared.

It almost draws all attention away from the Hawaiian tie-dye shirt he wore on picture day.

"I bet it was Stone," Ret accused. "He killed Quirk. Or at least got rid of him."

"Yeah," Ana concurred. "Probably pushed him overboard or something. Hope he did the same to Bubba, that lousy putz. He ruined Winter Formal for everyone!"

As Ana continued to complain relative to her "priorities," Ret's mind wandered in contemplation of what lay ahead for him. What element wished to be collected next, and where would he find it? When would another scar illuminate on his hand—in a few days, weeks, or years? And what sort of scheme did Principal Stone have in store for him, now that his bumbling buddy Quirk was no longer alive to slow him down?

But Ret was not half so much concerned about Stone as he was about Lye. Even though he saw no feasible way that Lye could have survived the total demise of Sunken Earth, Ret was not so naïve as to think an ancient lord of his caliber could be defeated so easily. Yes, Ret felt Lye was still alive—somewhere, somehow. He could feel it in the night; sense it in the shadows. What else could explain the frightful, eerie chills that haunted Ret amidst such pervasive heat?

CHAPTER 2

PLAN Z BACKFIRES

Although it was still quite a few weeks until they would officially be high school sophomores, the start of the next academic year also marked the beginning of the girls' volleyball season, and Ana and Paige were gearing up for the summer tryouts.

"Have I ever told you how convenient it is that your house has a huge gym inside of it?" Ana told Paige as they entered the southeast annex on the fourth floor of Coy Manor. It was almost every day now that they patronized the manor's facilities in preparation for tryouts. In an effort to be versatile, they would spend the first half of their routine playing on a traditional wood-paneled court, then, at the touch of a button, remove the floor to uncover sand and finish their practice beach-style.

"You're going down, girl," Ana teased Paige as they each took one side of the court. Ana, coordinated and competitive, loved volleyball, and since she was taller than most other fifteen-year-old girls, she had a knack for the sport. Paige, on the other hand, pretended to possess the same enthusiasm, but it wasn't exactly her favorite thing to do. True, she wasn't very good, and she would be the first to admit it, but she knew how much it meant to Ana, so she was willing to be a warm body to return her friend's serves.

"Nice bump," Ana complimented Paige, who had impressed herself by her own hit, "but not as nice as *this*." Ana spiked the ball into the sand on Paige's side. Another point for Ana.

"Do you think there will be many people at tryouts?" Paige asked as she went to retrieve the ball. The thought of lots of people watching her play volleyball had been haunting Paige for weeks, her nervousness building daily.

"Are you kidding?" Ana replied. "The whole *school* will be there. Everyone's dying to meet the new volleyball coach, *Miss Carmen*." Ana sneered upon saying her name.

"What, is she a bad coach or something?" Paige wondered, sensing Ana's scorn.

"Oh, I'm sure she's all that and a bag of Doritos when it comes to coaching," Ana said. "I heard she's even on some professional volleyball team in Chile, wherever that is." Ana sent another serve over the net.

"That's all fine and dandy, but all the guys can't stop talking about how gorgeous she is—slim and tan, with that whole foreign-exotic vibe going on." In her wrists, Paige could feel Ana's contempt building with every fireball she was sending her way. "And I'm sure she gets plenty of looks in her skimpy volleyball uniform. I mean, how can anyone feel comfortable wearing such short shorts? I'm so glad you found these extra long ones for us, Paige."

"Me, too. Is Ret still going to be there?"

"You know Ret," said Ana, "he *lives* at the beach. Why? Are you worried Tybee's new heartthrob might catch his eye?" She smiled slyly.

"I'm more worried he'll see me make a fool of myself," Paige fibbed, who was silently panicking over the probable flirtations of Miss Carmen.

As usual, the pair concluded their rigorous exercise by cooling off in one of the many bodies of water in the annex, whose multiple floors were more like terraces of varying heights within one massive room. On the top level, amid courts for volleyball, tennis, and basketball, sat the Olympic-sized swimming pool, one of whose sides came all the way to the edge of the floor where it spilled into raging rapids on their way down to the floor below. The second floor's pelagic pool, situated between a soccer field and a baseball diamond with a gymnast's paradise in one corner and a weightlifter's in the other, was deep to accommodate scuba diving, and the waterslides at its edge led to the third level. This next tier was home to a body of water that was more so a lake than a pool, as it had to be spacious enough for water-skiing, wakeboarding, and other aquatic and boating activities. Around the perimeter of the lake lay a racetrack for cars, cyclists, or runners, while a handful of floating islands with putting greens and colorful flags proved a challenging golf course certainly full of mulligans. A perilous waterfall plunged from the lake to the bottom level's fish-laden shallows, which licked the blades of a football field or zip-line landing or hang-gliding runway—or whatever purpose it happened to be serving. Not to mention walls made of rock for climbers, the annex contained the world's recreational activities all in one convenient—albeit gargantuan—room. Nothing less for Coy Manor.

Little did Paige and Ana know, however, that the fake duck in the nearby pool was watching them intently. Besides serving as a floating chlorine dispenser, the mallard's right eye had been replaced by a tiny camera, through which Mr. Coy was secretly peeking. To some, this behavior might seem creepy, but because it was Mr. Coy who was doing the creeping, it was quite normal.

"So *that's* why they've taken such a liking to volleyball," Coy whispered to himself as he overheard the girls' conversation. "They're preparing for tryouts— of course!" Then, upon hearing that Ret would be attending the tryouts, he said with glee, "I'd like to try out a few moves of my own." He leapt for joy in his faraway observation room. "Aha!" he cheered, "Peeping Tom, you've done it again, my feathered friend," he complimented the duck. "I don't care what they say about you: *I* think you really *are* all that you're quacked up to be."

Even before his yacht taxied into the manor's harbor, Mr. Coy was already focused on figuring out what element would be collected next. He had loved the adventure to Sunken Earth, as exploring and trailblazing were among his favorite things to do. Plus, it had kept his mind off other things.

However, instead of trying to unravel the riddle and collect the clues on his own (which was utterly unsuccessful last time), Mr. Coy had learned to pay a little more attention to his three teenage acquaintances: Ana, Paige, and especially Ret. Ret had proved to be the quintessential piece to their success in procuring the earth element—an obvious fact that Mr. Coy would not soon forget.

And so, after several more days of patient surveillance, Mr. Coy learned of the precise time and place of these tryouts, where he intended to make his move.

O   O   O

"Welcome, one and all, to Tybee High School's volleyball season kickoff," the announcer's voice bellowed from the modest grandstand on the sand. "As soon as everyone gathers in from their activities on the beach, we will introduce our new head coach," which words were greeted by hearty cheers and whistles from all the listening guys, while the girls sighed and rolled their eyes. "Then we will proceed to tryouts, and please make sure to stick around afterwards for the barbecue and dessert."

It seemed the scorching, mid-summer heat had kept no one away. As Ana predicted, nearly the entire school was in attendance, except for Principal Stone, whose absence might have been why everyone was so happy. Upon hearing the announcement that the kickoff was about to begin, the hordes of people made their way from the waves to the courts, seeking refuge under the many shady umbrellas.

"Your attention please, your attention please," the announcer's voice returned, quieting the crowd. "It is with great pleasure that we introduce our new girls' volleyball coach," he paused, asking for a drum roll while all the boys strained their necks, "Miss Carmen!"

A silhouette emerged within the shadowy veranda where the trainers and assistant coaches were seated.

Miss Carmen, full of poise and dignity, walked unhurriedly onto the center court. With remarkable balance, she strutted in the sand as if she were a model on a runway, penetrating her audience with a wanton stare that sent men's hearts swooning and women's brows furrowing. There was no denying she was fair to look upon, with a body built for volleyball, and there was a strong self-confidence in her dark brown hair and ruby red lips. Even the announcer seemed mesmerized by Miss Carmen's presence, as he fell mute for several moments.

"Uh...let's see here," he was heard at last, struggling to find where he had left off, "Miss Carmen comes to us all the way from South America, where she is the setter on the women's Chilean national volleyball team."

"You were right," Paige whispered to Ana.

"Yeah," she replied, "just look at those shorts! Ret's *boxers* are longer than that."

Paige blushed. "No, I mean about Chile."

"Girl, how can you think about food at a time like this?" Ana asked. Paige let it go.

"When she heard about the success of our volleyball program," the announcer continued, "Miss Carmen jumped at the opportunity to take over as head coach and fulfill one of her dreams to teach the sport she loves. And, having just celebrated her twentieth birthday, she's sure to fit right in at Tybee High. Please give a warm welcome to Miss Carmen!" The crowd again roared with thunderous applause.

"And what's up with everyone calling her 'Miss Carmen'?" said Ana, sounding put upon. "Doesn't she have a last name?"

It wasn't long after Miss Carmen's grand debut that the tryouts got underway. The first group on display was the remaining members of last year's team. Miss Carmen played a couple points with them, and Paige and Ana weren't sure if their purpose was to show off or intimidate the girls who would be trying out.

"Wow, she's really good," Paige admired Miss Carmen, whose superior setting skills proved to be the downfall of her opponents.

"Don't let them scare you," Ana cautioned, but the only person Paige didn't want watching her was Ret.

It was lucky for her, then, that Ret hadn't joined the festivities yet, preferring to play in the water a little bit longer. He was having too much fun, taking advantage of the day's unusually large waves, which only improved as the afternoon wore on. Before catching a wave, Ret liked to paddle a good distance offshore and lie on his surfboard, rolling with the approaching swells before they became breaking waves. It was in this position when, all of a sudden, something grabbed Ret's leg and yanked him off his board. Ret watched the sunlight at the surface gradually disappear as he was dragged deeper and deeper into the sea. Finding his bearings, he looked down to see what had latched onto him. Seeing no blood and feeling no pain, he wasn't very surprised to see the figure of a man. And then he recognized the subsuit.

"Mr. Coy!" Ret screamed, then abruptly stopped upon losing so much air. Knowing he would drown if he didn't halt Mr. Coy's dive, Ret spotted some rocks on the approaching seafloor and waved his fingers to propel them at Mr. Coy's grip. The pelted hand forsook Ret's leg, and he rushed to the surface.

"What's that guy trying to do, kill me?" Ret said to himself in between desperate gasps for air. "It's not like I have power over water," which was exactly what Mr. Coy wanted to find out.

Suddenly exhausted, Ret found his surfboard and slowly paddled to shore, frequently searching his surroundings for any more Coy traps. He collapsed on the beach and had only closed his eyes for a few moments when he heard the names of Ana Cooper and Paige Coy announced from the volleyball courts. They were in the next group to try out for the high school team.

Ret made his way up the beach towards the grandstand, where hundreds of people were still gathered, all watching the goings-on with rapt attention. From his vantage point in the very back, all Ret could see was the volleyball flying back and forth in the air from one side of the court to the other. As he reached and strained for a better view, he felt something like static moving up and down the back side of his body. When he turned around to see what was going on, he bumped into a man holding a metal detector.

"Oh, excuse me, pardon me," the intrusive man said gruffly through his thick mustache. When he scurried off, the breeze swept the wide-brimmed hat off his head, and Ret's suspicions were confirmed: Mr. Coy.

Ret knew that Ana would be mad if he didn't keep his promise and watch her performance at tryouts, so he set out to find himself a better seat. He snaked his way through the crowd, all the way to the bleachers. At the very end of the fourth row, he spotted a tiny piece of bench that a young woman was reserving for her purse. He decided to approach her and ask if he could sit there. Just before he opened his mouth to speak to her, however, Mr. Coy, concealed underneath the bleachers at precisely the end of the fourth row, released into the air an invisible cloud of helium from one of the kickoff's many balloons. So when Ret asked his question, his voice sounded like a chipmunk's.

"Is anyone sitting here?" Ret's eyes widened at the sound of his voice. He quickly covered his mouth. The young woman and her friends giggled but obliged.

Ret's frustration with Mr. Coy subsided as he directed his attention toward the tryouts. Ana, with a face full of determination, was bringing the heat and pleasing the crowd while Paige was buckling under the pressure. Once, when Paige was playing at the net, her curly hair got tangled in it, halting play. Then, when it was her turn to serve, she sent the ball directly into the back of Miss Carmen's head, which earned her an ugly boo from the crowd.

"Wow, she's terrible," Ret heard someone behind him say about Paige. Ret would have countered such a rude comment directed at his good friend, but he wasn't sure if his voice had returned to normal.

When the whistle blew to end their group's audition, an exultant Ana exited the court with Paige following behind, her head down. Ret hurried after them.

"Good job today," he called out before joining them by one of the few fire pits that had not been swallowed by the crowd.

"Yeah, good job today, Ana," Paige said sullenly, excluding herself from the compliment.

"I like the way you play," Ret said, trying to make her feel better. "I mean, not everyone's hair is so pretty that it disrupts the whole game."

Unseen to Paige, Ana shot Ret a confused glare, as if to say, "That's supposed to make her feel better?"

"So you think my hair is pretty?" Paige reiterated, suddenly perking up.

"Um, yeah," said Ret, looking to Ana's facial expressions for help. "Pretty...curly?"

"Oh, Ret," Paige smiled, "you always know how to make me laugh."

"So," Ret sighed, wanting to change the subject to something less awkward, "you're not going to watch the rest of the tryouts?"

"No," said Ana, "we've both had enough of Miss Carmen for one day. Besides, we wanted to claim a pit before they're all taken."

With the setting of the sun, the tryouts had been reduced to free play, although the only ones waiting in line were googly-eyed males whose lifelong wish, it seemed, was to play alongside Miss Carmen. Even though the temperature had scarcely slackened a degree or two, the fire pits were ignited, casting flickering panels of light in the growing darkness.

"Good evening, ladies and gentleman," a voice with a thick Italian accent greeted them. "May I take your order?" With a white apron taut around his waist and a poofy chef's hat on his head, the waiter stood with pen and paper, poised to write.

"Yes, I'll have one of the hamburgers," Ana stated quite instinctively, never denying the chance to be served, "but with no onions—you know, bad breath and all."

"Ah, but of course," replied the waiter, scribbling down Ana's order. "And to drink?"

"I'll take a diet…wait a minute," Ana stopped mid-sentence, "since when are there servers at a buffet-style barbecue?"

"Yeah," Paige joined in, "and why doesn't anyone else have a waiter?"

"My, my," the waiter said quickly, "looks like your fire could use some more fuel." The waiter bent over and picked up a fresh log from the wood pile.

"Dad!" Paige exclaimed, getting a better look at their server when he bent closer to the flames. "Is that *you?*"

The waiter made no reply but hurled the log into the pit, where the disturbed fire exploded into sparks and flames. Then, still bent over, he spun around until his backside collided with Ret, launching Ret forward into the blazing pit.

"Ret—watch out!" Ana cried.

But before Ret made any contact with the inferno, he subconsciously called upon all the sand surrounding the pit to come pouring into it, completely and immediately extinguishing the fire. Then Ret came crashing down on the sand, safe and unharmed.

"What on earth are you trying to do, Dad?" Paige interrogated her father.

"He's been harassing me all day," Ret explained.

"*Harass* is such a harsh word," Mr. Coy began to justify himself. Then, seeing the faces of his three young associates cloud over with silent perplexity, he turned around to see what had captured their attention. It was Miss Carmen. She had seen the whole thing.

"Who the heck are you?" Mr. Coy asked the snooping witness with no sense of propriety.

"Miss Carmen," she said sweetly. "And you must be Benjamin Coy," she assumed, analyzing his costume from head to toe with an air of ridiculousness.

"At your service," said Coy, regaining his posture and resuming his stance as a waiter.

"I am your daughter's volleyball coach," Miss Carmen informed.

"You mean she made the team?" Ret blurted out. Miss Carmen nodded.

"But she stinks," said Mr. Coy.

"She most certainly does *not* stink," Miss Carmen asserted, "and she and Ana will both make great additions to our team." She winked at Ana.

"Yes!" Ana celebrated, pumping her fist at the announcement. "Did you hear that, Paige? We made the team! Both of us." She hugged Paige, even though she didn't seem as thrilled at the news.

"Now would someone kindly tell me what just happened here?" Miss Carmen asked, staring at Ret who was still half-buried in the fire pit. The others looked at him as if they had forgotten all about him.

"Nothing that a sweet little thing like you should worry about," Mr. Coy told her coldly, turning his back to her to give her the hint that he wanted her to leave. For the next several seconds as she waited for an answer, Miss Carmen never took her eyes off Ret. She slowly analyzed his every feature while Paige followed her wandering eyes, unsure if the flames she saw in Miss Carmen's eyes were a reflection of the surrounding bonfires or the distaste swelling within herself.

"Fine," Miss Carmen finally concluded when it was apparent no one was willing to explain what had just occurred. Then, with her gaze still fixed on Ret, she said with an enticing grin, "All I can say is, I like what I see, Ret. I like what I see." She walked off.

"Well that's the worst pickup line I've ever heard," Mr. Coy said once she was gone.

"Yeah, looks like someone's got the hots for you, Ret," Ana observed. "I like her!"

"What?" a ruffled Paige interrupted. "All you've ever said are nasty things about Miss Carmen, and now you like her?"

"And she likes *me!*" said Ana. "Did you see the way she looked at us? And we know she likes *you*. I mean, you hit her in the back of the head during tryouts, and she *still* wants you on the team!"

"Whatever," Paige sighed. She knelt down to help Ret out of the pit.

"Have any of you been in your principal's office lately?" Coy asked another one of his off-topic yet loaded questions, something obviously on his mind. The three students shook their heads to tell him they hadn't; then they asked why he wanted to know. "Because I need to know if that second chest is still in his office."

"Why?" Ret wondered.

"Because I want to know what's inside of it," Coy responded in a condescending tone, as if Ret had asked a silly question.

"You mean you only looked inside *one* of the chests?"

"I ran out of time," Coy explained, "but I'm hoping its contents give us a clue as to what the next element is and where we can expect to find it because I'm all out of ideas. The fire pit was Plan Z."

"Why don't you break into his office like you did before?" Ret suggested.

"Because he's on to us now," said Coy. "He'll be expecting that. It needs to look natural—something that won't give him reason to be suspicious of us. Besides, there's no sense in going to the trouble of breaking in again if, in fact, the chest isn't even there."

"Here's an idea," Paige suggested as she brushed the last little bit of sand off Ret's arm. "How about you just look through his window?"

"No, he keeps the blinds shut," Ret remembered.

"You could pay off the janitor," Ana said.

"No, it needs to be one of you three," Coy decided. "One of you needs to get sent there."

"Once was enough for me," Ret said, counting himself out.

"I'm not getting in trouble," said Paige, unwilling to volunteer herself and mar her record.

"Oh, come on," Ana groaned at her friends' aloofness, "I'll do it. How hard could it be?" Then, turning to address Mr. Coy, she asked, "What did you have in mind, boss?"

He replied, "Look for the sign."

CHAPTER 3

A VISIT FROM LIONEL

It was the smell of sizzling bacon that awoke Ret from sleep. Theirs was the kind of house where they were always within earshot of each other, especially when Pauline took to cooking in the kitchen. The bang of bowls and clang of cutlery were not uncommon. Pauline was a regular souschef, capable of whipping up just about any dish on demand. She found great satisfaction in nurturing her children, and there was scarcely a meal eaten except together as a family.

Ret saw Ana whiz past his bedroom door, outfitted in her volleyball gear. At the scent of something peppered and oniony, he rolled out of bed and followed his nose, knowing the aroma portended delicious things. It was going to be a good day.

"Eat up, dear; you'll need your strength for practice today," Ret overheard Pauline say to Ana as he descended the stairs. "I still feel awful for missing your tryouts. It was poor planning on my part—you know, having met with the school board just a few days before." She wasn't telling them anything they hadn't already heard, but Ana listened politely, hoping it would help her mother feel better about the situation. "I wasn't feeling up to braving the crowd, especially one with so many people from school."

She turned from the stove and placed a skillet full of scrambled eggs on the table. Her apron, speckled with splatters, hugged her waist tightly. "Good morning, Ret."

"Good morning," he replied, taking his seat at the breakfast table.

"It's okay, Mom," Ana consoled, the same way she had before. Then she added, "Besides, Ret was there to cheer me on. And so was Mr. Coy, so you—"

"Mr. Coy was there?" Pauline asked in shock.

"Yeah, but not for the tryouts," said Ana. "He was mostly just bugging Ret the whole time, trying to figure out what the next element is going to be."

"He wasn't *bugging* me," Ret corrected, trying to downplay Ana's words since Pauline had a tendency to overreact, especially if Mr. Coy was involved.

"You said he tried to *drown* you—" Ana inserted.

"He did *what?*" Pauline balked.

"*—and* he pushed you into the fire pit."

"Good grief," Pauline said with frustration, "not *this* mess again. Will that man ever leave you alone, Ret? Hasn't he put you—us—through enough lately?" Her discontent was evident as she smashed her toast while trying to butter it. "Now he's conspiring behind my back again. I think it's time I marched to that mansion of his and gave him a piece of my mind."

"No, no," Ret protested respectfully, "I'm actually a little glad he did what he did." Ana glared at Ret with a mouthful of hash browns. "I've also been wondering what's next with the Oracle."

"Oh, Ret," Pauline sighed. "I think it would do us all some good if we took a break from that stuff for a while. It was quite the disruption to our lives, and I know you're still shaken up about what happened." She was right about that, at least. "Let's just leave it alone for a while. You're both going to be sophomores soon, and you need to focus on your schoolwork. Plus, I'm just ecstatic that Ana and Paige made the volleyball team, and we don't want anything getting in the way of them having a great season."

Pauline's words had a calming effect on the conversation. Soon, all that was heard was the scraping of silverware on well-worn plates, the kind with lots of gray marks in the center from countless uses. Pauline's attention shifted to the small stack of mail sitting beside her place setting.

"Oh," she said, "here's a letter for *you*, Ret."

"Ret got mail?" Ana asked incredulously.

"There's no return address," Ret observed, receiving the envelope from Pauline.

"That's sketchy," remarked Ana.

Ret eagerly tore open the envelope, for, as Ana had pointed out, mail for Ret was a rarity. Inside was a small sheet of yellow notepad paper, with a short message scribbled on one side in black ink:

Dear Ret,

I hope this note finds you well. I'll be in town this week and would very much like to speak with you. If possible, meet me at the Savannah River Delta Nuclear Power Plant this Thursday at noon.

Your friend,
Lionel Zarbock

P.S. Give my regards to Pauline and Ana.

"Now *there's* a role model if I ever saw one," Pauline said with confidence. "None of this secretive business or going behind my back—what a professional, what a gentleman! I hope you'll not let him down, Ret."

"Really?" Ret asked, surprised by Pauline's swift approval.

"Of course," she reaffirmed. "Lionel is exactly the kind of man you should emulate. He's intelligent and successful, very educated and levelheaded. Besides, maybe he'll even give you a tour of the plant."

"So I can go?"

"Certainly," Pauline smiled. "I'd be happy to drop you off. I know how much you love science. You might just learn a thing or two, and hopefully it'll take your mind off other things." Then, turning to Ana, Pauline continued, "I'm sure *you're* welcome, too, dear."

"No thanks," Ana declined, "I'm not one to invite myself to things. I'd never be caught dead in a nuclear power plant anyway. Why does he want to meet you *there*, of all places?"

"It must be for his job," Ret assumed. "Remember that story in the newspaper about how the UN asked him to report on all the power plants in the area?" Ana nodded her head in agreement. "I don't know how he found out where we live, though."

"*I* might have mentioned it to him," Pauline admitted, obviously pleased with herself. "You can never have too many good influences around you, children; remember that." She picked up their finished plates and deposited them in the sink.

As Pauline scrubbed the dishes, she beamed with joy at the thought of Ret spending time with Lionel. From their interactions in Sunken Earth, she had been quite impressed with Lionel—his sense of right and wrong, his willingness to stand up for what he believed in. She hoped that, by encouraging their association, Lionel would reinforce the ideals and morals that she so painstakingly tried to teach in the home. In some discomforting way, it bothered her that Ret felt so drawn to Mr. Coy. In her eyes, Mr. Coy was irrational and unpredictable, and his vocation was as ambiguous as his parenting practices.

Meanwhile, Ret shared Pauline's joy, though for different reasons. He could hardly contain himself in anticipation of his upcoming visit with Lionel. In just the few days when they rubbed shoulders in Sunken Earth, Lionel had proved to be a true friend of immense help, without which they may have never acquired the earth element. It pained Ret when Lionel left so abruptly. You'd think that, having no correspondence with one another all summer, they would have largely forgotten about each other, but, in fact, the opposite was true.

O   O   O

A mile or two north and west of Tybee Island, on a completely separate island called Cockspur where the river emptied into the Atlantic Ocean, sat the Savannah River Delta Nuclear Power Plant. Even though its domed containment structure towered unsuitably above the island's low-lying shrubs and oyster beds, the plant had been a part of the local landscape for as long as anyone could remember. Still, not many Tybee folks spoke of the plant. Some knew it simply as "the big thing that powers my TV," while others of a more opinionated nature maintained a sort of personal boycott towards the plant. By and large, however, most people had little knowledge of what it was or what purpose it served, which was why Ret was so eager to gather information first-hand.

Ret walked up to the main entrance with haste, partly out of excitement but mostly to escape the unbearable heat and humidity of another summer scorcher. Through a series of double doors, he entered the main office, where a security officer greeted him.

"Can I help you?" the guard confronted Ret in a deep voice. He was a large, imposing figure who didn't seem to take kindly to visitors. Ret read the uniformed man's name badge: Dread. With one hand resting on his firearm and the other on his bludgeon, Officer Dread waited for Ret to answer his question.

"I'm here to see Dr. Lionel Zarbock," Ret replied in a tone as if questioning his own response, hoping he had said the magic word. Apparently, he had, for as soon as Ret mentioned Lionel's name, Officer Dread's entire countenance changed.

"Oh, right this way!" Dread instructed politely. Ret stood still for a moment, in awe at the guard's transformation from cold-blooded officer to giddy museum docent, before hurrying after him.

Completely bypassing the security screening, Ret followed his escort into the belly of the plant. They cut through what appeared to be the plant's receiving sector on their way to wherever they were headed. Every few seconds, Officer Dread exchanged salutations with co-workers he passed en route, never failing to tell them he was taking Ret "to see Dr. Z." The mentioning of Lionel's name had the same, profound effect on everyone who heard it, and their faces, which initially probed Ret with a standoffish glare, suddenly became gracious and welcoming toward him as a visitor and newcomer. It was difficult for Ret not to let such star treatment go to his head, for it seemed that just by knowing Lionel, Ret shared his celebrity status.

At last, they arrived at their destination: a large control room of dizzying magnitude. Every square inch of wall and desk space was covered with buttons and bars, monitors and measurers, knobs and numbers. Ret was reluctant to even move, for fear of tipping some scale or adjusting some gauge. Things were blinking and spinning, buzzing and flashing. The only sight Ret could compare it to was the control panel inside Mr. Coy's helicopter, and even then it was a fitting comparison only if multiplied exponentially.

"Dr. Zarbock, sir," Officer Dread said respectfully, "there's someone here to see you."

A small huddle of scientists, hunched over some computer screen, quickly turned to face them. Their eyes first focused on the guard, then on the visitor.

"Ret!" Lionel emerged from the powwow and strode toward Ret. "It's so good to see you." He embraced Ret, which took Ret a bit by surprise, then grabbed his shoulder and turned to face his associates.

"Everyone," Lionel announced, "I'd like you to meet my good friend, Ret Cooper." Mostly middle-aged men with bald spots and eyeglasses, the other plant workers each took turns shaking Ret's hand. He couldn't help but notice the special outfits they were wearing, each highly adorned with protective gear. Ret wondered if he ought to be wearing such garb, but he didn't want to make a fuss or seem precocious. Surely Lionel would look out for him.

"The fact that you're here means you got my letter," said Lionel, his dark hair and eyes contrasting brilliantly against his white lab coat. "I was hoping you'd come." Ret smiled. "We were just finishing up here."

"Oh, yes, quite right," the others pattered in unison, getting the hint and submitting to their superior.

"Would you like to take a look around?" Lionel asked Ret, grinning because he was almost certain of the answer.

"Would I!"

They exited the control room and, squinting amid the bright afternoon sunshine, climbed a set of outdoor stairs until they were overlooking much of the facility.

"A *nuclear* power plant is very similar to most other types of power plants," Lionel taught. "Water is heated until it turns into steam." Ret followed Lionel's hand motions, moving from the river to the domed containment structure. "The high-pressure steam is channeled into the turbines, whose propeller-like blades spin to generate electricity." Ret's gaze continued to follow Lionel's gesticulations. "Then the electricity moves from the generator to the switchyard and, ultimately, to your living room." The countless wires and lines in the switchyard looked like an organized mess to Ret, who was all the more impressed.

Ret proceeded to ask the one question, despite a myriad of others, that was foremost in his mind: "But how—"

"But how is a *nuclear* plant different?" Lionel interrupted, knowing he had taken the words right out of Ret's mouth. "I'm glad you asked."

They descended from their viewpoint and started walking toward the massive containment structure.

"Power plants have to supply heat in order to change water into steam," Lionel spoke as they walked. "Some plants burn coal, others use natural gas or oil. Some even utilize geothermal heat. But a *nuclear* plant," he said, almost with affection, "—a nuclear plant, in this regard, is a whole different animal—the most beautiful of them all, in my opinion."

Arriving at one of the entrances into the containment structure, Lionel easily gained access and ushered Ret inside. For most Tybee residents, it was this—the power plant's concrete dome—that had come to symbolize the facility itself. By far, it was the largest and tallest edifice in town, with the exception of Coy Manor, of course. Adults passed by it on their commute to and from work, and youth saw it just as frequently from the school bus. But, apart from the science teachers and the few locals who worked there, no one really understood what took place inside the mysterious building, shaped like half a pill capsule. As such, Ret was ecstatic to find himself on the inside.

"Precautionary measures," Lionel remarked when he saw Ret studying the containment structure's outer shell, which consisted of multiple layers of concrete and steel, many feet in thickness. "It keeps harmful radiation in and things like crashing airplanes out."

A network of metal walkways, suspended in the air, carried them deeper into the circular room, their footsteps echoing off the rounded walls. Ret was surprised to learn the dome was hollow. The air felt damp, and a pervasive humming nearly numbed his ears. Besides a wide array of complicated-looking equipment, everything seemed to be built around a single, though stunning, apparatus in the middle.

"The reactor," Lionel whispered, as if paying homage to a shrine. Halting, they leaned over the railing of the walkway and looked below them. "This is the heart of the plant, Ret."

"It almost looks alive," Ret said of the scene below them, which glowed and vibrated with its own unique sort of energy.

"That's because it is," said Lionel. "Do you see those long, vertical rods down there?" Ret nodded. "Some of those are filled with uranium." Ret remembered learning about uranium in his science class last year. "This plant uses uranium-235, a heavy metal that can release a tremendous amount of energy: the nucleus of one U-235 atom contains 92 protons and 143 neutrons."

Ret added the two figures together in his head just to make sure their sum was 235. "That's a lot," he said, "compared to most of the other elements."

"Right," Lionel agreed, "but what also makes uranium special is that it can be split."

"Split?"

"The scientific term is *fission*," said Lionel. "Do you see that particle accelerator over there?" Ret pretended like he could distinguish it from the conglomeration of other devices surrounding them. "That accelerator shoots a neutron at the uranium. Then, when a nucleus of a U-235 atom captures the moving neutron, it literally splits in two!" Lionel was becoming more and more animated, as if retelling a great story. "In the process, energy is released, and the nucleus throws off a few neutrons of its own. Then *these* neutrons bombard other uranium nuclei, and thus a fission chain reaction is born."

Ret wasn't quite sure if he liked the sound of that. Or, perhaps, it was the sound of Lionel's tone that he didn't like. For several seconds, Lionel gaped at the reactor in silent reverence. The whites of his eyes reflected its blue gleam. His knuckles turned pale, so tightly did he grip the balustrade. It was as if he was absorbing some of the energy being released at the atoms' expense. Lionel was the perfect match for his job, Ret concluded.

"So why is this your favorite method of heating water into steam?" Ret inquired.

"Because of how effective it is," came Lionel's answer. "Just a single pound of uranium can generate more energy than thousands of gallons of oil or tons of coal."

"Yeah, but it seems kind of, you know, unnatural, don't you think?" Ret put forth. "I mean, how does something like this not get out of control?"

"Another great question," said Lionel, patting Ret on the back. "Let's get down a little closer; it looks like they're getting ready to refuel the reactor."

They stepped down a few stairs and arrived at a platform where a pair of well-clothed workers was inter-acting with the reactor like operators of a carnival ride. From the safety of their booth, they controlled the core remotely with a system of knobs and levers. Lionel led Ret to a front-row view.

"In between the rods full of uranium are other rods that contain certain elements that absorb neutrons," Lionel explained over the clinking and clanking of metal arms and gears. "When Dr. Rich here," Lionel pointed at one of the operators next to him, "wants to produce more heat, he lifts the control rods *out* from among the uranium, thus absorbing fewer neutrons. Or, to reduce heat, he can lower them *in*. Go ahead, Dr. Rich," Lionel addressed the operator, "let's see how you refuel. My friend, Ret, here would like to watch."

"Yes, Dr. Zarbock," Dr. Rich obeyed, "as soon as the control rods are fully lowered."

"Do it now, doctor," Lionel overruled.

"But sir—"

Lionel gave his protesting subordinate a patient

glare. "Do as I tell you," Lionel insisted calmly. Dr. Rich followed instructions. Lionel turned back around and mumbled to Ret, "You'd think *he* runs the place." Ret looked behind him at Dr. Rich, who reached for the clear mask atop his head and positioned it securely over his face.

Ret watched as the nuclear reactor came into view. He could easily discern which rods belonged to the control group because they were not fully lowered. As the distance between him and the core lessened, Ret could feel waves of energy on his skin, as if sitting in front of a roaring campfire.

"Can you feel it, Ret?" Lionel asked, his arms extended at his sides like a sunbather soaking up the sun's rays. "Pure nuclear energy—the product of millions of tiny things splitting into billions of tiny pieces."

By this time, the only thing that Ret was feeling was sick. Perhaps brought on by the heat, nausea had gripped his stomach while a headache surged in his skull. Drenched in sweat, he was beginning to feel light-headed, as if he might hyperventilate. He needed water, some place to sit down. He wiped his dripping forehead with the back of his hand—blood. Blood on his hand. He searched to find where it had come from. Then he saw small droplets of red on his arm—blood, coming through like perspiration!

Ret stumbled, fell to one knee.

"Ret?" he heard Lionel say. "Are you—"

His eyes were going dim, dizzy.

"He's bleeding! Quick, Dr. Rich, help me—"

Ret sensed he was being carried, his feet dragging behind him. A door opened—they were outside. The sun stung his eyes. He felt himself regaining consciousness, strength returning to his limbs. His rescuers stopped and leaned him against something.

"Here," Lionel directed, clasping Ret's hand around a cup, "drink this." Ret gulped some of the water, then splashed the rest on his face.

"Sorry about that back there," Lionel apologized, sounding winded and taking a swig of his own from what looked like a personal flask. "I should have realized getting that close to a reactor can be a little intense for a first-timer." He slipped the flask back into his coat pocket. "I didn't do so well my first few times either," he admitted. "Even now, I always make sure I stay well hydrated." He patted the pocket where his flask was deposited. "I do hope you'll forgive me, Ret."

"Of course," Ret promised, "it wasn't your fault. Besides, Pauline will be glad to hear you gave me a tour."

"Oh," Lionel chuckled, "and why is that?"

"She wants me to get my mind off the Oracle for a while," Ret said, his tone signifying he wasn't very fond of the idea.

"Well then," Lionel whispered, stooping down as if telling a secret, "you best not be telling her that's the reason I wanted to talk to you." He laughed.

"Really?"

"Really," said Lionel, helping Ret to his feet. "Ever since we escaped from Sunken Earth, I've been dying to know what happened down there. That civilization's collapse caused quite a disruption in the Atlantic, and I feel if I better understood what really took place after I left you at the foot of the mountain, then I could better substantiate my claims to the UN. What exactly was at the top of the mountain? Who was this 'Guardian' person you mentioned to me? And why—"

Listening to Lionel's questions, it occurred to Ret that he had never told Lionel much of anything concerning the Oracle, let alone the earth element. Ret almost chided himself for not including Lionel sooner, for someone as accomplished and knowledgeable as Lionel would certainly prove to be a great asset in their quest.

"Well, it's kind of a long story," Ret warned, though eager to fill him in.

"Then you can tell me while I walk you home," said Lionel. "You could use the fresh air anyway."

Leaving the power plant, they walked side-by-side along the only road that led from Cockspur Island back to Tybee. Ret paid attention to nothing but bringing

Lionel up to speed. He told him everything—the scar, the underwater road, Stone and Quirk, the element, the Guardian. He even fixed every pothole they passed along the road to remind Lionel of his power over everything earthen. Ret held nothing back because he could tell Lionel was sincerely listening to his every word. It wasn't like talking to Ana, who heard what she wanted to hear and then gave her two cents before moving on to something *she* found more interesting. Nor was it like trying to communicate with Pauline, whose own agenda and distaste for anything out of the ordinary prevented candid conversation.

It was different with Lionel. Here was a man of stratospherical repute—a mogul who dined with dignitaries, a genius who comprehended the cryptic—and yet, no one ever would have guessed. He wore fancy neckties, yes, but half-concealed by blue-collar philosophies. He claimed membership in the upper-echelon, obviously, but preferred to do lunch with the entry-level. A prodigy in knock-off penny-loafers, he was attractive and adored yet dictated by neither. Any other person with his accolades and acumen would never search out an adolescent, especially with the intent to be *taught* by him; such a person would have interrupted Ret not far into his narrative with exclamations of disbelief— "Preposterous!"—or with sentiments that trivialized teenage intellect—"You've a fine imagination, my boy."

But not Lionel. In a word, he was two-faced—he led two different lives and served opposing masters; he was double-minded with split personalities. But Ret didn't like to think of it in such negative and dishonorable ways, for he considered it Lionel's greatest quality: his ability to be *in* something but not *of* it—to possess something but not be defined by it. It was due to his pursuit to emulate such rare characteristics why Ret so enjoyed associating with Lionel, and he was grateful that he had spent enough time with him already to know somewhat of the differences between the men behind the masks. He felt sorry for others who remained perplexed with regard to the character of "Dr. Z": some would say he looked certainly kind but curiously unsettling; others, dark yet delightful; and the rest, though intensely intrigued and truly enticed by his enigmatic aura, would fail to quite put their finger on the man who was Lionel Zarbock.

But there was one thing that *was* certain: that hour, as the hot sun bore down on a prestigious physicist and a unique-looking schoolboy, royalty walked side-by-side with commonness—a major player in a minor league—the prince considering himself the pauper—and the mighty, the meek—while none of the drivers passing by could tell who was who.

"So now Mr. Coy is going to help Ana get in trouble at school so she'll get sent to Stone's office and see if the other chest is still in there," Ret explained, having told Lionel everything up to the present. "Coy thinks there's a clue in the chest that will tell us what's next, and I hope he's right."

"Ret, I want to help you in whatever way I can," Lionel announced, pledging his support. "I believe this is much bigger than any of us realizes."

"So do I," Ret agreed, "but I can't stand how it's taking so long. I mean, it took the whole school year to find just one element. We've been back from Sunken Earth for weeks now, and we don't know anything about the next one."

"Be patient, Ret," said Lionel sympathetically. "You can't force nature."

"But *you* can," Ret countered. "You do it all the time, in that nuclear reactor—forcing atoms to split like that."

"Touché," submitted Lionel, "you bring up a good point. Tell you what, I promise to make finding the next element one of my top priorities," he smiled, "how does that sound?"

"Great," Ret rejoiced.

"Here's my card." Lionel handed Ret a thick business card with his contact information. "Be sure to inform me whenever something happens, got it?" Ret understood. "Now, for starters, do you mind if I take a closer look at the Oracle?"

"Not at all," said Ret, "please do." They had just arrived at the Cooper home.

"I'll wait out here while you go and get it."

"Well, *I* don't have it," Ret informed. "Mr. Coy does."

"Oh," said Lionel, sounding a bit disappointed, "well that's okay, maybe some other time—"

"No, no," Ret insisted, desperate for some information, even if it was just speculation. "The Manor's just across the creek. Coy won't mind, especially if it's me asking. Come on!"

With reluctance, Lionel followed Ret to the backyard, down the wooden dock, into the kayak, and across the small inlet of water that separated the two islands. It might have been Ret's fastest time crossing Tybee Creek, so eager was he to learn what Lionel could deduce by studying the Oracle. Ret flew up the hillside, Lionel keeping pace, and approached the Manor's main gate.

"Is that smoke?" Lionel asked, directing Ret's attention to the west side of the Manor. They stopped and studied the broad but thin plumes of gray smoke, which quickly dissipated in the late-afternoon sea breeze.

"Come on," Ret beckoned, "I hope no one's in trouble."

Still outside the gate, they followed the fenceline until they arrived at the source of the smoke: a large and

well-defined swath of the Manor's grounds was burning.
Over the blackened bushes and charred dirt, Ret spied
the figure of a man standing about a stone's throw away.

"Mr. Coy," Ret yelled to get the person's attention,
"is that you?"

The silhouette only had to get a few steps closer to
confirm that it wasn't Mr. Coy. In fact, reaching the gate,
Ret had never seen this man before.

"No, I am Ishmael," said the man, "chief ecologist
and groundskeeper here at Coy Manor." He was a
middle-aged man, neither short nor tall, with olive skin
and what sounded to Ret like an Arabic accent of sorts.
"You must be Ret," he assumed with a pleasant smile.
"Miss Paige has told me much about you." Ishmael
seemed a gentleman, cordial and accommodating,
nothing like his employer. "Mr. Coy should be nearby;
would you like me to fetch him?"

"What exactly are you doing here?" Lionel
inquired, referring to the controlled blaze.

"The biannual purge," Ishmael explained. "We do
one now, near the end of summer, and the other one just
before spring."

"But only in this part of the property?" Lionel
pressed. The scientist in him demanded details.

"All of the plant species you see in this section are
illegal in this country," said Ishmael. "They are considered either to be invasive vegetation or to attract

invasive insects—you know, weevils and locusts and such—delicacies in *my* country." The thought resurrected Ret's nausea from the power plant. "Mr. Coy obtained permission from the government on the basis that he would purge the specimens at least twice a year to control growth and eliminate pests."

"Seems like a lot of work for some funny-looking plants," Ret remarked. He was referring to a few dozen shrubs and trees that clearly had been purposely allowed to survive the inferno. They were covered in some sort of transparent semisolid—a clear goo that oozed with tremendously high viscosity.

"Ah, yes," said Ishmael, "Coy cream. It's a special substance that Mr. Coy created to act as a sort of fire retardant. We spray it on delicate plants that are most vulnerable to intense heat. It's like applying multiple layers of water, which the flames slowly burn off, leaving the protected surface safe and cool."

"Excellent use of polymers," said Lionel, mentally studying the concept. Ret and Ishmael looked at each other, puzzled, and then shrugged their shoulders.

"Let me find Mr. Coy; you can compliment him in person," Ishmael offered, walking away. "He's manning the flamethrower—insists on being in charge of the fire; calls himself 'the torch bearer.' Be right back."

"Tell him Lionel's here and wants to see the Oracle," Ret instructed anxiously, gripping the bars of the gate with both hands and sticking his head through as far as he could.

"Do they always make their guests wait on the other side of the fence?" Lionel asked, trying to get a grasp on the architectural hodgepodge that was Coy Manor.

"At least the grass is greener," Ret joked, comparing the wild grass at their feet to the scorched lawn they could see through the fence.

They watched Ishmael trek across the grounds a little ways until he disappeared behind a large, burnt berm. Having found Mr. Coy, they must have been trying to talk over some loud thing, for Ret and Lionel could hear their entire conversation.

"Sir, there's someone here to see you," yelled Ishmael.

"Unless it's the pizza delivery guy," replied Coy, "tell 'em to beat it!"

"It's the Cooper boy, and some man named Lionel—"

"Lionel!" Coy shouted with fury. "What in the world is *he* doing here? Tell him to get off my island— now!" Ret winced.

"—and he wishes to see the Oracle," Ishmael finished the message.

"Oh, he wants to see the Oracle, does he?" There was a sudden change in Mr. Coy's tone of voice. Ret was hopeful. "Well, in *that* case," then returning to his original miffed tone, "tell him to get off my island right now or I'll come over there with my torch and burn his face off!"

"It's alright, Ret," Lionel sighed, "maybe some other time." He left Ret's side and started walking back the way they came.

For several minutes, Ret maintained his post at the gate, determined to succeed. He hollered at Mr. Coy, though to no avail, and then pled with Ishmael when he returned to relay what Ret had already overheard.

"What've you got against Lionel?" Ret complained to Mr. Coy, but there was no reply. "We have no leads, Coy—none! Why can't he just *look* at it?"

Though still starving—thirsting, longing—to know what the Oracle would have them do next, Ret trudged off. Concerned that Lionel was likely waiting for him, Ret hurried but was shocked when he got to the shore: the kayak was still there, untouched, but Lionel was nowhere in sight. Finding his departing footprints in the sand, Ret followed them until they disappeared at the water's edge.

"He didn't swim across the creek, did he?" Ret wondered in amazement. Had he not done so, choosing instead to take the kayak for himself, then *Ret* would have been the one compelled to swim across. "What a guy," Ret grinned at Lionel's selflessness. "No wonder Pauline loves him."

Ret hoped to find Lionel on the other side of the creek but wasn't surprised when he didn't, for such a quick getaway most certainly meant he was needed elsewhere. Ret secured the kayak, walked up the dock, and entered the house through the backdoor.

"There you are, Ret," Pauline greeted him cheerfully from the kitchen. "How was your day at the power plant?"

Exhausted in body and mind, Ret slumped into a chair. "It wasn't really what I was expecting, I guess," he said.

"I know what you mean," she said, rinsing some greens. "I still remember when I went there decades ago on a fieldtrip with my middle school. It wasn't exactly a pleasant experience, but I certainly learned a lot, although I can't seem to remember anything besides the fact that we went—"

"Ret!" Ana interjected in epiphany. "Are you *sunburned?*"

Ret looked at Ana like she was crazy. She shot from her seat and gently pressed her fingers on Ret's arm. Indeed, his normally pale and sunburn-resistant skin glowed with a bright, pink hue.

"Now I've seen everything," said Ana.

"Just what exactly happened at the plant today, Ret?" Pauline asked with interest.

Replied Ret, "Let's just say nuclear physics and I don't mix."

Little did he know.

CHAPTER 4

BACK TO SCHOOL
WITH A BANG

Nothing seems to put an end to summer better than the first day back to school. The recess transpired quite quickly for Ana and Paige, whose volleyball practices had consumed their last few weeks of it, but the time dragged on for Ret, agonizing every day over the lack of progress with the Oracle.

By and large, it was shaping up to be a painfully normal day. The ordinary, yellow bus came chugging down the Coopers' street at the usual time, its driver wearing his patch clasped over the same eye as always. As he had many times before, Ret wondered yet again how a person with an eye patch could get a job as a school bus driver. Then, finding their typical seat, they commenced the standard route to school, frequently interrupted by all of the usual stops, before arriving at Tybee High, which hadn't changed at all over the summer.

The only thing that felt out of the ordinary for Ret occurred when he spotted the power plant through his closed window on the bus. With his hand, he wiped away some of the condensation that had built up on his side of the glass, brought on by the humid air and body heat. Its domed containment structure rising above the tree line, the plant had never meant much to him before, but ever since his experience alongside the reactor with Lionel, the concrete monolith had taken on an unsettling meaning for Ret—like that feeling you get simply by looking at a food you once regurgitated.

Ret and Ana waited in line to retrieve their class schedules, then squeezed through the throngs of students in search of Paige.

"What class do you have first hour, Ret?" Paige asked as the two of them followed Ana to find their lockers.

"Trigonometry, with Mr. Jackson," Ret answered, studying his schedule.

"Trigo-what?" said Ana.

"You're taking trig as a sophomore?" Paige questioned with a mix of amazement and admiration.

"That's what it says," Ret said, consulting his schedule again to make sure he hadn't misread it. "Is that good or something?"

"It's great!" Ana cheered. "You can do my pre-algebra homework this year—yuck!" They had arrived at their lockers, three in a row. "I mean, why would I even want to *take* pre-algebra? Once I'm done with that, then it's on to actual algebra." With her textbooks piled in her arms, Ana moved to open her locker. "It's a conspiracy, I tell you. A never-ending—"

Ana gasped and slammed her locker shut. Her books crashed to the ground. Ret and Paige looked at her with alarm. A look of utter terror had seized her face. With both hands, she maintained pressure on her closed locker door. Paige bent down to pick up Ana's books amid curious glares from nearby students.

"Are you okay?" Ret asked Ana softly.

She mouthed her reply: "Bomb."

"What?"

"There's a bomb in my locker," Ana whispered slowly through her teeth.

"Let me see," Ret requested, somewhat disbelievingly.

Like peeking into the cage of a dangerous animal, Ret peered into Ana's locker, with Paige trying to look over his shoulder. Ana may have exaggerated in calling it a bomb, but it certainly was an explosive of some kind.

"It's not a *bomb,* Ana," said Ret, employing a confident tone that ridiculed her hasty jump to conclusions. "It's just a firecracker."

"Seems a little big for a firecracker, don't you think, Dr. Pyro?" she said doubtfully, calling Ret's bluff.

"Okay, okay," he admitted, "but it's no taller than your average bottle rocket, though it *is* quite a bit wider. And look: you don't have to light it—just pull this pin." Ret nearly removed the firework from the locker to show them its features, but Ana shoved it back into its hiding place.

"What, do you want the whole world to see or something?" she protested, shutting her locker sharply. A few students with lockers in the vicinity gave the trio peculiar stares.

"Wait, look!" said Paige with eagerness. "I saw something." With reluctance, Ana opened her locker just wide enough for their three heads to steal a glance inside. Paige pointed to the side of the unmarked firework, where a warning sticker read, "May cause serious injury or death." Then, below the statement, someone had scribbled the words, "'Bomb' voyage!"

"That's my dad's handwriting," Paige observed suspiciously, referring to the pun.

"Oh no," said Ana with utter refusal. "There's no way I'm going to set this thing off."

"But Ana," Ret pled, "remember when you said you'd get in trouble to see if the chest is still—"

"I said I'd get in *trouble,* not blow up the whole school," she pointed out. "For all we know, this could be a stick of dynamite." Her last word earned her some additional attention in the hallway, so she lowered her voice. "If *you* want to check on that chest so bad, then *you* can detonate Coy's bomb." The bell rang, signaling the start of the first class of the day, and Ana stormed off.

Throughout the day, Ret did all he could to wear down Ana's resolve. On the back of each new syllabus he received, he wrote her a note and slipped it into her notebook when their paths crossed between classes. "It's not a bomb," he wrote on the syllabus for his English class. "It's a harmless firework. Just light it outside. It'll go straight up and explode." Or, in between the grading matrix for his history class, he wrote, "Please, Ana! I need to know what's inside that chest. Remember: 'Cure the world'? It's for the greater good." By the end of the fifth hour, however, Ana had made no concessions, so Ret appealed to Paige in a note he gave her before the last class of the day began. "I need your help," he wrote. "Can you convince her? Please?"

With Ret's note in hand, Paige met Ana at their lockers to put their books away before heading out to volleyball. The firework stood in the back corner of Ana's locker, hidden behind her pre-algebra textbook.

"You know, Ana," said Paige, "I'm not encouraging you to get in trouble, but I think it would mean a lot to Ret if you—"

"Oh give it a rest, big P," Ana sighed. "I was always going to set off the bomb. I just like to give Ret a run for his money so that he thinks he owes me." Paige smiled at her best friend's cleverness. "After this, he'll be doing the dishes for months!" She grabbed the firework and concealed it in her bundle of volleyball clothes.

Once she had gotten dressed in her uniform in the girls' locker room, however, Ana was encountering great difficulty in hiding such an awkward object.

"Quick, Paige," bade Ana, "go and get me a ball or something so I can hide this thing." Paige scurried over to where the volleyballs were kept, snuck one out, and had almost returned to Ana when someone confronted her.

"Those stay here," barked Brittany Ashton, the volleyball team captain. "We're doing conditioning today." It was with considerable dismay that Paige and Ana accepted the news that Miss Carmen had selected Brittany as the new captain. Their first run-in with Brittany took place last year at the football game where Ret had first become aware of his powers and buried her in dirt. Yes, Brittany Ashton was the ticket-taker girl that night, and ever since that event, she seemed to harbor ill-will toward the three of them. In an unspoken sort of way, Brittany felt she could bully them out of prolonged blackmail since she was privy to Ret's secret, about which she apparently hadn't told anyone. For an upper-classman, she was certainly a person of low class.

"What have you got there, Cooper?" Brittany asked suspiciously of Ana, noticing her unusual behavior in the locker room.

"Oh, nothing," said Ana playfully. "Just my secret weapon. It's why I'm so good on the court." Brittany took a few steps closer until she was in their faces.

"I don't know how you two got on my team," she sneered threateningly, "especially *you,*" singling out Paige, "but I plan to do everything in my power to make sure you get kicked *off* my team —," then addressing Ana specifically, "even if you *are* Miss Carmen's favorite." They watched Brittany strut out of the locker room, then listened to the whistles and flirtations of the ogling jocks outside.

"I'd like to point *this* in her general direction," Ana said with scorn, clutching the firework.

"Come on," Paige insisted, rolling her eyes at Ana's emotions. "Wrap it in this." She handed Ana a page from the school newspaper sitting on the floor. "Let's get this over with."

They hurried out the door and ran off to join their teammates, who had gathered in the center of the football field amid runners on the track that encircled it.

"Now's your chance!" Paige instructed. "Do it now!"

"Now?" Ana worried, wavering in her resolve. "In plain sight? Everyone can see me!"

"Just pull the pin and drop it!"

"What is this, a grenade or something?" Ana said to stall. "There, I pulled the pin. Now what? *Now what?*" Her anxiety was making her irrational.

"GET RID OF IT!" Paige yelled. "Drop it! Throw it!"

Ana let out a terrified yelp before tossing the firework in a trashcan they passed as they continued their jog to the field. Not knowing what to expect next, she and Paige sprinted away from the explosive, out of breath by the time they joined their team on the football field.

"Excellent sprint, ladies," Miss Carmen complimented them. "You run like the school is on fire. Perhaps I'll have you demonstrate for us later. You can show your teammates how it's done."

"Sure thing, coach," Ana pledged between breaths. She could almost hear Brittany growling as she passed in front of her.

As the team continued to stretch, Ana and Paige looked over at the trashcan frequently, on pins and needles. They were just about ready to call the bomb a dud when they started to see smoke rising from inside the trashcan.

"Is it supposed to do that?" Ana whispered to Paige, who shrugged her shoulders.

A few seconds later, the trashcan erupted in flames, which swished and swirled as they consumed the rubbish within. Then, without any warning at all, the trashcan sped away across the ground. Remaining upright, it zoomed through the soccer field, knocking people over like a pinball machine.

"Did you throw it in sideways?" Paige wondered. Ana only glared at her with innocence and alarm.

As if under a magic spell, the flying trashcan, still standing up and flaming wildly, whizzed onto the baseball diamond, where it scooted into the pitching mound and fell onto its side. Now rolling uncontrollably, the trashcan was spewing its contents, leaving a trail of burning garbage in its wake.

Finally, the bewitched trashcan was stopped when it ran into the homerun fence of the baseball field, but the force of the firework's propulsion sent the projectile skyward. Like an infrared homing missile chasing a drunken bumblebee, the airborne trashcan looped and zigzagged above the fields.

At this point, the spectacle had drawn quite a crowd; in fact, every pair of eyes on the fields was watching the kamikaze garbage can with great interest. When the trashcan firework started climbing straight up, Ana and Paige breathed a sigh of relief, hoping it would finally explode. But then it made a sharp reversal midair and began hurtling downward. Screams filled the air as everyone scattered for shelter, no one knowing where it would strike. When it became clear the misfired rocket was heading straight for the football field, all the girls on the volleyball team scrambled chaotically to avoid the impending impact. With a rush of air and a flash of light, the trashcan collided with the earth, and the firework exploded in a wave of heat and sparks.

The members of the volleyball team had been thrown to the ground, where they now coughed and squinted amid smoke.

"Paige, are you okay?" Ana asked out loud.

"Yeah," her nearby voice wheezed.

All around them, the grass cackled and smoldered. While the breeze was blowing away much of the smoke, it was also fanning a fire on the ground. Soon, the whole field had taken fire, no thanks to the months of heat that had severely dried out the entire island. Backing away from the flames that surrounded them, the team met in the center of the field, unsure of what to do.

Meanwhile, Mrs. Murphy had just started explaining the curriculum for Ret's science class this year when the fire alarm went off. Ret and his classmates looked around, unsure if the alarm was part of a drill or a prank—or, most uncommonly, an actual fire. Then they heard a giddy student, skipping down the hall, shouting, "The school's on fire! The school's on fire!" Panic enveloped the school.

"Calm down, students," Mrs. Murphy said, trying to contain her part of the uproar. "Follow me on our evacuation route."

As the rest of the student body spilled out of the school, Ret set out in search of Ana, assuming she had set something on fire by detonating Mr. Coy's firework.

He rushed to the gymnasium, knowing she and Paige had volleyball during their sixth hour. It was empty. He struggled to think clearly with the fire alarm piercing his ears.

Ret dashed outside to the fields, determined to make sure Ana and Paige were safe. That was when he saw the football field, sending up a cloud of smoke from the fire that had encircled the volleyball team.

Ret hastened toward the scene. With nothing but grass for fuel, the flames were not very tall, but they were high enough to intimidate and prevent a band of high school girls from jumping across them, especially since they were outfitted in such short shorts.

"Ret!" Ana cried. "Help us!"

Ret raised his hands, intending to cast up streams of dirt to extinguish the fire by smothering the flames. But instead of commanding the dirt, he commanded the fire. Without really meaning to, Ret parted the flames like a curtain, creating a safe opening several feet wide. Ana and Paige were the first to pass through the gap, with the rest of the team following close behind.

By the time the last teammate had reached safety, the fire department had showed up and commenced putting out the fire on the field. The team members withdrew themselves from the action to a place away from the smoke where they could breathe fresh air and rest.

Amid so much excitement and danger, no one paid much attention to what Ret had done. But, with elation building in his bones, Ret looked down at the palm of his left hand and confirmed the thrilling news that he was suspecting.

"Is everyone okay?" Mr. Kirkpatrick, the assistant principal, asked upon arriving at the scene. Then, once it had been confirmed that no one was hurt, he inquired, "Does anyone know who caused this?"

"It was Ana," Brittany squealed, immediately stepping up with information. She pointed at the girl who she claimed was the culprit. "She did it." All eyes turned to Ana.

"Do you deny these accusations, Miss Cooper?" Mr. Kirkpatrick asked.

"Alright, I confess," Ana admitted dramatically, melting in her own self-pity. "I'm guilty. Take me away, take me away." Everything was going according to plan.

"The police will be here shortly to pick you up," said Mr. Kirkpatrick.

"The police?" Ana balked. "You mean I'm being arrested? What am I, a criminal?"

"We'll leave that for the authorities to decide." He escorted her back toward the school.

"Come on, Mr. K," Ana petitioned as the two of them left the scene. "It was just a harmless prank—you know, first day and all…"

The rest of the crowd watched as the pair disappeared into the school.

"Well this is bad," Ret mumbled to Paige, in awe at what had just taken place.

"Yeah," Paige agreed. "Mrs. Cooper's not going to like this."

Had the school not been evacuated, Ana would have made quite a scene as Mr. Kirkpatrick pulled her into the main offices. Apparently, no one had told her to come quietly.

"But sir," she begged relentlessly, "don't you think this is a little extreme? I mean, detention sounds more reasonable. I'll even compromise and settle with suspension. But arrest?"

"I'm sorry, Ana," Mr. Kirkpatrick sympathized, "but Principal Stone is not on campus today, and *he* is the one who assesses the severity of these kinds of violations and then extends the punishment—not me." Arriving at his office, he turned to face Ana. "In his absence, I have been instructed to turn wrongdoers over to local law enforcement until the principal takes action. Now please, wait here *quietly* until the police arrive." He motioned for her to sit in one of the chairs outside his office.

Ana slumped into a chair. "Just my luck," she murmured to herself. "I go to the trouble of setting his school on fire—the best prank this school has ever seen!—, and Stone's not even here to witness it. Well isn't this just great? I mean, what kind of principal skips the first day of school? That miserable little—"

"Quietly, Miss Cooper," an annoyed Mr. Kirkpatrick reminded her from within his office.

Ana spent the next several moments thinking how she might overcome the obstacle of Principal Stone's absence. In the midst of her scheming, she realized she was sitting directly in front of Stone's office. Then, noticing the small window installed within the door, she cheered, "Bingo!" She crept up to the door and peered through the window. But Stone's office was pitch black.

"Just like his heart," Ana muttered to herself. Had the drapes been drawn, there may have been enough light to determine whether or not the chest was still inside.

Even though she knew it was a long shot, Ana tried the doorknob. After tinkering with it a few times, she came to the unfortunate conclusion: "Yep, locked."

"What are you doing?" Mr. Kirkpatrick asked, appearing at Ana's side. She was still clutching the doorknob.

"Uh..." she stammered, "I thought I heard something—someone—in this office, here—right here, this office, in front of me." Mr. Kirkpatrick shot her a perplexed glare.

"There's no one in this office," he reaffirmed. "It's been locked all day."

"Are you *sure* about that?" Ana questioned him slyly, raising one eyebrow to remind him of her recent criminality. An air of suspicion came over him, and he unlocked the door to Stone's office. He opened the door and turned on the light just long enough to help him feel reassured. Then he quickly shut it, affording Ana more than enough time to see what she needed to see.

"Yes," he said assertively, "I'm sure. And there's the police now." Ana turned to see a pair of officers walking up to the front of the school.

○   ○   ○

"Ana Cooper!" Pauline announced as she stormed into the police station. "What in the world were you thinking, young lady? *Were* you even thinking at all? Why would you do such a thing? How did you *get* such a thing in the first place? No mother should have to bail her own child out of jail. I feed you, I clothe you, I bend over backwards for you, and *this* is how you thank me?"

If anyone had been sleeping at the time Pauline entered the station, they certainly weren't sleeping anymore. Pauline continued to rant at her child, much to Ana's embarrassment. Ana was well aware of her mother's tendency to overreact to new things, but

Pauline's reaction to the infraction was almost as uncalled for as the infraction itself. As Ana sat timidly by the front desk, she could spy out of the corner of her eye several police officers peeking into the room to see what all the commotion was about. Pauline's raving didn't stop until one of the officers asked her a question.

"Hey," he yelled so she could hear him, "aren't you that lady from the school board meeting?"

Pauline instantly fell silent, recognizing the officer as the guard who had carried her out of the meeting. All of the humiliation from her ill-fated faceoff with the school board suddenly returned. The frustration in her eyes faded into sadness as many of the other officers recognized her as "that crazy woman" or "Ms. Cooper, the loopy old bat."

"Like mother like daughter, eh?" the initial cop joked. Soon, the entire station was rolling with laughter. Pauline, feeling like a failure at home and in society, sunk into the chair next to Ana. They leaned against each other, waiting to see who would shed the first tear.

The last person either of the Cooper women wanted or expected to see waltz through the station door was Principal Stone. Tall and commanding, he burst through the double doors and marched to the front desk.

"Why is this young woman in handcuffs?" Stone demanded of the officer in charge. He was leaning over the counter so far that the officer bent backward in fear. "She is one of my students. This is completely inappropriate. I order you to release her, this instant." The cowering officer obediently unlocked Ana's handcuffs.

Suddenly, the police chief appeared around the corner. Not noticing Stone, he saw one of his men releasing Ana and slapped him upside the head.

"What do you think you're doing?" the chief interrogated rashly. "Fraternizing with the accused, are we?" When everyone remained motionless, he glanced at his officer.

"Stone, sir," the subordinate mumbled almost inaudibly to his superior, jerking his head slightly in the direction of the principal.

"Why, Principal Stone!" the chief greeted warmly, suddenly behaving as he ought to. "What brings you to our station this fine evening?"

"We were just leaving." Pauline and Ana rose from their seats and exited the building ahead of Stone.

"Don't think this changes anything, Stone," Pauline jeered. "Where were you when I spoke to the school board? Now this whole town believes I'm a lunatic! Why won't you tell them the truth? They all think you're some king when, really, you and I know exactly what you are: a liar, a cheat, a fraud!"

"You're welcome, ladies," Stone replied coolly as he stepped into his car. "Have a pleasant evening."

"You're the criminal here, Stone," Pauline continued to shout after him. *"You're* the one who belongs behind bars!"

Their drive home began in loud silence. As the car passed under each streetlight, Ana was given momentary glimpses of her mother's face. She looked old and worn—like a well-used pair of shoes. Heavy bags hung under her eyes, which she never tried to hide with makeup. Ana felt awful for the stress she had inflicted on her dear mother, but, at the same time, she defended her actions as a service rendered in Ret's behalf.

"Did Coy put you up to this?" Pauline asked, her voice void of any energy.

"Yes."

"Did you accomplish what you set out to do?" Her tone was one of pure exhaustion.

"Yes."

"Well then," Pauline concluded, "at least *some* good came out of this."

Ana waited for a few seconds before saying, "Mom, I'm sorry—"

"That makes two of us, dear."

As soon as Ana stepped inside the house, she called out for Ret.

"Ret, I have something to tell you."

"So do I," came his reply from upstairs.

Despite the tiring events of the day, Ana eagerly

climbed the staircase and pushed open the door to Ret's bedroom. Almost simultaneously, they spewed the exciting news that each of them wanted to tell the other.

Ana reported, "The chest in Stone's office is gone."

And Ret, holding up his left hand, said, "Take a look at this."

CHAPTER 5

STONE'S KEEP

It was late in the afternoon when Principal Stone finally packed his things and exited Tybee High at the end of his workday. Compared to the grimace he employed each morning upon arriving at work, his overall appearance seemed to exude a hint of cheer now that he was leaving. He walked to his car, an eye-catching and exceedingly shiny hot rod that was always parked in the space nearest the school's entrance on account of, as the students hypothesized, either seniority or display.

Sitting atop one of the many palmetto trees in the staff parking lot was Mr. Coy, determined to discover the new location of the second trunk after learning through Paige the results of Ana's mission. Having climbed to his perch early that morning, he was relieved to learn that Stone was leaving at last, as the spiky fronds were digging into his hindquarters. Noting which automobile belonged to Stone, Coy retrieved a small airsoft pistol from his pocket and fired a soft-shelled pellet at Stone's car, the faint noise of the impact being concealed by the slam of the driver's door. With impressive stealth, the pellet exploded into dust upon contact, coating Stone's car with a near-invisible, magnetic film not unlike pollen.

When Stone had peeled out of the parking lot and driven a block or so away, which didn't take long given his apparent need for speed, Mr. Coy carefully rose to his feet, put on a pair of sunglasses, and stuck out his arms like a swimmer preparing to jump from a diving board. In each hand, he gripped a sort of handle with a button, which he then pressed. A pair of long wings shot out from the pack on his back and adhered to his arms. As soon as the wings extended, they caught the wind, and Mr. Coy was airborne.

Coy would merely have been a thrill-seeking hang glider if it weren't for his special glasses. Besides allowing him to see the world in a darker shade, they also picked up the signals being transmitted from the dust particles on Stone's car, causing it to glow like neon in Coy's scope. High above the trees, Mr. Coy followed Principal Stone, looking like a soaring superhero but not a giant bird on account of his see-through wings.

Leaving Tybee, Mr. Coy had to pick up the pace as Stone entered the highway. After heading west, he went south for several miles, then turned eastward, crossed the bridge onto Skidaway Island, and disappeared soon thereafter. Coy's glasses went blank as Stone fell completely off his radar.

He tapped his glasses several times, hoping it was just a glitch. When it appeared his eyewear wasn't at fault, he complained, "Tracking dust is supposed to be superior—it's impossible to fully remove!" He began his descent, intending to land where he had last seen Stone's tracker on the map before it vanished. Just as his feet were about to make contact with the ground, his wings recoiled, and he immediately looked around to see where he was.

Mr. Coy was standing in the middle of a residential street—the kind that doesn't see enough traffic to deserve white or yellow lines painted on it. It was not a wide road, becoming ever narrower from the accumulating dirt and creeping weeds along its edges. The desperate roots of mighty oaks had cracked the asphalt in many spots, and their broad limbs cast shadows in the twilight that swallowed the road from view not very far in both directions.

Mr. Coy turned to his side to face the only house he could see for quite some distance, relieved to find Stone's car parked in the driveway. Visually, it was an impressively attractive establishment. The long driveway, outlined on both sides with box shrubs, led to a broad porch, where hanging baskets and flowerpots overflowed with colorful foliage amid rocking chairs that seemed hardly used. The home's brick façade, stacked with stones that appeared hewn by hand, gave the house a strong and sturdy appeal. Its large windows afforded its owners sweeping views of the perfectly manicured grounds. All in all, it was a property fit for a public-pleasing and educator-entertaining principal, though Coy found it painfully blah.

It was surrounded by an extensive fence whose sole entrance was the gate directly in front of Mr. Coy. Cautiously, he approached the closed gate, at the foot of which lay the ashen remnants of something that had been incinerated. Upon closer examination, he saw the remains of his tracking dust, a few of the particles twitching with their final breath of electricity.

His face just inches from the gate, Mr. Coy saw an insect fly past him and then through the bars of the gate. There was a tiny flash of electricity, followed by a noise like a cackle, and the bug, now reduced to ashes, flittered to the ground.

Mr. Coy took a wary step backwards, realizing the gate and the rest of the fence stood immediately adjacent to a wall of electricity—a blanket-like laser beam that scorched whatever passed through it.

"I wonder if he owns a convertible," Coy humored himself. "Now I know why his car is so shiny—must be

some special coating that repels electrical impulses."
Then, thinking for a moment, he said, "Either that or
some black market Turtle Wax."

Wanting to learn the extent of this obstacle, he
glanced upwards and watched as dozens of zaps were
taking place almost constantly due to insects and other
debris that were colliding with the invisible, protective
dome that covered the expanse of the property.

From the front pocket of his pack, Mr. Coy
retrieved two metal devices: one looked like a lead pipe
and the other resembled an extra large dinner plate. He
inserted the pipe through the hole in the center of the
plate and locked it in place. Pulling from both ends, the
pipe elongated several feet like a retractable antenna,
with the plate uncoiling and wrapping around the bottom
half of the pipe as an inclined plane. A cross between a
pogo stick and a screw, Mr. Coy stood atop his earth-
drilling auger and started manually rotating himself.
Each twist brought fresh dirt to the surface and sent him
a few inches deeper into the ground.

"Like I always say," he said to himself, now a few
feet under the ground, "I never was one to *over*achieve."

Not wanting to run the risk of getting fatally singed
by the front yard's force field, Mr. Coy set out to dig his
way under the fence, hoping he would reach safety on
the other side since Principal Stone apparently had.
Coy's head had slipped nearly a dozen feet below

ground level when his drilling suddenly became quite difficult and took on a much different sound. Wondering if he had struck a rock or perhaps the sewage line, he found he was still able to twist the auger. Without any warning, something gave way, and he came crashing down the hole, through a ceiling, and onto a floor.

A bit shaken up, Mr. Coy slowly rose to his feet and dusted himself off. He was quite perplexed to find himself in a room. The size of a small bedroom, it had a single light bulb that hung by a string from the center of the ceiling. Of most interest, however, was the stuff inside the room.

It was like taking a trip to the past. The walls were covered in articles and clippings from periodicals all across the world, collected from major cities and rural towns, written in a variety of languages. Yet each proclaimed the same headline story of man's first lunar landing. There was a cassette tape on a nearby shelf labeled "Copy of Nixon's Phone Call to Moon." Next to a schematic of some Soviet spacecraft called "Luna 15" was a map of Vietnam and a portrait of a General Wheeler. A letter, written in some type of Chinese dialect, had a note scribbled at the top that said its content pertained to the U.S. easing restrictions against Red China. A scorecard showed how Montreal beat the New York Mets 3-2. A model of an Israeli air fighter hung from the ceiling.

Even for a man as eccentric as Mr. Coy, it seemed odd for Principal Stone to have an entire room dedicated to what appeared to be the happenings on a single day in history. But in addition to the day's top stories, there was evidence all around that even the tiniest, most globally insignificant events had not gone unnoticed. There were index cards pinned to the wall that told how a specific person did a certain thing at this place and at that time. There were sticky notes listing the progress of a gang or the divorce of a family or the unresolved robbing of a bank. Mr. Coy opened a filing cabinet in which each country in the world had its own hanging file folder where scraps of paper, written in all kinds of different people's penmanship, were shoved like a receipt collection of a small business.

Despite its chaotic appearance, Mr. Coy had stumbled upon a masterfully organized system of record keeping. Every article and every picture bore evidence that it had been searched and scoured for the minutest clue or detail. Names of NASA employees had been circled and cross referenced, involving a complicated code that corresponded to other resources. Times of the Russian Luna's launch had been tracked. Attack plans had been pinpointed on the map of Vietnam, and potential flaws were noted next to Wheeler's peace plan. Attached to a write-up about an Australian mine blast was a thorough list of names and their biographical information. Hanging from the Israeli jet was a breakdown of real planes, Israeli and Egyptian, that had been casualties in the day's aerial conflict near the Suez Canal. The confidential itinerary of Nixon's upcoming visit to an all-star baseball game was given particular prominence.

All in all, it was an unsettling display of diligent stalking, a cross between the secret plotting of a mass murderer and a teenage fan's obsessive admiration of a famed star. And it acted like a bellows to Mr. Coy's suspicions. He made his way to the door and left the room. On the front of the door was the inscription "July 20, 1969." He turned around to read the caption on the door across the hall and found that it was occupied by memorabilia from another day in the same year. He glanced up and down the hall, which looked very much like it belonged in a hotel. Each room was reserved for a different day during the year 1969, never skipping or combining days. A kind of track ran down the middle of the floor as far as he could see.

Mr. Coy walked to the end of the hallway, where he encountered a walkway running perpendicular to him with the 1979 corridor beginning on the other side. He turned onto the walkway and proceeded in a direction so that the years were decreasing as he passed by them. Finally, with the 1960 hall on one side and the 1970 on the other, Mr. Coy stepped into a large foyer. It was in the shape of a decagon — a ten-sided circle with hallways beginning at the ends of each side. Directly across from him, he could see the 1910 and 1920 corridors. Each side of the room represented a decade, thus the entire floor encompassed a whole century. It was like a mind-boggling storage facility for a business conglomerate.

In the center of the circular room was a sort of unenclosed elevator shaft — a portal for a people-mover that not only traveled vertically but also laterally along the tracks that spanned all throughout the labyrinth of floors, halls, and rooms. Mr. Coy had ventured quite close to the portal when he saw the elevator coming quickly towards him. It descended from the floor above, then embarked for the 1980s.

Mr. Coy followed after the elevator. Locating it not far down the 1984 corridor, he peeked around the corner to see who or what was there. It was a woman — a very old woman whose back was so hunched that she stared at the floor when she walked. With a small stack of newspapers in her arms, she halted in front of one of the doors and rubbed her index finger across the inscription of the date. Then she opened the door and carried her load inside. When she reappeared outside, Mr. Coy watched as she seemed to spend a great deal of time feeling things. She had almost stepped into the elevator to fetch a few more things when she suddenly stopped.

"Is that you, Lester?" her feeble voice asked. Mr. Coy looked all around worriedly to see if Stone was present somewhere. When no one answered, she grabbed another load while saying, "I can hear you breathing."

Feeling relieved, Mr. Coy came out from hiding: she was blind.

"Why yes," he replied. Then, realizing his blunder, he coughed and attempted to impersonate Principal Stone. "Yes it is, uh...my lady," unsure of her name. "Please excuse my cold," he coughed again.

"Oh, Lester," she said endearingly, "how many times do I have to tell you to call me Charlotte?"

"Never again," he promised. "Once more was all I needed." He walked towards her as she continued to unload, making many trips on account of her frailty.

"Can I help you find something?" she inquired.

"Actually," Coy began thoughtfully, "yes—yes you can."

"Oh," Charlotte said, eager to help. "And what is that?"

"I'm looking for a chest—a trunk," he described, "similar to another I have."

"You mean the one you asked me to archive a few months ago?"

"Yep," Coy said anxiously. "That's the one."

"If I remember correctly," she recalled, "I filed that

in the nineteenth room of June—the day you gave it to me. Would you like me to take you to it?"

"Well of course I'd—" Mr. Coy said before catching his tongue, remembering to act like Stone even if he really had no idea how to navigate such a maze. "I mean, I'd love for you to take me to it, Charlotte."

Looking pleasantly surprised, she shut the door of the room, which belonged to March 3, 1984. Being the sightless senior that she was, Charlotte took her time stepping into the elevator. Mr. Coy extended a helping hand and guided her inside.

"Bless your heart, Lester," she said, sounding stunned. "Feeling chivalrous today, are we?" Coy deemed it best not to acknowledge his action, which was apparently uncharacteristic of Stone.

When they were both inside, the door closed, and Charlotte groped her way to the side panel. Expecting to see a huge array of buttons, Mr. Coy was shocked to see no buttons at all but instead a single clock whose face read thirty minutes past four o'clock. Confused by the time that this clock bore, Mr. Coy glanced at his watch, which differed in the amount of more than two hours later. Choosing not to vocalize his vexation, he watched Charlotte locate the hour hand by touch and then spin it clockwise.

"Let's see," she mumbled to herself, apparently thinking through something. "We need to go forward thirty-one years..." Making two full revolutions, she stopped about halfway into her third and situated the hour hand between the eleven and twelve. Each of the sixty tick marks along the circumference of the clock provided just enough resistance for her to feel her way around its face. "...Three months..." She then briefly spun the minute hand clockwise until it rested atop the nine. "...And sixteen days." Finally, she adjusted the second hand, which had stalled at forty-eight, by advancing it onward by sixteen seconds.

Dumbfounded, Mr. Coy stood in awe as the elevator departed from its previous destination of March 3, 1984, en route to the most recent June 19.

"Impressive," he remarked.

"Not bad for a blind old coot like me, eh?" she laughed, softly jabbing his side with her elbow. "When you've been doing this as long as I have, you pick up on a few things."

"Do you ever get lost?" Coy wondered, amazed by Charlotte's abilities despite her handicap. "You know, turned around?"

"Occasionally," she admitted, "but then I just clear the clock back to midnight and start fresh from today." Mr. Coy didn't quite understand.

The elevator returned to the twentieth-century foyer, then went up one floor, most of which had yet to be built. Upon arriving at their destination, the elevator door parted, and they found themselves facing the room that contained information pertaining to a day that had transpired just a couple of months ago: June 19.

"I'll be next door alphabetizing those records like you asked me to," Charlotte announced, hobbling into the room marked June 18.

"That ought to keep her busy," Coy muttered, feeling sorry that she was about to embark on a task that was impossible for her, though he was finally beginning to think like Stone.

Coy stepped into the room and found the chest sitting inside. He was quite relieved to have tracked it down at last. Kneeling in front of it, he reached into his shirt collar and pulled out a key that he was wearing on a string around his neck. It was the very key that had been discovered at the foot of the cell when Stone, Quirk, and Bubba had escaped from his yacht a few months ago. From the moment he laid eyes on it, Coy knew it was the key that would unlock Stone's second trunk. Eager to finally use it, Mr. Coy inserted the key into the large, rusted lock and turned it.

Nothing happened. It remained firmly locked. Mr. Coy was beside himself.

"Then what in the world does this key go to?!" he asked indignantly.

"You shouldn't need a key," Charlotte's sweet voice rang out from the next room. "All the doors are unlocked. You should know *that…*" Mr. Coy rolled his eyes.

He proceeded to pick the lock using the same putty that he had previously used to break into Principal Stone's office and snatch the contents of the first chest. But the semi-solid substance refused to harden; in fact, it melted soon after Mr. Coy inserted it into the lock.

"What the devil?" he muttered.

"Keep looking," Charlotte yelled. "I know it's in there."

Mr. Coy touched the chest: it felt warm. Then he touched the lock.

"Sweet mother of Abraham Lincoln!" Mr. Coy cursed upon making contact with the boiling hot lock.

"What's *she* doing in there?" Charlotte wondered of the former president's mother.

On the wall above the trunk was a handsome case containing an old hatchet. A note hanging from the wooden handle said it was purportedly the tool that George Washington used to cut down his cherry tree, sold on this day by one of his descendants at an auction. Mr. Coy ripped off the note and started whaling on the chest.

"Are you okay in there, Lester?" Charlotte asked upon hearing the sounds of wood cracking and splintering.

"Just doing a bit of remodeling," he hollered back. "That's all."

"It looked fine to *me*," she said.

Once he had cut out a large wedge from the top of the chest, Mr. Coy wrapped his hand in a nearby Lakers jersey and reached inside. He could feel the heat spewing out of the hole he had created. After a few seconds of groping, he came to the conclusion that there was only one thing within the trunk.

"Stone sure doesn't utilize space well, does he?" Mr. Coy said to himself, remembering how there was only a single piece of parchment paper in the first chest. "I bet he pays a fortune at the airport on checked baggage."

Coy removed the solitary item from the trunk. It was a rock—a large, round rock that was causing his hand to sweat. It was covered in tiny holes—pores where there had once been air bubbles—which made it not very heavy. But it was dark and almost seemed to glow. A little disappointed, Coy wrapped the specimen in the jersey and stuffed it in his pack.

"Smells like fresh hickory in here," Charlotte observed, appearing in the doorway and sniffing the air. "Did you find what you needed?"

"I certainly did," Coy said, trying to play it cool.

"Virginia just informed me that supper's ready," her hand still resting on a small wireless device clipped at her waist. She turned around, stepped in front of the elevator, and held out her arm, unlinked as if ready for Mr. Coy to assist her again. "Shall we?"

"We shall," said Coy, ready to make his getaway and glad that he wouldn't have to find his own way out of such a baffling network of doors, floors, and hallways.

Charlotte located the clock and began working its gears as the ones inside her own brain computed the math. She pushed the minute hand to the twelve, causing the hour hand to do the same, and then pulled back the second hand four notches. She had instructed the machine to take them ahead three months and back four days. Now Mr. Coy understood what she had meant by clearing the clock back to midnight: it represented the present day.

The elevator took them horizontally for a few seconds, then changed course and rose upward very briefly, passing through darkness. When it came to a stop, there appeared to be a tall and narrow doorway in front of them, as if they were standing inside some sort of glass cupboard. Charlotte led the way, stepping out of the elevator and pushing open the door. Mr. Coy mimicked her every move and realized, now on the other side, that they had just passed through a large grandfather clock whose time read twelve o'clock. They were standing in the living room of Principal Stone's house.

"Ingenious," Mr. Coy whispered in awe.

"You said it," Charlotte agreed, smelling delicious aroma in the air. "Virginia's lasagna is simply divine. You know, she once told me the secret is in the..." She continued talking as she slowly made her way to the dining room, Mr. Coy too enthralled in analyzing Stone's home to pay much attention to what she was saying. It was a delightful place, professionally designed and elegantly furnished. There was not so much as one smudge on the walls or a single crumb on the carpet. It was almost a bit too immaculate, as if they were trying to cover up something.

Mr. Coy wondered if dinner would be cold and stale by the time Charlotte arrived, so slowly did she hobble along. On their way out of the living room, Mr. Coy saw someone he recognized in a framed photograph sitting next to a lamp on a small table. He left Charlotte's side and went to examine it.

"Dr. Cross?" he said with great consternation. Then his attention shifted to the other person in the picture, the man with whom Dr. Cross was shaking hands. *"Stone?* What business does Dr. Cross have with *Stone?"*

Just then, a loud voice caused Mr. Coy to nearly drop the picture frame.

"Les, dinner's ready!"

"Coming, Virginia!"

Mr. Coy scrambled to hide as he heard Stone's loud footsteps coming up the hallway toward the living room.

Meanwhile, Charlotte was still babbling. "...And then she puts a final layer of cheese on top and broils it to a crisp! I tell you, Virginia is a magician in the kitchen."

"Charlotte," said Stone, arriving in the living room and finding Charlotte alone, "who are you talking to?"

"Why, Lester, I'm talking to *you,* of course," she said, a little offended.

Suspecting something out of the ordinary, Stone frantically began searching his house for an intruder. He stopped cold when he found Mr. Coy sitting peacefully at the dining room table. He had served himself a hearty helping of lasagna from the casserole dish, which sat in the center of the table between two lit candles.

"You know, Les," Coy said between bites, "I must say the extra ricotta is a nice touch, but do tell Virginia the sauce could use a bit more salt."

"What are you doing in my house?" Stone asked through his teeth, beside himself to find Coy sitting at his dinner table, eating his food. Virginia emerged from the kitchen to see what was going on.

"Your sweet Charlotte invited me to dinner," Coy explained unhurriedly, "but I think I'll take mine to go." Mr. Coy grabbed the casserole dish and flung its contents onto Principal Stone. Amid his shouts of outrage and Virginia's screams of fright, Coy pulled out two rocket boosters from his pack and strapped them to the long sides of the dish. Then he grabbed the candles, used their flames to light his fuses, and jumped into the dish, gripping the handles on its short sides and squatting to stabilize himself.

Mr. Coy turned to Stone, who was still wiping tomato sauce from his eyes, and asked, "Have you ever—*Ben Coy?*" The boosters ignited, propelling Mr. Coy off the table, through the window, and across the back lawn. Reaching the end of the grass, he held on for dear life as the terrain changed from land to water. He was now skidding across a murky swamp, dodging rotting tree stumps and thick patches of reeds. With his sights always set on the path ahead, Mr. Coy's heart sank when he saw the sky flickering with occasional pulses of electricity and remembered the laser bubble that enclosed the entirety of Stone's property. With a mere hundred yards to act, his distress doubled when a colony of crocodiles gathered to form an impassable line at the foot of the bubble.

Hoping it would prevent him from either being vaporized or digested, Mr. Coy pushed the front of the casserole dish down while simultaneously pulling the back of it up. He held his breath as he went underwater, passing under the crocs and the beam. He gradually tilted himself the opposite way until he had returned to the surface and was surfing safely away. Then he extended his wings and took to the skies, the casserole dish speeding out to sea.

"I suppose I owe Virginia a replacement dish," he smirked.

Mr. Coy soared northeasterly toward Little Tybee Island, a part of whose cliffside had been carved out to form a tunneled airstrip, its entrance masked by a hologram. He flew through the false wall into the enclosed passageway and landed on the runway.

Back at the Stone residence, Virginia was helping to peel large strips of lasagna noodles from her husband's face.

"My word, Lester!" said Charlotte, finally arriving in the dining room. "Can't your remodeling wait until after dinner?" She had heard the shattering of the window. "I mean, really, first the room in the Keep, and now this?"

CHAPTER 6

TRUE LOVE
BURNS DEEP

Ret had to brush a bunch of leaves out of the kayak before he and Ana could climb inside on their way to Coy Manor. This wasn't on account of infrequent use but rather that fall was in full swing. Yet, despite all the autumnal evidence around them, summer seemed to be clinging to the temperature. So far, it had been the hottest October the island had ever recorded, and although Ret didn't mind the prolonged warmth, it felt unusual to him, like something was askew. He wondered if nature might be trying to convey some message, like a parcel carrier returning day after day in waning attempts to deliver a package to an unresponsive addressee.

It was with a bit of suspense that Ret and Ana trekked up their usual dusty path on the east face of Little Tybee Island toward the Manor.

"Did Mr. Coy say anything about *why* he wanted to talk to us?" Ret asked.

"No, Ret," Ana replied, sounding as if she had answered the question before. "All Paige said was that her dad has something to show us."

"It probably has nothing to do with the scar since it stopped glowing before we were able to show it to him," Ret reasoned. "Do you think he found Stone's second trunk? Or maybe the Oracle did something new?"

"Whatever it is, we need to make it snappy," Ana ordered. "Paige and I have a big game today."

Having informed Paige of their proximity, they passed through the gate and hiked up the long walkway to the wide steps that led to the large double doors.

"Dad's in the planetarium," said Paige, greeting her friends in the semicircular foyer and quickly chauffeuring them through one of the many shadowed doorways along the arc of the entry. Ret purposely avoided the center of the room to keep himself from bumping into the invisible bust of Grandmother Coy.

They hurried down a long hallway. Their pace slowed, however, when the path ahead showed a sudden downgrade like a hillside. Since the walls were clear, it was quite easy to see that they were following the natural slope of the island. While the corridor was set in the ground, the ceiling stretched all the way to the dirt line, staying mostly covered with the exception of the occasional skylight. At the end of the hall, intertidal waves licked the other side of the transparent wall like a half-filled fish tank, informing them that they had reached sea level.

As their guide, Paige immediately started descending the spiral staircase, its first step flush with the floor at the end of the hallway. Ana did the same, but Ret paused for a moment to observe the large, glass pipe that was channeling ocean water through the side of the wall and down the hollow center of the spiral staircase. In a steady supply, the waves rushed seawater horizontally into the pipe and then vertically like some sort of freefall. Ret dashed down the stairs, interested to know the water's fate.

"I hope there's an elevator for the return trip," Ana moaned wearily as the staircase spiraled onward with its end nowhere in sight.

"It's warming us up for the game," Paige said brightly.

"If you say so, girl."

Meanwhile, Ret's gaze kept switching, back and forth, from his next step at his feet to the clear tube at his side. Its contents seemed to pick up speed every second, plunging downward like a bottled waterfall.

Reaching the end of the stairway, Ana let out a loud sigh of accomplishment. It was a small room, not unlike the bottom of a typical stairwell. There was a single doorway where a stiff curtain was drawn. The long pipe continued through the floor, where Ret could hear the loud sloshing of churning waters. Paige slipped through the curtain, and the Coopers followed.

They stepped into outer space—at least, that's what it seemed like. In a room that was at least the size of a sports arena floated a giant replica of the solar system. The only light came from a large sun, which rotated in the center while each planet, its size to scale with the sun, revolved around it. Thick pylons sat above and beneath the sun, connecting to it only with an electrical current that spanned the gaps. The perpetual current exhibited such great voltage and energy that it completely engulfed the sun in flames, making it easy to identify.

"What in the world?" Ana gasped, her hands frantically feeling her earlobes. "My earrings just flew out of my ears!"

"Oh, sorry," Paige apologized with a laugh. "I should've warned you: the walls are giant magnets." Ret looked around and was somewhat astounded to notice how the wall beside them quickly curved into blackness in all directions, making it impossible to see the floor or ceiling, not unlike true outer space. "It's how Dad's planets stay in orbit."

"Good thing I wasn't particularly fond of that pair," Ana said sarcastically, finding where her earrings had come to rest on the wall above their heads, out of reach.

Just then, Saturn passed right in front of them.

"Holy space monkeys!" Ana shouted, startled by how closely the large, ringed planet had rolled past them. "This place is a nightmare!"

"No, it's not, Ana," Paige said encouragingly. "This platform is magnetic, too." She tapped her foot to signify that she was referring to the small platform they were standing on, which jutted out of the side of the room. "It provides just enough attraction to pull each planet barely out of its individual orbit yet close enough for someone to get on."

"You mean you *ride* these things?" Ana asked, now beside herself. "Like a pony?"

"Of course," said Paige. Then, pointing to the other side of the room, she added, "Dad's on Uranus."

"He's on my *what?*" asked Ana alarmingly.

"Hello, fellow astronauts!" Mr. Coy shouted from across the solar system. He was affixed spread-eagle to one of the planets, looking very much like he belonged in the circus as the human target on the spinning wheel at which knives are thrown. "Go ahead, get on! Take one out for a spin."

Paige led them back through the curtain to a coat closet where she dug out three metal harnesses. She showed Ret and Ana how to slip the malleable harness over the shoulders, down the back, and between the legs. All of the straps met in the center of the chest and clicked together in one clasp.

"Sweet!" Ana cheered as her harness came together.

"Rule #1: In the planetarium," Paige instructed them, "we always stay behind the curtain until ready to jump. This curtain is coated in bismuth, which is diamagnetic, so it repels the magnetic pull of an approaching planet." Though Ret was enthralled by Paige's safety seminar, Ana was bored. "Which brings me to Rule #2: Never—"

"Sounds good, Paige," Ana said, brushing her off. "But Houston just cleared me for takeoff!" Ana passed through the curtain and jumped to the edge of the magnetic platform. Then she screamed as the planet Mercury pulled her onto its surface.

"Ana—wait!" Paige called after her. Instinctively, she jumped through the curtain in an effort to stop Ana. Upon realizing what planet she was on, Paige yelled, "That's Rule #2: Never get on Mercury because—" But Paige was interrupted when the next planet rolled by the platform. She turned and exerted herself against the pull of the magnetic planet. Still behind the curtain, Ret peaked through it and reached to grab Paige's hand but to no avail. Her escape was halted, then she stood motionless for a split second before being dragged away.

"Rule #3: Always avoid Pluto," Paige persisted as she floated away, sounding defeated. Just by observing Paige, Ret understood the rationale behind the third rule. True to its identity, the sphere representing Pluto in Mr. Coy's model was pathetically small—no larger than a basketball. With great difficulty, Paige clung to the planet she was coerced to ride, nearly enveloping it with her bear hug of a grip.

Ret remained behind the curtain, contemplating his own jump, but was greatly distracted by the warnings that Paige was desperately trying to give to Ana. Too busy enjoying the ride, Ana's shouts of jubilation drowned out her friend's cries of caution. Finally, Paige turned to Ret.

"Ret, you've got to help Ana," she pled. "Mercury gets too close to the sun!"

Ret knew what to do. He fled from behind the curtain and jumped onto the oncoming planet.

Meanwhile, Ana was beginning to sweat. She quieted her cheering and asked, "Is it supposed to be getting hot in here?" As Mercury continued to spin on its axis, Ana was brought to face the cause of her perspiration. A shrill scream filled the universe.

"Ret!" Ana yelped. "Help!"

With each rotation, the sun drew Mercury ever closer back to its proper place along the innermost orbit.

Ana employed a never-ending cry for help, a shriek that increased in volume every time her planet moved and positioned her facing the sun.

"Come on, come *on*," Ret worried, wishing his planet would revolve faster. Ana's, however, had returned to its orbit and was now nearing the stretch on its decreed course when it would be closest to the sun.

"Ret!" Ana squealed. "Now would be a good time to do something!"

Just as Ana was beginning to feel her hair getting singed, the wall of heat radiating in front of her suddenly went cool. She opened her eyes to see the smooth, flameless surface of the sun. She sighed.

With his left hand stretched out in front of him, Ret turned the palm toward him to confirm what he was hoping: the scar was glowing once again. He kept his concentration on sparing Ana of third-degree burns, and the flames, though still engulfing the rest of the star, ceased immediately about her person, following her through the end of her orbit. When Mercury had passed by the landing platform once again, Ana released her harness and slipped onto the stationary flooring. The first one back, she collapsed in exhaustion.

Next came Ret. He dismounted from Earth and hurried to Ana's side.

"Tell me, Ret," she begged earnestly, in between breaths, "are they gone?"

"What?"

"My eyebrows," she explained dramatically. "Did they get burned off?" Ret rolled his eyes.

"Well *that* was very entertaining," said Mr. Coy, approaching the platform at the completion of his orbit. "I'd say it was the most action this galaxy has seen since the Big Bang." He released his harness, slid off his planet, and walked through the curtain. They heard the closet door shut and then saw him return with something in his hand.

"This is what I wanted to show you," said Mr. Coy, coming in closer to them.

"Oh, nice!" Ana celebrated. "I love the Lakers."

"Not the jersey," Mr. Coy corrected her. *"This!"* He pulled away the sports jersey and revealed the artifact he had pilfered from Stone's chest.

"It's a rock," Ret observed, sounding unimpressed.

"Rocks are cool," Ana inserted, trying to keep Ret's hopes alive.

"Not this one," said Coy. "This one is actually quite *hot.*" He passed it to Ana. Caught off guard, she tried to get a grip on it. Then, when she finally did, she felt its heat and quickly abandoned it like a player in a game of hot potato.

"First the sun and now this?" she asked indignantly. "What are you trying to do, burn me alive or something?" Ana paused when she noticed how Mr. Coy had his eyes glued on Ret.

Ret was wide-eyed. As soon as he received the rock from Ana, it started to glow from the inside out. A red light began to smolder from within, each of the rock's tiny pores emitting a portion of the glow. In a matter of seconds, it changed from a dying ember to a live coal. When sparks began to pop, Ret dropped the rock out of fright. It fell to the floor without a bounce and quickly died. Mr. Coy scooped it up and rewrapped it in the jersey.

"What was that?" Ret asked, stunned by what just happened.

"'A rock,' to use *your* words," said Mr. Coy, still feeling cross from Ret's initial remark. "But to use *my* words, a clue—a clue to what, I don't know. Still, it never behaved that way while in my possession, so it must fancy your scar." Mr. Coy's eyes flew to Ret's palm. "So nice of it to light up again. May I?" Ret held out his palm for Mr. Coy's inspection.

"Your guess is as good as mine," Ret said.

"Well, *I* still think it looks like a gummy bear," Ana reaffirmed.

"A gummy bear?" Coy asked.

"You know," said Ana, "the candy."

"I *love* gummy bears!" Mr. Coy said, grinning at Ana. "What's your favorite flavor?"

"It's not a gummy bear," Ret insisted, perturbed by

his associates' flippant attitudes.

"Then what is it, Ret?" Ana wanted to know.

"I don't know," he said. "It looks like a—like a—a squatting man."

"Squatting man?" Coy repeated.

"That sounds like the name of some Indian chief!" Ana teased.

"Perhaps it's a squatting bear?" Mr. Coy suggested, trying to compromise.

"Give me a break." Ret retracted his hand, now considerably annoyed. Realizing the scar meant nothing to Mr. Coy either, he focused his attention on the rock.

"Where did you get that rock?" he asked.

"It was in Stone's trunk," Mr. Coy answered.

"Oh, so you found it, eh?" Ana wondered, suddenly interested since she previously went to great lengths to track it down. "Where was the darn thing?"

"In Stone's possession."

"You mean to tell me I went to jail for a rock?"

"Wait," Ret interrupted. "What do you mean 'in Stone's possession'?"

"I mean it was at his house," said Coy, clarifying as little as possible.

"You went to his house?" Ret asked with great intrigue. "What was it like? Did you find anything else? How did you—"

Mr. Coy held up his hand to stop Ret. "*I am going

to run some tests on this rock. In the mean time, why don't *you* concentrate on figuring out the squatting gummy bear man, hmm?"

"Sounds like a plan," Ana interjected. "We've got to get going anyway; don't want to be late for our big game today. Mom's been texting me, wondering where we are." Then she cupped her hands around her mouth and yelled, "Yo, big P—let's go!"

Paige was still clinging to Pluto, looking like a sloth wrapped around a limb. Her planet moseyed along, in no rush to return its passenger. Paige replied, "Coming."

As they waited for Paige to return from orbit, Ret could hear the faint rushing of the seawater that was cascading down the tube in the stairwell. He figured now was a good time to get some answers and finally put his curiosity at ease.

"Sir," he addressed Mr. Coy, who was standing at the edge of the platform and removing used harnesses as the planets came by, "what exactly is the purpose of that pipe full of water?"

"It spins the turbine to power the generator," he answered, with no intention of expounding.

"Turbine," Ret whispered to himself. "Generator—Lionel talked about those."

"Lionel did what now?" Mr. Coy probed, his curiosity piqued.

"Lionel—he mentioned something about a turbine and a generator when he gave me a tour of the power plant," Ret explained.

"Oh he did, did he?" Mr. Coy suddenly became very defensive. "Well, did *Lionel* also tell you how the high-velocity water strikes the turbine's blades enough to spin a copper coil which rotates between magnets within the generator, *and* that the magnets give off a magnetic field full of electrons that the wire scoops up and conducts to a network of circuits? *And* does *Lionel* have an in-home system that recycles seawater to generate electricity and store it in his *own* sun—enough to power his *own* house and be completely self-reliant? Eh?! Did *Lionel* tell you *that?!*"

Silence ensued. Ret and Ana were speechless. Mr. Coy, realizing his rashness, exhaled and then stubbornly stomped off. They listened until the sound of his footsteps up the stairs could no longer be heard. Paige arrived and dismounted but, noticing the disquieted expressions on her friends' faces, said nothing.

"What does Mr. Coy have against Lionel?" Ana asked Ret soberly.

"He's jealous," Ret said, obviously bothered. Inwardly, it angered Ret how much Mr. Coy loathed Lionel, a person who thus far had been nothing but helpful and friendly to them.

"Jealous of what?" Ana wondered softly.

"Jealous that Lionel is everything that he isn't."

Ret started for the stairs. Ana shrugged and followed. But Paige lingered, stung by Ret's cold words.

O   O   O

It was fortunate that Ana and Paige had to report to the game early since Tybee High's gymnasium was already nearing capacity when they arrived. The two of them ran off to join their teammates while Pauline, with Ret contemplatively trailing a few steps behind, scaled the bleachers and found a spot for the two of them several rows behind the home team's bench. As the girls warmed up on the court, Pauline waved repeatedly until her daughter located her in the stands. Ana replied with a flamboyant wave of her own while Paige scarcely fluttered her fingers, obviously nervous to be in front of so many people.

Ret sat hunched and leaning forward, his elbows on his knees and chin in his hands. He didn't bother to even pretend that he was at all interested in the big playoff championship tournament final game—or whatever Ana had called it. He could think about nothing except collecting the next element, which obviously was fire. Over the last few weeks, he had begun to see the world in a different light; indeed, in a more flammable guise. The more he thought about it, the more he came to realize the pervasiveness of fire. In just the last several hours, some degree of fire had been called upon to start the car, warm the bath water, and heat the stove. Even at the game, it was a flame that was cooking the hot dogs at the concession stand.

Yet this was to be expected; the very fact that he was to collect the six, most basic elements in nature portended that they would be ever-present. As such, it wasn't so much the identification of the element that was the crux of the mystery as it was the interpretation of the scar. But the scar might as well have never lit up, so unknowable was its design. At least the earth element's symbol had given them the unmistakable clue of a triangle. But *this*—this gorilla shrine, this ancient hunchback—Ret wondered if anyone could decipher it.

But, then he thought, maybe Lionel could? The idea flowed into Ret's mind like pure intelligence and blazed into an inferno, fanned by his hopes and optimism. Yes, Lionel might know. As soon as possible after the game, Ret would write him a letter.

Ret lost his focus when the gymnasium erupted into a frenzy of band playing and whistle blowing. The game had commenced, with Ana poised on the court and Paige contentedly on the bench.

After the initial fanfare, Ret's gaze quickly shifted from the floor to the stands. Crowd surfing with his eyes, he laughed at the petty rivalries, cringed at the competitiveness, and salivated over the buttery popcorn. Every fan seemed enveloped by the here and now — hurrah for the spike, boo for the miss. Was he the only person who wished to "fill the Oracle"? Did no one else care to "cure the world"?

It was during these moments of scanning the gym when Ret noticed a curious mark on Miss Carmen's back. Not very large, it was just below the nape of her neck but above her shoulder blades. Perhaps a tattoo, it was quite easy to spot since her hair was pinned up. It had the same general shape as his scar. Now very intrigued, Ret wanted to get a closer look.

Slowly, Ret inched closer to Miss Carmen. She was standing on the floor, of course, overseeing the game and straddling the sideline where the rest of her team was seated. Imperceptibly, Ret slithered from one bleacher to the next, moving longer distances during chaotic moments when the crowd jumped to their feet in applause. Unbeknownst to him, it was a very close and intense game, which allowed him to creep along without drawing much attention to himself.

Even though Ret had wormed his way to the first bench behind the team, Miss Carmen was moving around too much for him to make out the details of the mark. He thought they may have made eye contact for a brief moment, but he wasn't sure. One person who certainly *was* watching him, however, was Paige, still sitting in the same seat on the bench as when the game started. Silently, she wondered why Ret was so interested in Miss Carmen.

Suddenly, the entire crowd rushed onto the court. The game must have ended. Uninterested in which team was victorious, Ret utilized the sea of fans to secure an even closer view of Miss Carmen's tattoo.

Ret wiggled among the teeming celebrators, keeping his head down except when he occasionally looked up to learn the exact location of Miss Carmen. When he had at last forced himself immediately behind her, he couldn't believe what he saw. Her mark was more of a branding than a tattoo, about the size of a golf ball, and it was the same exact image as the scar on Ret's hand. He carefully studied this magnified version of his scar, and he noticed a detail that he hadn't seen before: on the lower abdomen of the squatting man—or whatever it was—there was a jagged semicircle. It resembled a rough, unfilled dot with one very pointed tip pointing upward. Ret glanced down at his own scar, and there indeed was a tiny speck inside the body of the symbol.

When Ret looked up from his hand to further analyze Miss Carmen's mark, he was mortified to find she had turned around. Ret returned her satisfied smirk with his dropped jaw. Many of the bystanders, most of whom were young men who merely desired close proximity to Miss Carmen, began to watch what they were doing.

"Come by my office sometime," Miss Carmen lulled with a seductive smile, "and I'll give you a closer look." She brushed his face softly with her hand before walking away. Several guys in the vicinity gave Ret a rousing cheer before following after Miss Carmen. The spectacle fled with her, and she soon disappeared behind her office door on the other side of the gym.

When Ret turned from watching her, he found Paige and Ana standing nearby, having witnessed the whole thing.

"Shouldn't you be following *Miss Carmen?*" Paige sneered.

"Paige!" Ana gasped, surprised by her friend's words.

"What?" she snapped back. "He couldn't keep his eyes off her the whole game."

"Paige, look," Ret began, trying to defend himself, "I can explain—"

"Really, Ret?" Ana asked, shocked by Paige's accusation.

"It's not what it seems," Ret petitioned.

"So now you're checking out my coach, are you?" Ana surmised, crossing her arms.

"No—"

"Come on, Paige," Ana said with closure. "Let's find my mom." Together they stalked off, leaving Ret alone in the dispersing crowd.

Across the gym, through a gap in the blinds of her office window, Miss Carmen grinned.

CHAPTER 7

PARENTAL
PERSUASIONS

Ret dreaded the end of the calendar year. Though he found the first month or two of winter to be the dullest of all, the last several weeks of fall were somewhat more unpleasant to endure because each day reminded him that colder days were around the corner. There was little reason for him to venture outside, a sad sentiment that may have been different if he lived in a place that actually saw snow. Instead, he tried his best to appreciate the nip in the air; the chill in the water; and, perhaps worst of all, the growing brevity of daylight.

From his favorite retreat on the southern tip of Tybee's coast, Ret watched the sun dip even further south than it had yesterday along its ever-changing path in the increasingly grayer skies. As much as he preferred the warm seasons of the year, he remembered there was the whole southern half of the world that needed its turn to bask in the life-giving rays of the sun. He smiled, wondering what it would be like to live in that hemisphere, celebrating the winter holidays in summertime heat or shoveling fresh snow in July.

But his playful smile soon faded in contemplation of the earth's sheer enormity and vast diversity. How was he ever going to "cure the world"? He hardly knew anything about it! He possessed neither a degree in global affairs nor a well-used passport. He was a self-taught homebody who could count the number of times he had left the island on one hand—insofar as he could remember, of course.

Still, perhaps a more baffling question was *why* "cure the world." Was it sick? Yes, apparently so, but in what way? Would it soon fall ill to some pandemic plague? Was it already now diseased by some civil and cultural cancer? Could it be that filling the Oracle would rid the globe's inhabitants of their most distressing social ailments? Such thinking didn't seem logical, given the geographical nature of the Oracle.

As such, maybe filling the Oracle would bring about the cessation of natural disasters, which atrocities, as explained by the Guardian, had been introduced by the ancient scattering of the elements. Did the Oracle mean for Ret to erase fault lines and raise flood plains? Halt tempests and refreeze icecaps? Snuff out fires and shore up mudslides? Although these conjectures sounded more reasonable, they hardly seemed plausible after the natural disaster Ret caused when he collected the earth element.

Ret's head started to hurt. Obviously, he had no idea, and it was driving him mad! But who could blame him? He was like a stranded astronaut, lost in space, desperately trying to maneuver himself toward his unseen destination but lacking the one, all-important, do-or-die provision that fatally distinguishes a once-cosmically marooned survivor from an eternally galactic drifter: a push in the right direction.

Out of the corner of his eye, Ret saw someone walking towards him. It was Pauline, bundled up in a light jacket against the late afternoon's strengthening sea breeze. Without saying a word, she sat next to him in the sand.

"A letter came for you today," she informed Ret, extending a small envelope toward him. Ret's heart leapt with excitement. Pauline asked, "Is it from who I think it's from?"

"Lionel!" Ret replied enthusiastically, noticing the familiar handwriting and lack of return address that were becoming characteristic of Lionel's letters. With great eagerness, Ret tore open the envelope. He had written his letter to Lionel weeks ago, reporting on recent events with as much detail as possible: his control over fire both on the football field and in Mr. Coy's planetarium,

the curious rock that Coy had retrieved from Stone's
trunk, and the mark on Miss Carmen's back that was
identical to the scar on his hand. Ret even included a
photograph of the new scar, finding his written description to be quite unhelpful.

Anxious, Ret read the letter aloud:

Dear Ret,

*Thank you for your letter. I'm afraid your scar
doesn't strike a chord with me; however, your description of Mr. Coy's rock matches one of my own. It's the
only rock I've ever come across that emits heat. I found
it years ago on a research expedition in the Nazca
Desert of southern Peru, where I think we might find
some answers. If it's okay with Pauline, I'd like to take
you there during the winter holidays. Let me know.*

Your friend,
Lionel Zarbock

*P.S. I've included a small piece of my rock with this
letter.*

Given the several random burn marks on the paper,
Ret looked inside the envelope to locate the small rock
Lionel had included. Fortunately, Lionel had astutely

sent the letter in a decorative envelope—the kind with a semi-metallic liner—thus preventing the rock from burning through and getting lost in transit. Ret held the sliver in his hand and watched it come alive, similar to what Mr. Coy's rock had done but to a lesser degree. It even caused his scar to faintly glow.

Meanwhile, Pauline watched in silence, sitting patiently with an amused smile on her face. She was waiting for Ret to remember her presence. When he finally did, he looked down with a tad of embarrassment, realizing how foreign and alarming all of this must have appeared to her.

"When are you going to start telling me about these things, Ret?" she asked, employing her special tone that demanded respect but in the gentlest of ways. Ret sighed, trying to hide how glad he felt that someone was actually coming to *him* and asking for *his* take on things. "All I ever hear is what Ana tells me," she explained. "I want to hear *your* side, too."

Ret obliged. Not only was it a topic that he was happy to discuss but he also knew he needed to pour out his heart if he was ever going to win over Pauline (and convince her to allow him to travel to Peru!). Even after all they had witnessed together, Pauline was still not a full supporter of the Oracle. It was too adventurous for her blood; too at odds with her upbringing; too out-of-the-ordinary for her inside-the-box mentality. Had it been, say, more of a hobby—a weekend pastime— maybe then she could get behind it. But, instead, it was to her a time-consuming escapade that disrupted the norm and disregarded her comfort zone. She was perfectly content to live and die in Tybee—cooking meals, cleaning house, and raising a virtuous posterity.

And, in just about any other situation, Pauline would have been right. But not this time. It was the reality of this real-world fantasy that she couldn't quite convince her mind to accept.

"I know it all sounds so...so bizarre," Ret admitted, having summarized his perspective on the events of late, "but when I hold this rock, I feel happy— I feel at peace." He held Lionel's rock in his hand, outstretched toward Pauline, hoping its miniature fireworks show would further prove his point.

"So you weren't flirting with Miss Carmen at the game?" Pauline put forth, wanting to revisit the subject just to make sure.

"Of course not," Ret reaffirmed. "I just wanted a closer look at the mark on her back."

"Oh, good," she sighed, though she was never really worried. "You might want to let the girls know. They're still pretty shaken up by the whole thing."

"I've tried," said Ret, "but they always leave when I try to tell them. And then, when I *do* tell them, they pretend not to hear me."

"You can tell them until you're blue in the face, Ret," Pauline said in a matter-of-fact tone, "but until you *show* them, they're still going to be upset."

Ret gave her a confused stare.

"Paige adores you," Pauline blurted out. "Surely you've noticed−"

"I know, I know," said Ret, more annoyed than flattered.

"Well, do *you* have feelings for *her?*"

"She's a...well...," Ret said uncomfortably.

"Oh, Ret," Pauline said with a defeated chuckle. "Maybe while the girls are in Chile, you'll come to appreciate them a little more. Absence makes the heart grow fonder, you know."

"Chile?" Ret questioned astonishingly. "Ana and Paige are going to Chile?"

"Didn't they tell you?" said Pauline, surprised that Ret had not been informed. "Miss Carmen is playing in some fancy volleyball tournament during winter break, back in her hometown in Chile, and she invited Ana to go with her. Ana told her she wouldn't go without Paige, and Miss Carmen acquiesced."

"And they both want to go?"

"Personally, I think Paige couldn't care less, but Ana? Does she ever!" Pauline continued. "She agreed before she even thought to ask me. Of course, I was not exactly gung-ho about the idea. We had quite the talk, she and I—you know how stubborn that girl can be sometimes." Ret thought Pauline was one to talk. "In the end, I told her the only way I would allow her to go running off to some exotic land with that wanton coach of hers was if *I* went with them."

"I bet she *loved* hearing that," Ret remarked, rolling his eyes.

"As a matter of fact, she hated it," Pauline retold, "and she hasn't stopped whining about it since. But she accepted my terms, even though she told me I need to be more like Mr. Coy: I guess when Paige asked her father, he granted his permission before she even finished asking—no questions asked."

"So you're off to Chile, eh?" Ret said with a sly grin, knowing it wasn't her cup of tea.

"The things I do for my children," she said tiredly. "True, it's not my thing, but it helps that it's all paid for. Plus, considering what you just told me about the mark on Miss Carmen's back, I'm glad I'll be with them in case anything unusual happens."

"I'm shocked you're still going to go," Ret admitted. "I don't think it's a coincidence that her mark is the same as my—"

"Then it's a good thing I don't think much of these scars then, isn't it?" Stung, Ret left it at that.

Silence prevailed for a few moments before Ret asked, "So does this mean I can go to Peru with Lionel?"

"I was wondering when you might ask that," Pauline confessed with an air of disdain. "I suppose it wouldn't be fair if I didn't let you, would it?"

"So I can go?" Ret asked, on the verge of keeling over with joy.

"I guess," she smiled.

Ret burst into cheers. "Oh, thank you, Pauline! Thank you so much!"

"This whole Oracle thing really means a lot to you, doesn't it?" she deduced, happy that he was happy and that she had helped make him so.

"It means the world to me," he stated, still ecstatic.

"Well, keep in mind," she added, "the only reason I'm granting your wish so willingly is because you'll be with Lionel. He's a good man with a good head on his shoulders. I trust him, and you would do well to learn from him."

"I will," Ret promised.

"Now, if this adventure was being headed by Mr. Coy," she said warily, "then my answer would be a resounding *no.*"

As if he heard Pauline say his name, Mr. Coy appeared on the beach, a considerable distance away from where Ret and Pauline were sitting. Seeing something moving in their peripheral vision, the Coopers were both taken back to find the town hermit out in plain sight. In a very small way, they were glad he was walking towards them since they were very curious to learn the reason why he was strolling along the shore.

"Who's that other man?" Pauline asked Ret, noticing a second person following Mr. Coy.

"Ishmael," Ret answered, recognizing the man. "He's the groundskeeper at the Manor."

Though brimming with anticipation, Ret and Pauline feigned a collected and uninterested façade as Mr. Coy and Ishmael approached them. This was a most unusual meeting, and the Coopers were on pins and needles to find out how Mr. Coy would explain himself or if he might ignore them altogether.

Finally, he stood before them and asked, "Have either of you, by chance, seen a casserole dish around here?" Pauline unsuccessfully suppressed her shriek of a laugh.

"Are you joking?" she asked.

"He's not," answered Ishmael.

"Look, Mr. Coy!" Ret said. "Lionel responded to my letter and sent me this rock." He presented the sliver to Mr. Coy who took it begrudgingly. "He said it might be identical to the one you have." A frown formed on Mr. Coy's face, and it quivered with rage. "He said it's from the Nazca Desert in southern Peru, and he wants to take me there when school's out."

On account of his own innocence, Ret was unaware of how easily his report was misconstrued as a direct assault against Mr. Coy. Coy knew Ret was privy to his disgust toward Lionel, and now he felt as though Ret was rubbing it in his face.

"Darn it, Ret!" Mr. Coy shouted. "If I hear *one* more thing about Lionel, I swear—" Mr. Coy turned and threw the piece of Lionel's rock out to sea.

"Mr. Coy!" Ret gasped. He instinctively shot out his hand to stop Mr. Coy's rash move. Just as the skipping rock had bounced across the water for the third time, it stopped and came rushing back toward them. It flew directly into Ret's hand, and he clasped his fingers tightly around it. Everyone stood frozen for a moment.

"I...I knew—figured—that would happen," Mr. Coy fibbed, floundering for words to explain away his temper. "I was just surprised," he persisted, trying to appear rational, "by...by how long it took Lionel to come to that conclusion." He convicted himself of his lies by the way his voice wavered. "I've known for weeks that the rock originated in southern Peru."

Ishmael chimed in, "No you—"

"Quiet!" Mr. Coy interrupted for the sake of his rationalization, delivering a hearty punch to his associate's shoulder. "Even now, my hot-air balloon stands ready to take us there as soon as school lets out for the holidays."

"You intend to travel all the way to Peru in a hot-air balloon?" Pauline asked incredulously.

"Well, after considering a layover in Bogota," explained Coy with a hint of sarcasm, "we've decided to make it a nonstop flight."

"I think it's fine the way Lionel has it planned, Mr. Coy," Pauline insisted. "I'm sure Ret will tell you all about it when he gets back."

Mr. Coy swallowed and dug his feet a bit deeper in the sand, ready to engage in a war of words.

"You know," he said, unprovoked, "a mother as sweet and compassionate and understanding as yourself would—"

"Don't patronize me, Coy," she urged.

Coy blinked a few times before continuing unabated. "I was merely going to point out that *you,* of all people, ought to sympathize with a fellow parent's desire to accompany a minor on such an extended, overseas excursion. Remind me again of the ultimatum you gave your daughter Hannah?"

"Ana," Ret mumbled.

"—Right, Ana?" Coy continued.

"Were you listening to our—" Pauline started.

"And riddle me this, oh hypocrite," said Coy, despite Pauline's hot displeasure. "Why do you think so little of the coincidence between Ret's scar and pretty-faced Miss Carmen's body art, but you don't even bat an eye at a much more alarming and foreboding coincidence—namely, that our dear friend Lionel possesses the same artifact as your bosom buddy, Lester W. Stone?"

For being such a dopey fellow, he had certainly made a sobering distinction.

"Fine," Pauline finally said, throwing up her arms. "What do *I* know? I'm just the mother, after all."

"Don't let her guilt trip you, Ret," Mr. Coy whispered to him. "My mother used to tell me the same thing all the time."

It was puzzling to Ret that no one bothered to ask his opinion on the matter. Truthfully, he was not opposed to Mr. Coy's accompaniment on his journey with Lionel; unlike Pauline, Ret found Mr. Coy to be a valuable asset, with his innumerable collection of gadgets and gizmos. Still, Ret's reservations stemmed from Mr. Coy's incurable distaste for Lionel. He worried that Mr. Coy's temper might get the best of him and thus spell the worst for the rest of them. As such, Ret's only hope was that Mr. Coy and Lionel would work together to foster a spirit of synergy rather than vicious and villainous calumny.

Not exactly reciprocating the kindest of feelings, the small huddle on the beach dispersed.

"All my kids are running off to South America," Pauline summarized as she walked off, clearly dissatisfied with her own approval of it all. Ever since Ret had pointed out the unexpected synchronism of his scar and

Miss Carmen's mark, Pauline had begun to feel a bit uneasy. By the time she reached the house, however, her uneasiness had progressed to full-blown dismay because of the eerie truth that both Lionel and Stone possessed the same rare rock—although she wasn't sure what made her more aggravated: the coincidence of the rocks or the fact that Mr. Coy was the one who had shrewdly pointed it out.

At the same time, Mr. Coy and Ishmael had left Ret's company, striding across the sand toward the Manor. Coy didn't fret nearly as much about Miss Carmen as he did about Lionel. He didn't trust him, and he wasn't about to let Ret—or the Oracle—go gallivanting to Peru without himself coming along to keep Lionel in check.

"Make sure to pack all your potions, Ishmael," Mr. Coy instructed as their silhouettes were swallowed up in the evening shadows, "especially plenty of integritas extract."

CHAPTER 8

THE LINES
IN THE DESERT

The happy day at last had come when school let out for the holidays. With unusual enthusiasm, the Cooper kids hopped off the afternoon bus and hurried home to finish packing in preparation for their trips abroad. Neither of them was envious of the other's travel plans, as both were perfectly content with their own, each bound for an exotic land at the side of their respective role model. It was like a dream come true—for Ret, and for Ana.

The first ring of the doorbell came by way of Paige, who rolled her one piece of luggage into the house and refrained from making herself comfortable since her arrival meant it was time for the women to depart for the airport, where they were to meet Miss Carmen.

"Ana," Pauline called to her daughter from downstairs, "Paige is here. Time to go!" From Ana's room came the deep, guttural sound of a strained zipper coming together to enclose a bulging suitcase, followed by the rhythmic thuds of small luggage wheels crashing on each stair. Reaching the bottom floor, Ana dragged her suitcase into the entryway and parked it next to her other three pieces of overstuffed luggage.

Noticing Paige's light load, she sighed, "Good," sounding winded, "you can carry some of mine."

Now that it was time to part ways and bid farewell, the awkwardness that Ret and the girls were dreading was beginning to set in. Ana and Paige were still giving Ret the cold shoulder, and Ret wasn't exactly willing to stoop to groveling in order to rekindle any flames. So it was quite a relief for all of them when the second dingdong of the doorbell revealed Lionel on the porch, ready to accompany Ret to Coy Manor.

"May I help you ladies with your things?" Lionel offered with smoldering chivalry. Happy to avoid the uncomfortable setting, Ret followed Lionel's lead. Then, when finished, Ret quickly waved his general goodbye and started for the Manor.

"What was *that* all about?" Lionel asked when he had caught up with Ret.

"What?" Ret wondered defensively, though well aware what Lionel was referring to.

"Back there," Lionel explained. "You hardly said goodbye to them."

"It's complicated," Ret said.

"I'm a smart guy," Lionel pressed. "Try me."

While rowing the kayak across the creek, Ret described the situation to Lionel. He probably provided a bit more detail than his listener desired, but Ret couldn't help himself: he loved how Lionel seemed to be so interested in his life.

"If you ask me," Lionel observed at the end of Ret's summary, "it sounds like Paige just wants to know she's not invisible to you. I remember watching her in Sunken Earth: terribly shy—always in Ana's shadow. Why not tell her how you feel about her?"

"Why does everyone keep saying that?" Ret wondered with a tinge of annoyance. "What if I don't *feel* anything towards her?" They had secured the boat and commenced their climb up the hill. "I don't want to think about that stuff right now. All I want to concentrate on is finding the five remaining elements and filling the Oracle. Once I've done that, then I'll worry about my 'feelings' for Paige."

Lionel opened his mouth to respond but held his tongue, unsure if now was the right time or if Ret was yet ready for what he wanted to tell him. Personally, Lionel was growing a bit leery of what he perceived was Ret's gradual preoccupation with the Oracle.

Approaching the entrance to the Manor, Ret could see Mr. Coy and Ishmael out on the front lawn, not far from the main gate. Ishmael was handing different items to Mr. Coy who, standing on a ladder, was then loading them into a sort of raised basket.

Ret recalled Mr. Coy's plan to ferry him and Lionel to Peru via hot-air balloon. It seemed that such an airship lay before him, but, as with most of Coy's creations, Ret had to literally stop and intently focus on the situation in front of him in order to better understand (and believe) what he was seeing.

The raised basket was actually floating a few dozen feet above the lawn, held down by a couple of cables that were staked into the ground. It was a typical wicker basket, the most common breed of gondola for hot-air balloons, and it looked as though it might accommodate quite a few riders. Attached at the base of the basket was a sort of engine, the kind you'd expect to see on a jet airplane. Still, what puzzled Ret was the apparent absence of the actual balloon—the envelope in the shape of an inverted teardrop.

"They are here, sir," said Ishmael, informing Mr. Coy that Ret and Lionel had arrived.

"Let them in," said Coy, taking a handful of provisions from his assistant.

Remotely controlled, Ret heard the gate unlock and pushed it open. As they walked toward the scene, Ret noticed how there was a huge piece—in the shape of a balloon—missing from the background, replaced by the partly cloudy, afternoon sky. Something was up, and Ret secretly loved getting to the bottom of Mr. Coy's, well, coyness.

"Greetings, Ret," Mr. Coy said cheerily, jumping down from the ladder. Then, with dead seriousness, he and Lionel forced salutations by uneasily exchanging surnames.

Said Coy, "Zarbock."

"Coy," Lionel replied, employing a more pleasant tone. "I must say," Lionel continued, hoping a compliment would foster friendship, "I am intrigued by your balloon."

"As you should be," said Coy, turning to ascend the ladder into the basket. "Not only is it stealthily disguisable but also fully self-sustainable. Instead of the traditional envelope of rainbow-colored gores and annoyingly-cutesy designs, *my* balloon is covered in hundreds of lightweight solar panels." Climbing inside the basket, Mr. Coy reached high above his head and tapped on the balloon, producing a sound as if he were rapping on plastic. "The energy garnered from the sun is stored in this battery." He pointed to a large, blackened brick, hanging above the basket and half-concealed within the throat of the balloon. "Atop the battery is a hot plate, which not only keeps the cabin warm and toasty but also heats the air inside the balloon, allowing the craft to rise amid the colder air around it—just like any other balloon. But *unlike* any other balloon," he said with visible self-gratification, *"mine* traps the hot air enough for condensation to build up inside the balloon, then water drips down onto the hot plate, thus becoming steam and keeping the hot air flowing." He pried the base of the envelope away from the battery just enough to release several streams of water and a few puffs of steam in an effort to illustrate his lecture.

"*Also* unlike other balloons," he pressed on, "this baby can travel at speeds up to ten times faster, thanks to my repurposed jet engine—also powered by solar energy." He leaned over the side of the basket to take an admiring look at his handiwork.

"Why not just travel by plane?" Lionel inquired, asking the question that had been on his mind ever since Ret informed him of Mr. Coy's intention to go by balloon.

"Because public transit just doesn't fly with me," Coy explained, wincing, "and even if I wanted to take one of *my* planes, there's the hassle of clearance and registering—you know, the legal way of things. Besides," he shrugged, "then everyone would know what we're up to, and that makes me terribly uncomfortable."

"Hence the camouflage," Ret stated, ready for some answers in this regard.

"Right, Cooper," said Coy. "The silicon mixture inside the solar cells is a special solution that reflects its surroundings like a mirror while still absorbing the photons from the sun. In this way, the entire balloon takes on the appearance of whatever it is near. Blue during the day and black at night, we'll be as difficult to spot as a tiny basket, floating in the endless sky."

After mulling it over for several seconds, Lionel concluded, "It seems a bit risky, if you ask me."

"Then it's a good thing *you're* full of hot air," Coy teased. Lionel rolled his eyes. "Besides," he continued, motioning to Ret, "we'll have a human sparkplug onboard."

"I know he's nuts," Ret whispered to Lionel, "but his work is actually quite genius."

"If you say so," he obliged, his reluctance succumbing to his trust in his teenage friend.

When every bag, bundle, and body had been brought aboard, Ishmael reeled in the guy-lines, and the balloon bobbed free. Mr. Coy increased the heat available to the hot plate, which appeared to behave much like a pot of simmering water. The condensed water collected in a shallow pool at the bottom of the envelope; thus, by turning up the heat, Mr. Coy was able to burn off a greater proportion of the water and funnel hotter air into the system.

Higher and higher, they rose above the island until clearly discernible features had been reduced to mere specks on a checkered landscape. In Ret's limited estimation, the wind didn't seem to be blowing them in the southern direction he knew they needed to take.

"Fire up the engine, Ish," Coy ordered.

"Right away, sir."

Expecting a deafening roar and a sudden jolt, Ret was surprised to find that the engine hummed quietly and propelled gently. Standing in the center of the basket, Mr. Coy gripped a wheel that rose up from the floor and allowed him to control the position of the engine.

"Good thing we added that extra dampener," he remarked to Ishmael, pleased to find the engine's roar not altogether unpleasant. He maneuvered the engine until it was taking in air from the direction they needed to go, expelling it behind them in the ever-increasing distance from Tybee.

In an effort to keep from being spotted from the ground (especially since their shadow was not as easy to camouflage), Mr. Coy bent their course out to sea. Soon, the only thing to look at was open ocean, though such a view was not too bland or boring for Ret, even in the waning daylight. However, as they started to pass over the Caribbean islands, Ret's heart began to sicken at the memory of Sunken Earth. He retired from his sightseeing, slunk into one of the corners of the basket, and drifted off to sleep.

○   ○   ○

Like a rooster, Ret awoke with the rising sun. Though a bit startled to arise amid such unusual circumstances, his fears quickly faded when he saw Mr. Coy and Lionel still fast asleep, with Ishmael steadfastly manning the wheel. Quietly, Ret rose to his feet, stretched, and looked around to see if he could determine where they were.

Feeling the warmth of the sun on his back, Ret saw large, forested landmasses approaching them in all directions but north. Continuing this westward course, Ret watched raptly as they began to pass over land. Lush greenery covered most of the landscape, with many bodies of water twisting like veins around vegetated hills. After only a few minutes, however, Ret could see the abrupt end of land and the return of vast ocean. He was confused; if they were flying over a large island, why was there a waterway that ran the entire width of the land, from ocean to ocean?

"The Panama Canal," Lionel said with a yawn, as if he had read Ret's mind. He appeared at Ret's side and leaned over the side of the basket. "But I'm sure you already knew that."

Ret smiled, preferring not to fess up since Lionel was someone he always tried to impress.

"So we must be close," Ret deduced.

"Sort of," said Lionel. "It looks like Coy is keeping us just off the coasts, and we've still got to go through Columbia, Ecuador, and then all the way down Peru." Hoping he hadn't crushed Ret's enthusiasm, he added, "But we're getting there."

"You must come here a lot," said Ret.

"I've spent quite a bit of time on this continent," Lionel admitted. "It's played a big role in my research."

"Where *haven't* you been, Lionel?" Ret asked rhetorically, in awe at his travelogue.

"The women's restroom," he replied. They both laughed. "I've been blessed to have a career that has taken me all over this earth," said Lionel. "I feel sorry for people who, for whatever reason, can't or simply choose not to travel the globe, consigned to experience the world through a one-dimensional map their whole lives. Do you know what I see when I look at a map, Ret?" Ret remained silent. "Lines." He stopped for a few moments before saying, "There are so many boundaries and borders. I mean, look over there." He pointed to the South American continent to the east. "Do you see any lines on those hills? Can you tell which way national borders run, or at what point the soil stops being Ecuadorian and starts being Peruvian?"

Ret said nothing.

"Neither can I," said Lionel. "That's because borders and boundaries are manmade. Sure, they may organize and systematize things, but lines also separate and categorize—they stereotype and segregate. Boundaries beget blocs. Borders create unseen stumbling blocks. Lines in the sand are born from lines in our hearts. You see, what lines do is make us unequal. Never underestimate the hidden meaning of lines, Ret."

For a moment, Ret's mind reflected on the delineated society of Sunken Earth, which had been divided into stark classes of differing equality. He remembered the first time he gazed upon the civilization—how it looked so amicable from a distance but, up close, was actually a corrupt and fallen culture.

"But when I'm way up here," Lionel resumed, "when I remove myself from the deafening noise of the day-to-day and the blinding static of the here-and-now, I no longer see the varied lines and differing brushstrokes that define life; instead, I see the whole image—one grand and glorious painting—the big picture that defines existence. If large cities and diverse states can live by the same laws and philosophies in peace and harmony, then why can't whole countries—even entire continents? Through geography, Mother Nature made them contiguous; why, then, can't man, through sociality, make them continuous?"

"Good question," Mr. Coy interrupted, having snuck up behind them during Lionel's monologue. "I'll be sure to ask the Wizard of Oz when I reach the

Emerald City at the end of the yellow brick road." Ret and Lionel looked at him with flustered perplexity on their faces. "Look alive, kiddos," Coy hollered, returning to the controls. "Peru approacheth."

Now that they were a considerable distance down the South American coast, Ret noticed a significant change in the topography of their aerial, panoramic view. Whereas the shoreline and subsequent inland expanse were once bespeckled with greenery, the entire landscape had turned a dusty brown. From the waters of the Pacific to the feet of the Andes, this high-desert plateau stretched long and thin from north to south. Ret had no memories of traversing through deserts, and this one looked wildly unforgiving and unappealingly dead.

"There's Lima," Lionel pointed out. It was a sight that couldn't be missed. A truly enormous metropolitan area sprawled in every direction, threatening to spill over the Pacific coast. It was a sea of concrete—a dense grove of skyscrapers and buildings. Still, it paled in comparison to Sunken Earth.

Soon, the cement of the city gave way to the dust of the desert. Mr. Coy adjusted their course to gradually take them inland.

"Where would someone start looking for these incendiary rocks?" Mr. Coy asked aloud as they flew ever nearer toward the far-reaching Nazca Desert.

"I suggest we start at the north end and work our way down," Lionel replied.

"In that case," said Coy, "we'll start at the south end and work our way up."

Though Ret frowned, Lionel shrugged his shoulders with lightheartedness.

The cloudless sky provided ample sunshine as the balloon resumed a land route. The ground was all sand and rock, constituting a barren wasteland. In some areas, hills sat like burnt potato chips; in others, more mountainous patches resembled the scattered vertebrae of some ancient behemoth.

Plunging further south, Ret noticed the presence of several geometric designs in the flat, prairie-like regions of the desert. They were a series of incredibly straight lines, crisscrossing in no particular order, like the residual imprints of some giant's game of pick-up sticks. He had almost convinced himself to think nothing of the curious lines when he saw a drawing in the dirt.

"Look!" Ret shouted. "Look at the ground! There's a hummingbird!"

Everyone rushed to Ret's side of the basket and peered over the ledge. Indeed, a massive drawing of a hummingbird had been etched into the surface of the earth. With clearly drawn wings and elongated snout, it was an astounding discovery. More impressive still was the fact that it had been scratched into the ground in a single, continuous line, the whitish color of which contrasted distinctly against the brown land.

The party scarcely had enough time to gather their thoughts when a second geolyph could be seen ahead. It had a lanky body, with four appendages, a stuck-out tongue, and a long tail curled into a large spiral design.

"That almost looks like a...like a," Lionel said, astounded, "a monkey!"

"Yeah," Ret agreed with childlike fantasy, "a monkey!"

"And look!" Mr. Coy hailed, looking off to the east. "There's a dog over here!" He conducted the balloon eastward to follow the giant sketches in the soil. The canine lay conspicuously before them, each toe of its four long legs accounted for, the entire outline completed in one, unbroken line.

When the dog had passed, only the abnormally straight lines remained, stretching out of sight. The lull in the caricatures provided an opportunity for the group to discuss the unexpected phenomena.

"I've never seen anything like *this* before!" Lionel confessed, obviously excited. "I mean, I'd heard there were rumored markings in the Nazca Desert, perhaps from ancient tribes, but I had no idea they were anything like *this*—full-blown drawings of animals."

"Never mind *you*," Coy insisted. "What could this mean for *us*—for the Oracle?"

"Well," said Ret skeptically, "unless there's a drawing of a flaming rock or a fiery, six-sectioned sphere—or even a squatting man—I doubt these lines mean anything for us."

"Well, I can't tell if he's squatting," said Ishmael, "but there's a man over here."

Still reluctant, Ret dubiously crept to where Ishmael and the others were standing, crowding around the east side of the basket. Ret gave the spectacle half a glance. On a long and gently sloping hillside, there certainly was the figure of a man etched into the ground. Similar to Ret's scar, the body was rounded with a long torso and pronounced eyes, but this graphic looked more like a suited astronaut. What's more, he had one hand raised, as though he was waving to them—trying to win their attention, beckoning them thither.

While the others gawked, Ret consulted the palm of his left hand. There was no activity whatsoever. His scar was neither lit nor tingling—nothing like when they saw the shadow of the submerged road that led to Sunken Earth. Ret retreated, his incredulity confirmed.

Just then, Mr. Coy released a great deal of steam from the balloon.

"What are you doing?" Ret asked, assuming Mr. Coy's intention to descend.

"Taking her down for a closer look, of course," Coy explained.

"But it's nothing," Ret debated. "It's not identical to the scar or Miss Carmen's mark, and it doesn't even have anything to do with fire."

"But it *does* bear a striking resemblance," Lionel added.

"No, this isn't how it works," Ret persisted, unwilling to give in. "When we were in Devil's Triangle and saw the road from the helicopter, I felt something in my hand. When the road became a downward stairway, it was because I felt something in my hand when I waved it over the symbol on the stone. From that moment until we left Sunken Earth, I felt something *in my hand.*"

"So I'm guessing you don't feel anything in your hand," Mr. Coy gathered sarcastically.

"Not a thing," said Ret definitively.

"Ishmael," said Coy, "prepare for landing."

Ret threw his hands up in defeat. Was he not the quintessential element? Then why did no one seem to value his opinion?

Noticing his frustration, Lionel put his arm around Ret's shoulder and gave him the counsel that he had withheld from their previous conversation about Paige. Said he, "Just because you can't feel something doesn't mean it's not there." It was a statement that Ret didn't exactly want to hear at the moment.

As they approached the ground, Ishmael rolled a ladder over the side of the basket and climbed down to secure the guy-lines. They were near the top of the hill on whose wide and semi-flat face was the carving of the man. Mr. Coy powered down the balloon and then anxiously exited the craft with Lionel close behind.

"Still a naysayer about lines?" Mr. Coy muttered to Lionel, referring to the conversation he had overheard earlier. Lionel feigned a humored grin.

Ret was, by far, the last to descend the ladder. With heavy footsteps, he made his descent onto the desert floor, the rocky dirt crunching beneath his feet as if walking on loose gravel. The air was dry and windless. He took no more than a few steps before coming to a stop and sitting down. He put his face in his hands.

"What are we doing here?" he murmured to himself. "We're halfway across the world, in the middle of some forsaken desert, looking at scratches in the dirt. They're about as useful as children's chalk drawings on a playground. We're wasting time." He would have felt differently about his current situation had his scar demonstrated even the slightest hint that they were on the right track.

Like most seated wallowers, Ret was rather involuntarily grabbing handfuls of whatever lay in front of him and letting it sift through his fingers. The coarse soil consisted of reddish-brown pebbles, quite easy to excavate. After several scoopfuls, he noticed a whitish layer about five inches below the dirt.

Suddenly, Ret felt something wet invading his seat. He quickly stood up for an assessment. The hot-air balloon was leaking water profusely, as Mr. Coy had left the envelope to drain and condensation was still occurring within. Ret watched as the water flowed into the stray geometric lines that had been etched into the hillside. Like a system of rain gutters, it seemed these trenches were purposely configured to catch water and channel it in some predetermined route. Ret followed the flow of the runoff as it percolated into the furrows and trickled chaotically, intersecting like a family of air hockey pucks.

Enthralled, Ret followed the general flow of the water in hopes of discovering the final destination of its drainage. He was careful not to step on any of the lines, now aware how delicate they were. Each one led to the giant geolyph of the man, though they all made contact with it at different points and from different angles. Ret halted near the man's head and watched the lines funnel water into those that outlined the man.

But the water's journey did not end there. Without abatement, it continued to flow toward a central point in the man's torso where, like the pointed symbol on the belly of Miss Carmen's mark, there was a separate etching within the sketch of the man. Unlike the other lines, however, here the water came to rest and filled up the trenches without moving onward.

The water show had also attracted the attention of Mr. Coy, Ishmael, and Lionel. They left their former spots of analysis and hurried to the belly of the man in order to see what design had been outlined in his torso. Ret hastened to join them, anxious to learn what the lines had to say.

CHAPTER 9

THE CITY
IN THE MOUNTAINS

"Machu Picchu!" Lionel shouted.

"Gesundheit," said Mr. Coy in response to Lionel's epiphanic exclamation.

"It's the Machu Picchu skyline," Lionel continued giddily, undeterred by his associate's sarcasm, "as seen from the south. Can you not see it?" He took a step closer and bent down to the ground.

Like a broadside portrait of a small automobile, the design was about half as tall as it was wide and sat in the giant figure's lower abdomen, about where you'd expect to find his belly button. With half a dozen or so indiscriminate lines feeding into the system like a major freeway interchange, the outline was quickly filling up with water runoff from the balloon. The late morning sun shone brilliantly upon the water, which accentuated even more the whiteness of the lines against the dull dirt of the parched desert—like wax amid watercolor.

"This is the residential district, right by the main entrance," said Lionel who, with his finger, pointed to the bottom-left portion of the outline. "And here's the main plaza." His hand moved rightward along a vacant stretch in the center. "This is Huayna Picchu, of course," he said, identifying the large, conical mountain in the background.

"Oh, yes; of course," Coy remarked quietly to Lionel, as if the features of the ancient city were common knowledge.

"Over there is the industrial zone," Lionel's gesticular tour resumed, "which rests across from these sacred sites. It doesn't show everything, but it's clearly Machu Picchu. Wouldn't you agree? It's one of the most famous skylines in the world, you know."

"Yes, we know," came Coy's irked assertion. "Thank you very much, King Inca."

"Do you think it could have something to do with the scar?" Ret asked, his mind clearly focused on one thing. "Or with the element?"

"It's certainly a possibility," said Lionel. "Not much is known about the pre-Columbian city or why it was abandoned, which is why I find it more and more fascinating each time I visit it. In fact," he paused, surveying the horizon as if to orient himself, "it ought to be only a couple hundred miles to the east of us."

"Let's check it out!" Ret rejoiced, ready to go. "Come on!" He was about to make for the balloon but stopped when he caught Mr. Coy's skeptical eye. Ret braced for some disparaging comment from him that would likely be at odds with Lionel's judgment.

Amid silence, Mr. Coy glanced at Ishmael, who returned his boss' glare with his usual look of pleasantly obedient servitude. Though there was no exchange of words or reciprocation of winks, some reassuring fact seemed to be communicated between the two of them.

"Well then, what are we waiting for?" Coy asked with an acquiescent smile. "All aboard!" Ret cheered inaudibly while Lionel shrugged, satisfied yet surprised by Mr. Coy's approval. Ret led the way back to the balloon, several eager steps ahead of the rest of the group.

"Next stop: the city in the mountains," Mr. Coy announced soon after disconnecting his airship from the earth. Like a fishing float, the balloon bobbed above the desert floor until the heating system provided enough lift to raise them heavenward. Ret watched as the departing figure of the giant man on the ground gradually became smaller and fainter until it could no longer be seen. With his raised hand, the man seemed to be waving goodbye to them, as if his purpose had been fulfilled.

Ret's attention turned eastward. As they sailed further inland, the evolving landscape foreshadowed the drastic change of scenery that their destination would bring. Like frills on a woman's garment, the terrain had become exceptionally rugged, with innumerable mounts—ruffled and jagged—butting up against each other for miles. Void of vegetation, though replete with bronzed and ashen rock, the scene came to resemble one of Pauline's platters of no-bake cookies. It was no mystery that the elevation was steadily increasing. Occasionally, the balloon would come quite close to scalping a high-rising peak, prompting Mr. Coy to increase the craft's altitude.

Poking at the horizon were numerous snowcapped mountaintops, and snow meant moisture. As their slopes steepened and colors deepened, the Andean alps assumed a lush and living appeal. Greenery replaced barrenness. Rivers flowed where hillsides converged. The forested regions sang of fauna. Ret marveled at the prodigious difference made by a fair bit of water.

"There it is!" Lionel proclaimed. "Just beyond that ridge." He pointed to yet another bluff in the endless expanse of the mountain range. The ridge petered out into a shallow ravine on its southern side, so Mr. Coy steered the balloon to the right to pass through it. As they rounded the side of the ridge and floated into the gully, the ancient city finally came into view.

Like the saddle of a pack animal, the ruins of Machu Picchu sat in a wide-bottomed trough, cradled between two crests, with a large summit on one side and a shorter one across the way. Ret thought of it in terms of a recent lecture in science class, classifying the scene as a wavelength that was low in both frequency and amplitude—for it truly rested at the top of the mountain, whose sides were more like sheer cliffs than steep slopes. In fact, the whole operation appeared as if it might slide off like sheet cake at any moment. Unlike most of the surrounding mounts, Machu Picchu was a tad shorter and considerably more isolated, like a butte in its own valley. Its tall precipices met the ground in a healthy river that encircled the mountain on nearly all sides.

Ret groped for the right word to describe the sight before his eyes. It certainly was breathtaking, in might and majesty, but it was also curious, nontraditional, and downright unusual. It seemed one of the worst possible locations to build a city, at least for practical reasons, but quite ideal for protection against armed conflict or concealment of hidden treasure. Still, its utter remoteness was a suspicion too glaring to be overlooked. It was as though it had purposely withdrawn itself nigh out of existence—perhaps to be out of sight also meant to be out of prying minds—and even if it had been newfound, it was no easy task simply to get to it. Secluded, excluded, precluded—*that* was the story of Machu Picchu. But Ret wanted to know the *why*.

Mr. Coy maneuvered the balloon up onto the southern end of the saddle. Ishmael heaved the ladder over the side of the wicker basket and climbed down to the ground to secure the guy-lines.

Anxious, Ret skipped the last few rungs of the ladder when it was his turn to descend and jumped onto the mountain soil. He turned northward and stared at the panorama of the lost city. It was not an entirely new sight, for directly in front of them lay the skyline that had been bored into the belly of the giant figure at Nazca. It was the spitting image of the desert lines; there was no mistaking it.

Like a child amid his slew of birthday packages, Ret looked to his scar, anticipating good news. Nothing. No glow, no numbness, nothing. He sighed with dejection.

The curious quartet set out to explore their surroundings. The rich dirt beneath their feet was largely blanketed in grass, brightly colored and thick as hair. A gentle breeze blew an occasional cloud into the mountainsides, temporarily veiling the city and shielding it from the warm sun in its strikingly blue sky. Despite the elevation, the air was warm and moist, which were conditions much enjoyed by the tropical flora. The calls of exotic birds rang among the forested cliffs, and the elongated neck of a sunbathing llama stretched above the low-growing ferns and orchids nearby.

The architects' use of stone was quite impressive. Although not a place of many roofs, the walls of homes and buildings were expertly crafted using stones of all shapes and sizes but without requiring any kind of mortar. With trapezoidal frames and even modest windows, the structures were clearly built to withstand the tests of time—either that or seismic shifts. At times, browsing the ruins felt like walking a tightrope, so vertiginous and dizzying were the constantly changing levels of varying heights. One misstep near the city limits could lead to a grave freefall of thousands of feet. Where the boundaries didn't end in precipice, the still-steep slopes bore the workmanship of terracing, which, as if stairs for giants, spanned up and down and all around the mountainsides like a modern stadium, each terrace's dirt retained by the same stone-walled and mortar-free building technique.

There was not a soul in the whole compound. Walking through the narrow alleys between the rows of cold dwellings, it felt more like touring a former concentration camp than the hidden jewel of a once-great civilization. Why was this place, which had been so painstakingly constructed, now utterly abandoned?

While the others roamed the site in pursuit of personal fancies, Ret wandered aimlessly in the forsaken city. For a brief time, he stood under the leafy boughs of a lone tree in the central courtyard, which seemed as out of place and on its own as he felt. Then, as his three separated comrades individually began to gravitate toward him in their continued combing of the community, Ret set out in search of a more solitary place to be alone with his despondent thoughts, which he didn't wish to share with anyone.

Ret noticed a sort of hill at the upper periphery of the property and started climbing a set of irregular steps at its base, hoping to secure solitude somewhere along the way. Reaching the top of the hill, he entered a shoddy enclosure. Though roofless and sporadically walled, Ret found a large block of white stone inside, one side of which had been cut out to form an ideal bench. Ret sat down with a frustrated sigh.

"What a bust!" he lamented. "A total waste! We've come all this way, and what do we have to show for it? Nothing. Absolutely nothing." In his self-defeatism, he kicked a clump of small rubble in front of him, as if it was in his way. "All this time, all this effort, all this worry—and for what?"

He stopped his whispered dialogue at the sound of approaching footsteps on the dusty stairs. Someone was climbing toward his private enclave.

"Hey, Ret!" Lionel greeted with wonder in his voice. "Pretty amazing place, huh?"

"I wouldn't say it's *amazing,*" Ret said bitterly.

"Oh? And why not?"

"Well, have you found anything related to the Oracle here?" Ret asked.

"No, not yet," Lionel answered sheepishly, sensing Ret's displeasure. "Have *you?*"

"Not a thing," said Ret, his disappointment apparent, "which is why I'm sitting on this bench, waiting until we leave this place."

"First of all," Lionel said in an upbeat tone, noticing how Ret needed some cheering up, "*this* is not a bench. It's the Intihuatana Stone, one of many ritual stones in South America, carved out of the rock of the mountain itself. We're not entirely sure why the ancient cultures built them, but the answer may lie in astronomy."

"What did you call it?" asked Ret, backtracking to the unfamiliar term he had heard Lionel say in his spiel, to which he wasn't really paying much attention.

"The Intihuatana Stone," Lionel repeated, amused by Ret's naïveté in the field of ancient archeological artifacts. "I know; it's kind of a funny word, huh? It comes from the local Quechua dialect and means 'the place that ties up the sun' or something like that." Lionel commenced a methodical walk around the large granite block, sliding his fingers along its rough surface. "This top piece," he said, reaching to touch the rectangular prism in the center, "was carved so precisely that each of its corners points in one of the four cardinal directions." Ret didn't bother to turn around and look behind him at the object of Lionel's lecture. "Twice a year, on the equinoxes, it supposedly 'ties up' the sun—pointing directly at it and, therefore, casting no shadow. It's also rumored to share some special significance with each of the solstices." As though intrigued by a word spoken from his own mouth, Lionel paused to check the date on his cell phone. "If I'm not mistaken, *today* is the winter solstice—which means it's the summer solstice in *this* hemisphere, of course." He studied the stone with greater thoroughness upon this realization, squatting for different perspectives and squinting in search of finer details. "But I'm not sure what I ought to be looking for."

Ret wondered why Lionel was telling him so much about a lame rock that wasn't even very comfortable to sit on. "Well, it'd be nice if it could tell me where to find the next element."

Cringing at Ret's sour attitude, Lionel completed his walk around the stone and then sat down on it next to Ret. Motionless, they sat in silence for a few moments. Then Lionel opened his mouth to tell Ret something that had been on his mind.

"Ret," he said, in a tone that wasn't altogether pleased, "it seems to me as though you're a little obsessed with this Oracle business."

"Well yeah," said Ret as if Lionel had stated the obvious. "Filling the Oracle is my top priority. I want it more than anything else."

"That's what worries me," Lionel admitted.

"Why?" Ret asked incredulously, almost offended. "Is that bad? Is it bad to want something so much that you'd do anything to get it?"

"Depends," Lionel replied, somewhat to Ret's chagrin. "Does 'anything' include being willing to do without it?"

In his vexation, Ret made no response, waiting for Lionel to explain his conundrum.

"Ret," Lionel counseled, "there are some things in life that you can't have unless you're first willing to *not* have them." He paused to let his words sink in, knowing such maxims hadn't the tendency to initially strike very forcefully the chimes of youthful inexperience.

Shaking his head, Ret replied, "Lionel, that doesn't make any sense—"

"I know, I know," Lionel agreed. "At first, it seems self-contradictory. But think about it for a while, and, by and by, I think you'll come to understand the truth behind it. It took me a long time to figure out that lesson, but I thought I'd share it with you—you know, to give you the upper hand."

"So if I want something," Ret said dubiously, attempting to repeat the perceived paradox in his own words so as to better understand it, "the trick is to *not* want it?"

"Yeah," said Lionel, more or less agreeing. "That's the gist of it. It's a universal principle; what it means for you is up to *you* to figure out, Ret."

"Then what am I supposed to do," said Ret, suddenly jumping to his feet, "just walk away from it all?" He took a few haphazard strides forward to ridicule the concept presented in his words. "Shift gears? Change course—180 degrees? Forget all about my scars and the Oracle? Pretend Sunken Earth never happened? Is that what you're telling me?"

"What I'm telling you, Ret," said Lionel, remaining calm, "is that you need to learn to control your passions." Ret put his hands on his hips and looked at the ground with dissatisfaction. "It's not a bad thing to have desires—wants, ambitions—even strong ones. But when they consume us—when the fire of our passions burns everything we touch, singes every thought we think, scalds every person we know—*then* there's a problem: a raging inferno that gags the voice of reason and blinds the clearest vision. So the 'trick' is to discipline yourself—to control the burner, to limit the fuel, to bring out the fire extinguisher—and not let your passions control *you*. That's the secret to success: giving it all you've got without letting it take all you are." Ret's pensive gaze remained fixed on the ground.

"In the meantime," Lionel advised, "don't overlook the joy that's to be found in the journey. Don't see through the people you see all the time."

"You mean Paige?" Ret said with a pinch of contempt.

"Maybe the reason you lost your past is because you already spend too much time in the future at the expense of the present."

"But it's always on my mind, Lionel," said Ret earnestly. "What's the next scar? Where's the next element? What does the Oracle want me to do next? I can't enjoy today because I'm so worried about what's next—wondering why I'm not getting any help from my scar, whether or not I'm in the wrong place, how in the world I'm going to find these elements." Then, with a face of pure desperation, Ret said, "I just want the reassurance that I'm on the right track. What if I made a wrong turn somewhere along the road? It's hard to 'enjoy the journey' when I'm not sure if I'm making the right one."

Lionel smiled and asked, "Do you know what faith is, Ret?"

Ret thought for a moment, though unable to come up with his own definition. "Believing is seeing," he replied, employing the traditional, though hardly understood, cliché.

"That's the gist of it," said Lionel, again.

Recognizing the repetition, Ret tried to restrain a smile, grateful for Lionel's patience. "Faith means believing something even though you don't really have any proof. It's hoping and trusting when the evidence is not there. It's not the easiest thing to do; it's uncertain, and risky."

"Like you riding in Coy's balloon," said Ret.

"Right," Lionel said, glad Ret was following. "I had never seen Coy's balloon in action, but you told me to trust him, so I put my faith in your good judgment. But people don't want to *believe;* they want to *know.*"

"So you're saying I need to have more faith?"

"Have you ever heard the old Quechua fable about the man with no shadow?" Lionel asked. Ret shook his head, so Lionel proceeded. "In his quest for completeness, a good man chased Sun to escape Shadow for so long that, upon finally finding no Shadow around him, he wondered wither the Sun had fled."

Ret waited for a few moments and then asked, "That's it?"

"Almost," said Lionel. "You see, shadows have a bad rap. They're dark and scary, synonymous with doubt and mischief. But as undesirable as they may seem, shadows can also be very helpful because they reveal where light is. When we have faith, we step into the unknown—into darkness, into shadow. The man in the fable was so bent on fleeing his shadows of doubt and uncertainty—so consumed by his passion to supplant faith with knowledge—that, when he at last got to that point, he wondered where the Sun had gone," and then Lionel recited the last line of the fable, "unaware that it was directly above him."

Lionel slowly stood up to finish his lesson. "We can't outrun faith in our search for knowledge, Ret. You can't know something unless you're first willing to not know it, or, in other words, unless you're first willing to have faith. Oftentimes we think we've wandered way off the deep end because we can't even see our own shadow, when actually quite the opposite is true: we're so on track but don't realize it because we're standing right under the light."

Lionel stepped close to Ret. He put his hand on Ret's shoulder, and they stared at each other for a moment. A slight frown had grown on Ret's face, the kind brought on when youthful inexperience rears disgruntled ambition. As if it reminded him of a former time in his own life, Lionel returned Ret's minor scowl with a tempered smile, the kind that bespeaks tenderness and seasoning gained in the refining rotisserie of life.

Then, with his charismatic smile that could garnish even the darkest of lies with truth, Lionel concluded, "We all need a little shadow to show us our next move."

Across the complex, Mr. Coy and Ishmael stood behind one of the many unfinished walls, concealing themselves from plain sight. They were keeping a close eye on Lionel's interaction with Ret at the Intihuatana Stone.

"Lionel sure has been talking to Ret a lot lately," Mr. Coy spoke softly as he watched Lionel take his hand off Ret's shoulder and start down the stairs. "You're positive he's been drinking the extract, Ishmael?"

"Without a doubt," Ishmael affirmed. "I pour a dose into his personal flask every chance I get. So far, I've been undetected, sir."

"Well done," Mr. Coy complimented. "Keep up the good work. Thanks to you, I can sleep at night."

Though Lionel had excused himself and started down the stairs, Ret stood in place, contemplating the possible meaning of Lionel's parting words. Ret looked down at his own shadow. It lay on the ground to his right, a bit behind him, short in length since it was still early in the afternoon. Almost out of instinct, Ret glanced to his left, a little in front of him, then heavenward. As he knew he would, there he found the sun, directly opposite the slant of his shadow. It was a commonsense fact that he had never thought much of before: how a shadow gives away the location of its light source. But there had to be more to it than that, for the depth of Lionel's lessons were never so shallow.

Still standing and engrossed in thought, Ret stared purposelessly at the Intihuatana Stone in front of him. He hadn't paid much attention to it until now, and he was somewhat intrigued by its erratic shape. Overall, it looked like a deli sandwich with an extra thick toothpick stuck through the center: there was an upper slab stacked atop a lower one, as well as a stunted pillar-like piece jutting up from the top in the center, curiously carved to serve the sundial-like functions that Lionel had alluded to.

The recollection of its potentially astronomical purposes prompted Ret to take a closer look at the peculiar top piece, a rectangular block sitting on its short side. The prism was not shadowless, which made sense since the nearest equinox was months away. In fact, a waxing shadow was already present behind its eastern side. If the rumors were true, as Lionel had mentioned, that the block held some affinity to the solstices, then the phenomenon would have to include the presence—not the absence—of shadow.

It was at the end of this maze of thought when the mouse of Ret's reasoning reached its cheesy prize. With swelling interest, he studied the shadow of the upright brick, which would have been quite ordinary had it not been for an inconsistency in the tabletop. A large portion of the top layer had not been made level with the rest of it, so it rose like a step, as when a tree root abruptly forces a sidewalk slab upward. This disparity in depth distorted the shadow. With wide eyes, Ret gaped at the shaded image before him: it was his scar.

With restrained excitement, he manipulated the shadow to make sure he wasn't imagining things. He passed his hands in and around and through the dark figure, only to confirm its authenticity. At one point, he grasped the stone itself to test its mobility. Though it refused to budge, as soon as Ret touched it, the stone began to spark and smoke. In fact, it put on the same spectacle as had both Mr. Coy's pilfered rock and Lionel's airmailed sliver. This time, however, Ret retained his grip.

The block erupted into a smoldering mass of flames and steam. Despite the blinding effervescence, Ret maintained his hold on the prolonged and miniature explosion, well aware that the combustion was a result of his tactile stimulus. Unharmed by the incineration, Ret could feel the stone lessening in size as it was reduced to ash and vapor.

Meanwhile, the pyrotechnic display had not gone unnoticed. Ret's three companions saw the unintentional smoke signals and came running. Lionel was first at the scene, followed by Coy and Ishmael. They dared not say a word, too enthralled by the show. Though his body was nearly engulfed in smoke, the fizzing fire and sputtering sparks lit up Ret's glowing face.

Soon, the charring ceased and smoke dispersed. The rectangular rock having completely disintegrated, Ret found himself gripping what appeared to be a pair of shoes affixed to the top of the Intihuatana Stone. Though made of rock, they were apparently unresponsive to Ret's touch. They constituted a pair of very unique footwear, consisting of an unenclosed sole with nothing but a cupped toe to keep it from slipping off. Combined with a set of sturdy spikes underneath, they were a cross between a flip-flop and a cleat.

"I wonder if they come in my size," Mr. Coy whispered hopefully to Ishmael.

"What happened here?" Lionel asked urgently.

"The stone," Ret began to explain, blowing ash from his face. "It cast a shadow that looked just like my scar, so I started fiddling with it. Turns out, it was the same kind of stone you two have." He singled out Mr. Coy and Lionel. "So when I touched it, it started to burn, and this time I didn't let go."

Lionel, upon realizing at least some of his allegorical advice was making a difference, beamed at Ret who, soot-faced, grinned back.

"So what are the shoes for?" Ishmael inquired.

"Wearing, of course," Mr. Coy said mockingly, leaping onto the granite slab. "Although, my impeccable sense of fashion tells me these are *so* Stone Age." Despite his critique, Mr. Coy attempted to slip his foot into one of the shoes, only to find it wasn't his fit. Finding all eyes on him, he blushed and pulled away. "Come and take a look at these, Ish," Coy said, calling him onto the stone. "Something from your country, perhaps?"

Ishmael joined Ret and Coy on the rock for his requested examination. "They're nothing I've seen in all my years," Ishmael confessed. "Then again, I'm an apothecary, not a podiatrist."

"Yes," said Coy, "but you *do* make a mean cherry cobbler."

"Mr. Coy is right," Lionel interrupted, not wishing to be left out of the impromptu council meeting.

"I am?"

"Yes," said Lionel, lunging onto the sacred stone. "These shoes are obviously meant to be worn." Then, urging Ret toward them, he added, "Worn by Ret."

Mr. Coy quickly shot Ishmael a look that demanded reassurance. Ishmael gave an imperceptible nod, and Mr. Coy's concerned face melted.

"Of course they are," Mr. Coy said confidently. "Go ahead, Ret. Give them a try."

Despite the oddity of Mr. Coy and Lionel actually agreeing on something, Ret didn't have to think twice about their suggestion. There wasn't a sound in all the Andes as Ret slipped his right foot into the right shoe, then his other foot into the one that was left. All four men held their breath, bracing for the unknown. None of them—not even Ret—could feign a foothold on what would happen next.

CHAPTER 10

UNEXPECTED
CONNECTIONS

Pauline was grateful they had arrived at the airport with time to spare since it took longer than anticipated to check Ana's slew of luggage, which came at a price that was as hefty as the bags themselves. Fortunately (and to Pauline's great relief), Miss Carmen graciously footed the bill, which also included a nice meal at an overpriced restaurant near the international terminal plus some last-minute snacks in preparation for the long flights ahead of them.

"I've flown this route enough times to know that some peanuts and a couple swigs of soda aren't exactly enough to satisfy an appetite," Miss Carmen told them, deriding the scanty in-flight service as her fellow travelers covered the concession stand's checkout counter with a bounty of goodies.

As it was the first time they had spent any real quality time together, Pauline was finding Miss Carmen to be a surprisingly pleasant woman. She was kind and generous, certainly interesting to talk to, not to mention her stunning beauty, which the vain tend to repel out of covetousness but the homely befriend from flattery. What pleased Pauline most, however, was Miss Carmen's increasing interest in Ana, and though obviously reciprocated by Ana herself, it came at the expense of Paige. Of course, the daughter of Mr. Coy didn't make a fuss about being shoved to the side. She was more or less content to walk alongside Pauline, pulling her friend's extra carryon bag behind her, both silently overhearing the more important conversation strutting in front of them. It was long ago when Paige first learned the sad truth that, for some unfortunate reason, there's room for only two peas in a pod because three's a crowd.

Contrary to their expectations, the plane they boarded was not very large. About three dozen rows were divided by a narrow aisle with a pair of seats on each side. Miss Carmen led her guests toward the back of the cabin, where she and Ana sat next to each other on one side of the aisle with Pauline and Paige doing likewise on the other. With the volleyball stars chatting away, Pauline lost herself within the pages of a thick cookbook while Paige stared longingly out the small window. Once the thrill of takeoff had ended and the aerial views had been swallowed by thick layers of clouds, Paige's mind turned to Ret and stayed there for a long time.

"What's on your mind, Paige?" Pauline asked, closing her book and shaking Paige out of her trance-like pondering. Paige had been so enveloped in her thoughts that she wasn't aware that over an hour had transpired since their departure.

"Oh, nothing," she fibbed. "Just mesmerized by the view, I guess." Paige glanced out the window to find the unsearchable sky black with night. She smiled hopefully at Pauline, who couldn't be fooled.

"You should get some sleep, dear," Pauline suggested, proffering a plastic-bagged pillow.

"No thanks," said Paige politely. "I've never been able to sleep much on planes—even when I was little."

"Did you travel a lot when you were a kid?" asked Pauline, who hadn't done much flying in her adult life, let alone her childhood.

"Tons," Paige replied. "Mom and Dad were always going somewhere."

At the mention of Paige's mother, Pauline was suddenly extremely interested in the conversation, which enthusiasm she tried to downplay. "You know, I don't believe I've ever met your mother," she said. "What is she like?"

"Oh, she's wonderful," said Paige with eager fondness. "Everyone loves her. She makes friends wherever she goes. She's super intelligent and very pretty. People compliment her all the time on her long, blonde hair—curly, which is where *I* get it, I suppose." Paige patted her hair with pride. "She's always happy and loves to cook—oh, you'd love her, Mrs. Cooper."

"Without a doubt," Pauline agreed. "She sounds delightful. I'd love to meet her."

"Well, that's not really possible," said Paige.

"Those are the exact words your father said to me," Pauline recalled, a little perturbed, "and I'd really like to know why—"

"She's dead."

Pauline instantly fell mute, as if some force had just tightly grabbed her lungs. For several breathless seconds, she was thrown into a kaleidoscope of emotions. Finally, she thought to say, "She's...she's what?"

"She passed away about ten years ago," Paige said, her emotions stable.

"Oh, Paige," Pauline said consolingly, "I'm...I'm so sorry. I had no idea."

"It's okay, Mrs. Cooper; you didn't know."

Pauline utilized the next few moments to contemplate the best way to continue extracting information on such a delicate subject. "If I may ask," she gently pressed, "why do you speak about your mother as though she's still...you know...still alive?"

"Because she is," Paige admitted quite candidly. "Well, don't get me wrong; I know she's gone: I remember laying a flower on her casket. I just don't know *where* she's gone. She went somewhere— somewhere I can't follow until I die, too. It's kind of like when the sun sets: even though you and I can't see it anymore, another part of the world is saying 'good morning.' So I keep my memories of her alive to remind me that she's not dead forever—sort of like you and Jaret." Pauline cringed at the unexpected reference to her husband. "Deep inside, I know I'll see Mom again— somewhere, somehow. Death can't kill a love like ours. That's what I feel, anyway."

Pauline was completely beside herself. The revelation of Mrs. Coy's death was one thing, but the apparent insensitivity with which Paige had relayed it was quite another. Had Pauline been Paige's deceased mother, she would have been insulted, for here was her daughter talking about death as though it was just a natural part of mortal life. Where were her tears? Where was her sorrow? Why was there neither grief in her tone nor mourning in her attitude?

"It must be on account of her age," Pauline thought within her mind, the one territory where no one could say she was wrong. "I mean, to lose your mother so early in life is tragic, of course, but certainly not without its advantages: their relationship still being developed, the depth of their love not fully realized, the innocence of childhood, the lofty hopes of youth, the forgetfulness awarded by the passage of time." The voice in her head spoke even more quickly than that of her throat. "Yes, the cheeky girl is simply too young and inexperienced to know what true love is and how crushing it is to lose it. One day, she'll have to wake up and face reality."

The truth, though unacknowledged by herself, was that Paige's confident composure had quite the unsettling effect on Pauline because it clashed with the way she preferred to handle her similar situation. If anything, Paige's burden was harder to bear since her loved one's demise was confirmed, and, yet, instead of sorrow, there was strength—prudence in place of passion, faith in the face of fear. And although it worried Pauline—troubled and taunted her with the threat of demolishing her remorseful retreat—there was something attractive, contagious even, about Paige's earned equilibrium, so much so, in fact, that the more rational part of Pauline, as small as it was, wanted in on it.

"So, Paige, dear," said Mrs. Cooper, trying to extend herself beyond her comfort zone, "how...uh...how exactly did your mother...you know...die—er, pass away?" In her nervousness, she was subconsciously tracing never-ending circles with her finger along the slight indentation on the tray table where a cup is meant to sit.

Paige did not rush to reply as she had previously done. Instead, she leaned forward and looked around in every direction. The travelers in her immediate vicinity were either napping or tuned into media via earphones, and both Ana and Miss Carmen were sound asleep, the one leaning on the other for support. Finding the area free of possible eavesdroppers, Paige proceeded.

"Well, it might help if I give you a little background first," she said in hushed but willing tones. "I was pretty young at the time—five years old when Mom died—so some of the details are a little fuzzy." ("Just as I thought," Pauline's psyche echoed within.) "I can remember a few things about Mom, but most of what I know I've learned from the staff at the Manor since Dad never talks about her and forbids us from doing so—" then, smiling, "—at least in his presence."

"I learned that the hard way," Pauline mumbled, rolling her eyes in recollection of her ill-fated attempt to strike up conversation with Mr. Coy about his wife that day not too long ago on the yacht.

"Before Mom got sick," Paige continued, "it seemed like we were always on the move, always going somewhere. I only remember scenes: Mom trying to occupy me in airplanes, Dad cradling me on nauseating trips at sea, a scary-looking military general with a mustache who tried to get me to smile but just made me cry, fancy dinners where I always spilled things, men in white coats letting me hold one of their lab rats, riding a bumpy camel in the desert (which I think is why I have a phobia of getting sand in my hair)...lots of random snapshots like that, almost like pictures in a photo album. At the time, I was just along for the ride, thinking I lived a normal life."

"But the maids at the Manor have helped fill in the gaps," Paige said. "As it turns out, my parents were both pretty famous people. Dad was one of the top dogs in the government or the military—or both; we're not really sure—and his love of math and engineering led him to invent lots of things. Mom was a world-renowned scientist who had won awards for her research and earned all kinds of recognition for her philanthropic work. She helped discover vaccines, relieve suffering, and improve societies all over the globe."

"Wow," Pauline commented, "impressive."

"And that's just the beginning," Paige stated with admiration in her eyes. "When Mom and Dad met and got married, they became an unstoppable team. They were the perfect match, both incredibly brilliant, both endowed with a love for helping others. One of the maids told me Mom and Dad were pressured not to have any children because a family would impede their work, but they obviously disagreed." Paige beamed. "And when I came into the picture, they didn't slow down a bit. In fact, my birth opened even more doors and softened even more hearts."

"It must have been the curls," Pauline said playfully.

"I just remember life being so good," Paige reminisced fondly. "We were so happy—all three of us, all the time. I still don't know where our home was, we traveled so much. But it didn't matter because we were together—always together. In every photograph I have, we're together, smiling. They could have left me at home, called a sitter, hired a traveling nanny. But they didn't. There's a picture from when we met the Prime Minister of India, and Mom's shaking hands with him while holding me in her arms. There's another one from when we met a tribal leader in the jungles of Africa, and Dad's carrying me on his shoulders, and I'm holding his machete."

"I may not have known where we were going or what we were doing," said Paige, "but I always knew my parents loved me. There was never any doubt in my mind. I could feel it. They treated me like a princess (and they met quite a few real ones over the years). And I loved them back, knowing their love for me stemmed from their love for each other. I was young then, just a kid really, but the example of my parents' love has stayed with me all these years—true love, the kind where you care more about the other's happiness and well-being than your own. I'm sure you know what I'm talking about."

It was in this moment when Pauline began to take back the hasty judgments she had mentally made of Paige just moments earlier. She had always known Paige to be a lovely young woman, and now she was learning something of her exquisite beauty—not so much the visible attractiveness of her appearance as her far fairer and richer inner beauty.

"And then, all of a sudden," Paige continued her narrative, "Mom got sick one day. We had just taken a trip to an exotic island, I think—a really weird-looking place where Mom and Dad had found some new thing that they were anxious to research. But she became very ill, and no one could figure out what was wrong with her, not even this special doctor we went to—Cross, I think was his name. Anyway, they tried everything, but she only got worse. And then she died."

Paige looked down, but Pauline still could not detect any tears.

"And that's when life stopped being so good and happy," said Paige gloomily. "Dad changed overnight. He went from fun to weird to weirder. I never saw him smile again; in fact, I almost never saw *him* again. Tons of people started coming into our lives: maids and nurses, butlers and chauffeurs. They took care of me while Dad did…well, did other things. It was like he didn't want to see me, didn't want to be around me, didn't want to be my dad anymore. At night, I would cry for Mom, scream for Dad, but the only ones who came to my rescue were strangers. I felt so alone."

"Oh, Paige," Pauline wept, pulling the poor girl into her shoulder with love.

"That's why I'm so glad I met Ana," Paige carried on optimistically. "Yeah, she can be a little rough around the edges," they both glanced at Ana lovingly, still snoozing across the aisle with her mouth wide open, "but she has such a big heart. She's such a good friend."

"And you've been a truly outstanding friend for her, Paige," Pauline informed. "I mean it; whether she realizes it or not, Ana adores you. And so does Ret."

"He does?" Paige exclaimed with astonished glee.

"Well, maybe not in quite the same way," Pauline reasoned, "but he certainly does care for you, I'm sure. Please be patient with Ret. He's been putting himself under a lot of pressure because of this Oracle business. You do realize he was only staring at Miss Carmen at the end of your championship game because of the mark on her back, don't you?"

"I know, I know," Paige confessed in a manner that could have knocked Ret over with a feather. "It's just that I've been trying to get him to notice me for such a long time, and then some hot momma comes along and earns his immediate attention." Paige peered over Pauline to make sure Miss Carmen was still asleep. "Hopefully Ret's noticed that I've been ignoring him."

"There's no doubt about that," Pauline told her. "I'd say your silent treatment is having its intended effect."

"Well, it's not that I'm trying to be difficult," Paige explained. "It's more that I'm learning to control my feelings and remind myself that I can't force someone to love me. Life's taught me not to be a very passionate person; if there's something I really want but can't have, then I need to change what I want."

"Well, I hope Ret comes to his senses soon," said Pauline tenderly, shifting in her seat to get comfortable, "before he misses what's right in front of him. There aren't too many girls as special as Paige Coy." She embraced Paige again and handed her a pillow. "We'll kindle a fire inside of that boy yet; just you wait and see."

"I sure hope you're right, Mrs. Cooper," Paige grinned, and they both closed their eyes to rest.

○　　○　　○

"Please, Mom," Ana begged, half-conscious, "just five more minutes."

"I'm sorry, Miss, but the pilot's orders are to prepare for landing."

Ana felt the tray table in front of her fold up. She opened her eyes in alarm just as the stewardess was returning Ana's reclined seat to its upright position.

"Oh, sorry," Ana apologized as the stewardess walked away. Stretching and yawning loudly, Ana noticed her three travel partners were staring at her. "Buenos días, everyone!"

Paige returned her eyes to the window. With fascination, she watched as the thriving metropolis of Santiago came into view. The Chilean capital sat in the center of a large, bowl-shaped valley, surrounded by towering mountains on all sides. As impressive as it was to Paige, it seemed to her a mere barrio compared to Sunken Earth.

Their first step inside the airport reminded them that they were far away from home. Despite their good grades in Spanish class so far this year, Ana and Paige were lost linguistically.

"Looks like we're not in Kansas anymore, Toto," Ana observed, gripping Paige by the arm. "It's like everything's in a different language or something."

"Sí," Paige replied.

Pauline was faring even worse than the girls, for all she recalled from her foreign language education eons ago was how to say the hardly helpful question,

"Where is the library?"

"Biblioteca," she said aloud with pride in an attempted but terrible Spanish accent.

"The hills with the library," Ana said with desperation. "All I want to know is where the English *bathroom* is. I need to pee like a—"

"Baño!" Paige cried. "There it is!" She pointed to a sign bearing the internationally known, though faceless, man and woman, hanging above two doorless archways.

Recognizing the caricatures that symbolize restrooms, Ana hurried in that direction, mumbling, "I hope the ladies wear dresses here, too."

As the rest of the party waited for Ana just outside the bathroom, they heard a flush, followed by Ana's exclamation, "Hey, guys, the toilet bowl water really *does* flush the opposite way south of the equator."

"That's my girl," Pauline sighed with amusement, just happy that no one walking by seemed to understand what the American girl in the middle stall had to say.

Needless to say, Paige and the Coopers were relieved to have Miss Carmen as their guide.

"Stay close to me," the Chilean native advised them as they approached customs. "I don't want to lose any of you."

Like a slithering serpent, they held hands and weaved in and out of the throngs of travelers on their trek from the international terminal to the main concourse.

"I've arranged for our luggage to be brought to the hotel," Miss Carmen explained, "so let's pile it all here while I locate our transportation." She pointed to a spot near the sky concierge.

"Talk about five-star service," Ana cheered.

Standing on the edge of a noisy street in the warm summer air, Miss Carmen flagged down a taxi, and all four of them crammed into the backseat. Miss Carmen barked orders to the driver in Spanish, and they sped away.

Even though Paige and the Coopers had no idea where they needed to go, they glanced at each other with puzzlement when their driver turned onto a restricted driveway and entered an extension of the tarmac. They rolled underneath the bellies of parked planes, mail jets, and sundry aeronautical vessels. Coming to a stop inside a dark hangar, Miss Carmen immediately got out of the taxi and shut the door behind her. Paige gulped, and she and Ana glared at Pauline with worry.

"Maybe she went to get some money to pay the cab driver," Pauline suggested, trembling.

"Don't you worry your little head, Pauline," the driver said in a voice that sounded unpleasantly familiar. Turning around to face his passengers, the driver removed his shawl-like hood and hissed, "This ride's on the house." The girls gasped: it was Bubba.

Her shock quickly giving way to rancor, Ana immediately punched him in the nose. Caught by surprise, the blow sent Bubba backwards into the steering wheel, whose horn bellowed for several seconds.

"And don't even think about asking what *that* was for," she threatened.

"Take them away," Bubba ordered, massaging his nose.

Like chauffeurs for criminals, a group of thugs opened the rear doors, grabbed the girls, and tied them up as if they were unruly swine.

"Miss Carmen!" Ana shouted, hoping her coach could hear her, wherever she had gone. "Miss Carmen! Watch out—there's…"

Ana fell silent when Miss Carmen emerged from the lowered cargo lift of the small jet not far from them inside the hangar. Her high-heeled shoes rapped the metallic lift, sending echoes of betrayal throughout the hangar. Ana stared at her with utter bewilderment.

"Did you see the pure-blood I captured?" Bubba asked as Carmen approached the group.

"All strapped in and ready to die," she answered affirmatively. "Nice work, captain." Miss Carmen twirled a lock of Bubba's fire-red hair with her finger and then delivered a juicy kiss on his crimson lips without a trace of abashment.

"My one native is nothing compared to your catch," Bubba said, pulling away.

"Oh, it was easy, really," Miss Carmen sighed, "thanks to this one." She kicked Ana's foot. Then she turned to the muscle and instructed them, relative to the girls, "Put these next to the sacrifice!"

"Sacrifice?" Paige yelped as the thugs dragged her and the Cooper women into the aircraft, Ana still enveloped in her astounded stupor.

"I demand to know what you intend to do with us," Pauline asserted. "This isn't the first time you've tied me up, Bubba, you little wart. Mark my words, you won't—"

"Drug 'em!"

At the command, each of the girls' menacing escorts produced a cloth and shoved it in their squirming hostages' mouths. With each inhalation, the world turned more blurry and distorted. Finding themselves lying on the cold, hard floor of the cargo hold, they saw next to them an olive-skinned man, already unconscious. The lift rose until it shut, the engines started with a roar, and the girls' vision went black.

○   ○   ○

"Paige!" Ana called out, awaking from her brief coma. "I just had the weirdest dream. We were riding in a taxi, and Bubba was the driver! Then he tied us up and—" She stopped upon realizing that her hands and feet were bound. "Oh," she deduced, "so it wasn't a dream. I hate waking up!"

It was the rough landing that had put an end to their blackout. Sitting up to take stock of their plight, they were startled by a sudden jolt as the rear of the grounded plane began to open. They squinted as abundant sunshine poured into the cargo hold, at whose mouth several large silhouettes appeared and advanced toward them. Half blind and still enchained, the captives were hauled into some sort of crude land rover, their native counterpart wailing as if cognizant of his fate.

On account of their blanched vision, Paige and the Coopers had to rely on their other senses for information pertaining to their new location. A hot sun baked their skin whenever the cool breeze died down. The crisp air tasted of salt, and the faint crashing of waves was heard in between the grunts and jeers of their captors. The terrain was very bumpy, and occasionally wafts of disturbed dust filtered into their nostrils.

In no time at all, the road assumed an incline. As the view to one side had become quite dark, the girls steered their sights in that direction to finally give their eyes ample time to adjust. After a few moments, they could see that they were part of a convoy, climbing a spiraling path that wound upwards along the side of a mountain. In the other direction, ocean stretched infinitely, brilliantly reflecting the tropical sunlight.

At length, they arrived at the summit, where the caravan stopped and became ambulatory. Bubba and Miss Carmen led the procession, with the prisoners being prodded forward behind them and a gaggle of jubilant ruffians bringing up the rear.

Without any warning, the ground beneath their feet shook violently. Then a large plume of smoke shot up beside them. Everyone except the female hostages quivered and cowered with fear as if in sudden, remembered reverence to some divine, displeased deity. It was at this moment when it became unmistakably clear that they were walking along the rim of an active volcano.

When the shaking had subsided, the group pressed on. Eventually, the prisoners were brought to a landing where a part of the crater's cliffside extended furthest out, creating a miniature jetty much like the infamous plank of a pirate ship. Paige peered over the edge into the volcano's throat. Through the smoke and steam, she could see a tumultuous bed of churning lava, bubbling and gurgling. It was like peeking into a stifling oven, so powerful was the heat against her face.

"Take a seat, blondie," Bubba hissed, grabbing Paige by the shoulder and shoving her into Ana and Pauline. Bubba then seized the man they had called "the pure-blood" and towed him toward the crater's edge.

The native, who resembled Miss Carmen's general appearance, squirmed and struggled intensely as Bubba lugged him away. Aided by another disorienting tremor from the agitated volcano, he managed to wiggle himself free from his bonds and struck Bubba, who forsook his grip. The noble man ran for his life but could not evade the nimble guards. With a guard clutching each of his arms and legs, the near-escapee was brought back to Bubba, face to face.

Suddenly, the volcano rumbled yet again. The same reverential attitude fell over the audience. The quaking lasted much longer this time. When it concluded, Bubba stuck his bruised face within inches of his prisoner.

"The good news is you ought to appease the volcano just long enough until our more worthy sacrifice arrives," Bubba sneered, glancing at the girls to make sure they had heard his words, which pertained to them in part. "The bad news is," he continued, glaring at the native with pure hatred, "I won't have a reason to sacrifice any more of your kind—or what's left of it," he smirked, "you miserable—"

The brave native spat in Bubba's face.

After a few unnerving moments, Bubba spoke up. "You know, I was only going to *enslave* the rest of your race," he said, wiping his fuming face, "but now, thanks to you, I think I'll keep killing them until they're extinct!

Throw him in!" Amid blood-curdling shrieks from the doomed and ritualistic chants from the goons, Bubba's minions heaved their human sacrifice over the edge to his death. The girls looked on in speechless terror as the volcano belched a plume of smoke and then became still.

"Well, we've had quite the change in travel plans, haven't we?" said Miss Carmen pleasantly, striding up to the girls. "I forgot to tell you about our connecting flight to beautiful Easter Island—or, as we like to call it, *Fire* Island. Silly me!"

She reached inside Ana's pocket and retrieved her cell phone without any resistance. Searching through the list of contacts, she found the name she was looking for and initiated a call.

"Now then," said Miss Carmen, turning the dialing phone to face the girls, "which one of you would like to inform Ret?"

CHAPTER 11

THE BELLY
OF THE LAKE

It was like something out of a movie. As soon as Ret slipped both of his feet into the stone shoes, the world became one great blur. While Ret, Lionel, Mr. Coy, and Ishmael stood motionless, the entire earth flashed before their eyes as its motion was expedited exponentially. Like an accelerated flipbook, the sky alternated between day and night multiple times, while the indiscernible terrain shifted back and forth from land to sea even more frequently. It seemed, in a very literal sense, the shoes had flipped the fast-forward switch on the reel of time.

After only a few seconds, the world resumed its normal pace. The four men took a moment to regain their bearings, each having been thrown a bit off balance from their high-speed voyage. They were facing a landscape of rolling hills, brown and dusty with scant vegetation. A warm sun combined with brisk air to create one of those confusing climates in which the body flirts with perspiration. Ret was about to write it off as a terribly bland place when he turned around and discovered an enormous lake in their immediate vicinity. Startled by such an unexpected sight, Ret took a few steps backwards. Suddenly remembering he was still wearing the shoes and realizing they were now moveable, Ret's footing floundered, and he fell to the ground.

"These were obviously *not* made for walking," Ret concluded as he removed the shoes from his feet. Though they slipped off very easily, their long and thick spikes created a platform that would have presented trouble for even a life-long wearer of high-heeled shoes.

"Let me carry those for you, sir," Ishmael volunteered, graciously securing the bulky shoes in his pack.

"Thanks, Ishmael," said Ret, rising to his feet and dusting himself off. "So where are we?"

"*I* can answer that," Mr. Coy promised proudly. He whipped out his cell phone, pressed a few buttons, and held it up toward the sky. After a brief pause, he lowered the device and glared at it. Obviously unsatisfied, he repeated these steps. Still unhappy, he waved his phone all around, apparently searching for a signal. "Lousy service," he grumbled, still gesticulating like a chorister.

Finally, he cheered, "Aha! My satellite navigator says we are still in Peru, right next to—ah, yes," he smiled, "right next to Lake Titicaca." He chuckled, "You never forget a name like that."

Lionel, who had yet to say a word, was visibly engrossed in thought, trying to find a rational explanation for the unique form of travel in which they had just participated. At Mr. Coy's pronouncement of their new location, Lionel took out his own phone. With a quizzical look yet urgent voice, he asked, "Coy, what date do you have?"

In a debonair tone, Coy responded, "Oh, she's a real fox: brown hair, hazel eyes; not the sharpest tool in the shed, but certainly the shiniest, if you know what I—"

"No," Lionel interrupted, "I mean what do you have *for* the date?"

"Well," Coy carried on, "I thought we'd start with a nice candlelit dinner and then maybe catch a flick." Not amused, Lionel stared at the ground with strained patience. "It's the twenty-sixth," Coy groaned, finally answering the original question. "Lighten up, you stiff."

"Well soak me in brine and call me a pickle," Lionel said, his face lighting up with awe. "I think we just experienced time travel!" The claim was greeted with stares of disbelief.

"How do you figure?" Ishmael queried.

"Instead of *us* coming *here*," Lionel postulated, "*here* came to *us!*" His listeners' puzzled looks requested explanation. "Think about it: *we* didn't move an inch, right?" The others nodded in agreement. "But everything else moved, right?" Again, nods. "That's because the earth is constantly in motion. It revolves around the sun *while* rotating about its axis *while* tilting back and forth—all at the same time. If we were to stand still in a vacuum, the earth would roll right along without us, which is precisely what just happened. The spot in the universe where we're standing right now is the exact same spot where the Intihuatana Stone at Machu Picchu was just a few days ago."

"So it's like a time-warp!" Ret deduced.

"Yes, and it's absolutely brilliant!" Lionel gloried, brimming with wonder now. "Of course, I have no idea *how* it was done—how we defied gravity or how time sped up—but still, we're here, aren't we?" That was a fact no one could dispute. "Now the question is why did the earth bring us *here?*"

During the next few moments of pensive silence that followed, Mr. Coy, scratching his head and rubbing his stomach, asked, "So *who's* got the pickle?"

Lionel brought up an excellent point: while wondering the *how* would certainly lead to thought-provoking theories, to ponder instead the *why* would hopefully reveal life-changing truths. Why, of all places, were they sent to this place? Despite the list of unknowns, Ret took comfort in the bolstered likelihood that they had been on the right track all along. Now, the task was to ensure no deviation. He glanced at his scar; there was no sensation, as he half expected, and yet, as a result of the application of Lionel's recent counsel, the same could be said of his leveling temper. Time travel, Ret concluded, ought to be proof enough.

Just then, they heard rustling in the nearby brush. Ret's heart jumped with both excitement and apprehension. Something had stirred within a patch of dense shrubbery and, now having mistakenly brought attention to itself, fell silent. Mr. Coy exchanged a soundless glance with Ishmael, as did Ret with Lionel. With suspended breath, the four of them slowly crept toward the bush in question, whose noiselessness screamed as loudly as sirens.

Suddenly, a man jumped out from behind the brush. Without a word, he raced away from the quartet, who recoiled defensively at the emergence of a swift-footed person. Immediately, they engaged the runaway in hot pursuit, with Ret quickly taking the lead.

"Wait!" Ret called out. "Don't leave!"

The fugitive flew down the hillside, headed straight for the lake. Reaching the water's edge, he hopped into a small boat and frantically began paddling away from shore.

"Wait!" Ret tried again. "Come back!" But the man persisted.

Not willing to be outrun, Ret zoomed down the hillside. As he approached the lake, he leapt onto a wet rock and manipulated it to become a sort of trampoline, launching him forward. He soared well beyond the gentle waves lapping the shore and fell into the fleeing boat.

Scared beyond his wits, the man forsook his failed flight by boat and prepared to abandon ship. Just before his dive, Ret caught hold of his leg and prevented his escape. The trembling man scrambled, rocking the boat violently, but Ret retained his grip.

"It's okay, it's okay," Ret coaxed, with a voice as soothing as balm. "I won't hurt you. I'm your friend."

With a face still stricken with terror, the man ceased his unruliness and stared timidly at Ret. He saw in Ret's eyes proof of the truthfulness of his words. Then, looking at Ret more closely, a feeling of relief washed over the man, as if he had initially mistaken Ret for someone else. With lingering caution, he picked up his oar and started to row further into the lake.

"Wait!" Ret protested. "What about my friends?"

The man looked back at the shore. Lionel and Ishmael were standing with Mr. Coy, who had his hand extended with the thumb raised like a hitchhiker. Expressionless, the man obliged. Warily, the three new riders boarded the boat, partly leery of the intentions of its oarsman but mostly of the integrity of its construction. The canoe-shaped vessel was entirely made of reeds—long, bendable reeds, yellow in color, that had been stitched and tied together tightly and thickly enough to keep out water. It was like floating in a buoyant basket.

Their ferryman made no attempts at conversation. Standing at the helm, he kept his back to his foreign passengers, although he rather frequently turned his head just enough to keep a suspicious eye on them. Initially, Lionel rattled off salutations in multiple languages and dialects, hoping to stimulate dialogue. After about a dozen tries, the man made a sharp, convulsive sound.

"Hmm," Lionel thought, "I'm not sure what *that* translates to."

"That's because it was a sneeze," Mr. Coy informed him.

The lake was remarkably placid. Except for the occasional flip of a fish or flit of a fowl, there was nothing but the gentle wake of their boat that disturbed the dark, deep water. As they ventured farther from shore, the vastness of the lake became more apparent with every stroke of the paddle. Much longer than it was wide, its entire circumference was dominated by great hills and mountains. Ret was accustomed to seeing such isolated and attractive locales thronged by carefree recreators and lined with busy marinas.

But not this place. A solemn fear enshrouded every breath, as if a piercing eye monitored every move. One felt to curse the sun for revealing hideouts and distrust the wind for carrying whispers. It was a palpable veil that thickened like fog as they floated deeper into the heart of the lake, enough to cause a visitor to wonder if a more appropriate name might be Eerie and if its gondoliers had interned at Styx.

Eventually, Ret began to see large deposits of floating debris in the waters ahead. From far away, they looked like random heaps of accumulated rubbish, but as they drew nearer, Ret recognized them for what they really were: floating, inhabited islands. Totaling more than three dozen, each island measured about the size of a cul-de-sac in a modern subdivision. Everything, from the thick foundation to the crude but comely huts, was made of the straw-like reeds that were so prevalent throughout the lake. Maintenance seemed a constant battle, as residents were transporting harvested reeds and laying them down in low spots. All in all, it seemed a very primitive and precarious place to live, where the greatest threat was likely either rough and turbulent weather or the huffing and puffing of a Big Bad Wolf.

The man rowing the boat took them a good

distance into the colony, passing several islands along the way. Ret and his associates studied the island dwellers as intently as they did their intruders. The natives were short and stout. The women sported bright-colored skirts and long-sleeved blouses, their dark hair worn in long braids. The men were also fully clothed, and everyone seemed to don a hat. Their skin was dark, either from sun exposure or heredity. Children clung to parents as all eyes fell upon the strangers. Ret wondered if any of them knew how to smile.

At last, their boat came to a stop alongside one of the islands, and the man leapt onto its thatched floor. Extending his hand, he helped his four riders in their climb out of the craft and onto the raised island. With each step, Ret sank a few inches, and it felt as though he was walking on a waterbed. In very little time, a group of armed men emerged from among the huts and advanced towards the newcomers. One individual, who by far was the most decorated, stepped forward and addressed them.

"What business do you have with my people?" the chief bellowed, in a most unfriendly manner.

Lionel, surprised to hear a familiar tongue, answered respectfully, "No business, sir, but to learn and be on our way."

Just then, the oarsman appeared at the chief's side and whispered in his ear.

"My spy tells me you carry the cleats that belong to the man with flaming hair," the chief accused.

"Cleats?" Ret asked, turning to Lionel.

"He must mean the shoes," Lionel assumed.

"Man with flaming hair?" Ishmael wondered of Mr. Coy.

"Poor guy," said Coy. "Must've sat too long under the dryer at the salon."

"Are you referring to *these,* sir?" said Lionel, lifting one of the shoes out of Ishmael's pack. The entire crowd let out a frightful gasp at the unveiling of the footwear. "We found these at Machu Picchu."

"You mean the city in the mountains?" the chief asked earnestly. "Tell me, are the people safe?"

"People?" Lionel said with consternation. "Sir, no one has lived there for centuries."

Sorrow engulfed the chief's countenance. He rested his large arm on the man next to him for support as he digested the news.

"Good chief," Lionel crooned, "who is the man with flaming hair?"

"The enemy of our peace!" roared the chief, his fists clenched. "Our ancestors came from a volcano-island, far beyond where sea and sky meet—a place they called the Navel of the World. They lived in harmony until they were discovered by a man with flaming hair who believed there was a great treasure hidden within the island's mighty volcano—a treasure that he would share with our ancestors if they helped him uncover it. He flattered them into joining his cause. As the generations passed, each aging man with flaming hair passed his power to a younger man with flaming hair, each more ruthless than his predecessor. Their dark reigns saw the exploitation of the island's limited resources, the starvation of its people, their shipment as slaves to foreign lands, the spread of strange diseases, sacrilege, and deadly skirmishes."

"That sounds terrible," Ret grieved.

"But the volcano fought back," the chief continued. "It came alive to defend itself. The man with flaming hair claimed only one of pure blood could subdue the volcano, survive its heat, and locate the prize. He tricked them into believing that all who tried to tame the beast were heroes—that any attempt was worthy of honor. Using the very rock and ash they excavated from the volcano, our people built great statues as a tribute to their martyred relatives and positioned them facing inland so as to watch over and protect the living."

"But they were deceived: it was really an act of suicide. When our dwindling ancestry finally realized the trickery, the man with flaming hair began to sacrifice our people without restraint—men, women, and children."

Lionel cringed with disgust.

"Knowing the man's insatiable passion would spell their extinction," said the chief, "our people gradually began to escape, secretly fleeing the island in small groups in boats of reed." He pointed to the canoe they had arrived in. "Many died at sea, but those who reached land began new lives. Some settled in the tops of the mountains. Our parents found refuge at this lakeside. I suspect more are scattered in every part of the land."

The chief's tone seemed to soften until he added, "But the man with flaming hair continued to haunt us, thirsty for our blood. One day, he appeared on our shores, drunk with revenge and still in search of human sacrifices. He and his men pillaged our homes; burned our crops; and kidnapped our people, who were never to be seen again. We never know where along the beach he and his forces will surface, but they always depart at the Sacred Rocks on the island in the belly of the lake." He motioned to a distant island, far from them on the other side of the lake. "In our extremity, we have built these floating islands, which make it difficult for our enemies to reach us. We have enjoyed relative peace but know we must be vigilant if our race is to survive."

The chief's sobering narrative cast a pall on the already sullen surroundings. In a sweeping yet searching stare, Ret surveyed the island community and its hosts of vulnerable vagabonds. They were a suppressed people, acquainted with injustice, not unlike the destitute hordes of Sunken Earth: largely unlearned, clearly unmoneyed, and with no apparent beauty. They wore homespun fabrics, ignorant of current fashion trends. They ate reeds and tubers on crude cookery. Their shanties were but overturned wicker baskets, free of modern conveniences. No cars. No restaurants. Not even a toilet.

Ret knew something of despoiled societies: the exploited and extradited, the oppressed and ostracized, the war torn and wiped out. He had read about enslaved races, genocidal purges, tyrannical takeovers. He had heard of rioters, criminals, anarchists. But such atrocities hardly seemed real to him—as intangible as headlines, never anything that related to his here-and-now. They were tales from history books—accounts of a different time. They were stories for news anchors—reports from distant places. In hindsight, even the tragedy of Sunken Earth seemed otherworldly. In fact, all of these exotic destinations—with their inflated histories and deplorable societies—differed so radically from the norms of Ret's day-to-day life that he was beginning to think that maybe *he* was the one who lived outside the real world, ignorantly encapsulated in the isolated bubble of his disconnected life back in detached Tybee.

Ret felt something vibrating in his pocket. His phone showed an incoming call from Ana. Although he wondered why she would be calling him during their respective trips, especially when their relationship was still on the rocks, Ret ignored the call, since answering it would certainly be a rude gesture in his present situation. A few seconds later, his voicemail chimed to inform him that Ana had left him a message, which she almost never did.

"Would you excuse me, please?" Ret petitioned, stepping away from the group to listen to the message privately.

He was surprised to hear Paige's voice, trembling and urgent: "Ret!" she throbbed. "The volleyball tournament was a setup; Miss Carmen's a fake. She and Bubba captured us and took us to an island where they're going to throw us into a volcano if you don't come." She was clearly in great distress. "Don't come, Ret! It's a trap—"

"Alright, alright," Miss Carmen's villainous voice was heard. Taking command of the phone call, she snarled, "Come to Easter Island now or your next call will be the screams of your dying friends. Bye-bye!"

Stunned, Ret stood in shock for several seconds, in disbelief of what he had just heard.

"Are you still there?" his phone asked in its female, computer-generated voice. "Press 1 for..."

Ret saved the message and then returned to the group.

"I'm sorry to interrupt, but would you excuse *us?*" Ret requested of the chief with a broad smile, grabbing his three cohorts and pulling them aside in a huddle.

"Listen to *this,*" Ret whispered soberly. He played the message for all to hear. When it concluded, he waited, eager to listen to their observations.

Mr. Coy was the first to speak up. "Wow," he said with wonder, still staring at Ret's phone. "Who's your service provider?"

"Who is Bubba?" Ishmael wondered, disregarding Mr. Coy's immaturity with a more appropriate question.

"It's a long story," Ret sighed, "but let's just say he's a man with flaming hair." A light bulb went on in Ishmael's head.

"What do you think we should do, Ret?" Lionel asked.

"I've been thinking," Ret said, overjoyed that someone was asking for his opinion. "When we found the lines in the Nazca Desert, where was the outline of Machu Picchu?" Lionel and Ishmael waited for him to answer his own question while Mr. Coy was, once again, wildly waving his phone. "It was in the figure's belly—or his navel." Now a light bulb was flickering within Lionel. "And where does Bubba go to leave this lake?"

"To the belly," answered Lionel slowly, catching Ret's drift, "or the navel."

"Right," Ret agreed with growing anxiousness. "And what did the chief call the volcano-island?"

"The Navel of the World!" Lionel declared with joy.

"Right!" Ret rejoiced.

"Of course!" Lionel exulted. "Why didn't I see it before? The original Polynesian colonists named the island *Te Pito O Te Henua,* which literally means 'The Navel of the World.'"

Although all were stunned by Lionel's vast knowledge, it was Mr. Coy who asked, "Have you ever thought about going on Jeopardy?"

Puzzled, Ishmael questioned, "Then why did that lady tell you to come to *Easter* Island?"

"I can answer that!" Mr. Coy blurted out. He held out his phone for all to see. "Because Easter Island *is* the navel of the world." His screen showed a map with a tiny speck in the middle of the vast Pacific Ocean, thousands of miles west of the South American continent.

"That's where we need to go," Ret instructed. Everyone glared with awe at the idea of traveling to such a remote place.

"I hope those shoes of yours are waterproof," Lionel grinned.

Returning to the group of natives, Ret proclaimed, "Can you to take us to the Sacred Rocks on the island in the belly of the lake."

The chief gasped with fear, with his men belatedly following his example.

"It is forbidden!" the chief refused. "We never set foot on that island."

Frustrated, Ret noticed a dying fire in a pit outside one of the nearby huts. He stretched forth his hand and called its waning flames into his palm. Then, holding the fire before the chief, Ret repeated, this time a bit more sternly, "Take us to the belly of the lake."

The chief gladly obliged.

With swiftness, he and his men boarded a boat and escorted their insistent guests toward their requested destination. Although it was quite a distance from the floating community to the lake's navel island, the voyage was quite brief, for not only were there several more rowers but they paddled hastily as if trying to get the job done as quickly as possible. As soon as they were close enough to the island, they dropped off their one-way riders and returned from whence they came. Void of farewell salutes but full of dismayed grunts, the natives promptly disappeared in the increasing fog.

Unlike its reed-made counterparts, this island was neither artificial nor floating. In fact, comparatively it was quite large and hilly, though very rocky and inhospitable. Except for sparse brush, there were no signs of life.

"So we're looking for Sacred Rocks, huh?" Mr. Coy said glumly as his eyes fell upon the innumerable

rocks that littered the island. "This should be easy."
Then, kicking a pile of pebbles directly in front of him,
he said, "Found some."

The group split up, with Mr. Coy announcing
every few seconds that he had "found some." Given the
land's bareness, it didn't take long for the search party
to stumble upon a curious formation of unusually large
rocks situated in a small plain in the upper portion of
the island. Its foremost feature was a great, rectangular
slab, raised off the ground with the support of a square
rock at each of its four corners. Strewn around the
altar-like centerpiece was a handful of other large,
square rocks, almost like tree stumps or places to sit. In
many ways, the arrangement mimicked the Intihuatana
Stone.

As their one and only lead, Ret leapt onto the slab
and stared at the others with a look that beckoned them
to do likewise.

"How do you know this is the site of the Sacred
Rocks?" Lionel asked as he climbed aboard.

"I'm open to suggestions," said Ret sarcastically,
knowing there were no other immediate options.

"If it's not," remarked Ishmael, helping his boss
onto the rock and handing Ret the shoes, "we'll certainly
be quite an odd sight."

"Rub a dub dab," Mr. Coy rhymed, "four men on a
slab." The others looked at him a bit awkwardly. Then,

nestling himself into the snug group, he announced, "The Navel of the World or bust!"

As soon as both of Ret's shoes made contact with the stone, it immediately became clear that they were at the right place. Once again, the scene around them rolled into an unidentifiable smear as the earth sped up its motion. Unlike the former occasion, this time the landscape skyrocketed in the opposite direction. Like viewing video while rewinding, they crossed the continents and sailed the oceans amid sunshine and moonlight. Its duration but a few seconds, their supersonic journey concluded only when the earth had returned to the point in time and the place in space when Easter Island had been where Lake Titicaca would be.

Given the optical chaos of their trip and the luster of their new setting, Ret was having a hard time getting his vision to refocus. As his eyes realigned, they zeroed in on a sharp, shiny object, positioned directly in front of his face. It was the tip of a spear, poised and steady.

"Well," Mr. Coy said woozily as the lag of their ride wore off, "now I can check off 'walk on water' from my list of things to do before I—" He stopped abruptly, also finding a blade between his eyes.

"—die," his voice quivered.

"And just in time, Coy," Lionel muttered, the four of them retreating until back-to-back, surrounded by an

armed and angry battalion of advancing foes, each
wielding an unyielding weapon.

CHAPTER 12

THE NAVEL
OF THE WORLD

A grunt escaped from the austere lips of the guard in front of Ret. At the signal, a crew of footmen emerged from within the squadron and bound their captives' hands. Instead of rope or chains, they employed a sort of clamp made of rustic rock, a light and sponge-like stone that Ret had seen before. An acute sensation throbbed in his hands as the clamp closed tightly over them.

"Ret!" Ishmael whispered to get his attention. The four were still standing with their backs to one another, forming a sort of inverted huddle. Peripherally, Ret noticed how Ishmael had slipped off his pack and stealthily placed it on the ground directly behind Ret.

"Shoes," Ishmael instructed like a ventriloquist, motioning for Ret to include the footwear with his effects. Imperceptibly, Ret quietly drew back each foot and easily flopped the shoes into Ishmael's bag, the

entire bundle now concealed from view by the tall
grass.

When the prisoners had been cuffed, another grunt
sent the entire party into a brisk march.

"What'd you do *that* for?" Lionel quietly asked,
glancing back at the pack hidden in the grass.

"We don't want any of those things falling into the
wrong hands," Ishmael explained with gravity.

Like the queue to board the Ark, the entourage fell
into ranks, parading two-by-two in a long, unbroken
line. The soldiers looked nothing like the natives at Lake
Titicaca. These men were tall and strong, with broad
shoulders and sturdy legs. Their fair skin and bright
features reminded Ret of the soldiers in Sunken Earth,
but the resemblance stopped there, as these guards were
not nearly as advanced militarily. Although their blades
and battleaxes were inarguably lethal, they also had been
crudely smithed. What's more, their armor, though
consisting of all the typical pieces, had been forged from
a most nontraditional material—dark and claylike, as if
once a sooty, bubbly plaster. It was the same pumice-like
material, in fact, that composed the clamps that had been
clasped over their hands

Ret wondered if the guard had fettered him too
tightly, so hot and uncomfortable did his hands feel.
Suddenly, the rock around Ret's hands began to crack
like the splintering shell of a hatching egg. Smoke and

sparks were expelled through the fissures, emissions from the combustion within. Chunks of fragmented rock broke away and fell to the ground, where they were trampled under the heavy feet of the advancing brigade. As if holding a firework, Ret was reminded of his very similar experience with the Intihuatana Stone.

It was in this moment when Ret realized why the material of the clamps and armor looked familiar to him: it was the same as the rock that Mr. Coy had retrieved from Stone's trunk and the sliver that Lionel had sent to him— the same volcanic rock that reacted with Ret's hand.

When the final pieces had peeled away, Ret was perplexed to find that his left hand still felt strange. During his attempt to learn the source of the poignant numbness, he discovered something shiny in his palm.

"My scar!" he cried. "My scar!"

"Is it illuminated?" Coy asked eagerly.

"Yes!" Ret cheered. "Finally!"

"Then will you take care of these guys already, Ret?" Mr. Coy appealed quietly, the guards shuffling them forward. Ret knew what he was referring to; he himself had thought to call upon his powers to level their antagonists but decided against doing so when it became clear that the guards' objective was merely custody and not brutality.

"Let's see what they intend to do with us first," Ret replied, to Mr. Coy's displeasure.

Still, Ret wasn't opposed to the idea of practicing his newly-acquired firemanship skills on their less-than-hospitable captors. With a quick twirl of his finger, he spun the helmet of one of the guards in front of them until it sat on his head backwards, covering his face. Confused, the guard muttered a few grunts before setting it aright. Then Ret sent the same guard's head crashing into that of his neighbor, who shrugged it off with a displeased grunt.

Enjoying the show, Mr. Coy suggested, "Make him do the Macarena!"

Obeying the whims of Ret, the guard's arms extended in front of him as his hips caught the rhythm of the Spanish salsa. The guard next to him glared at his dancing neighbor with a look of consternation, which only grew when the backsides of the two guards in front of him erupted in flames (thanks to Ret). Hastily, the bewildered guard began swatting the guards' burning derrieres, prompting them to turn around, only to see one of their cronies dancing. Since Ret had cut off the fuel to their posterior blaze, they, too, caught on to the groove, which spread through the entire platoon like wildfire.

"Does anyone know what the date is?" Lionel put forth when the entertainment had died down. He was curious to know where in the past or future their most recent bout with time travel had taken them.

"Hold on," said Coy, "I'll ask." His hands bound, he stuck his head in the gap between the shoulders of the two stern guards marching in front of him. "Excuse me, gentlemen," Coy greeted politely, "but do either of you happen to know what day it is?"

The guards moaned angrily and moved closer together to snuff out Mr. Coy.

"Is that what you'd call the cold shoulder?" Ishmael quipped.

"I got it," Ret pledged, retrieving his phone from his pocket since he was the only one with a free hand. "It looks like it took us to the past, right where we left off— so back to the present, then...I guess."

"Oh, good," Mr. Coy sighed with relief. "Back at the lake, I was afraid I'd missed the season finale of my favorite soap."

True to its ancestral name, Easter Island really was the navel of the world—insofar as Ret could tell, of course. In every direction, the boundless belly of the Pacific Ocean stretched out of sight, its shimmering waters rolling infinitely toward the nearest inhabited landmass, more than a thousand miles away. Still, it was not exactly a small island; in fact, it was many times larger than the tiny Bahamian island of Bimini, in whose waters once rested the submerged road to Sunken Earth. Easter Island was triangular in shape, with a coastline of rough, black rocks. Hilly yet flat, the ground was covered in little more than grass and gravel.

Coinciding with the chief's record, Easter Island looked overwhelmingly exhausted—overused and underappreciated. A casualty of deforestation and subsequent erosion, the terrain seemed almost incapable of supporting life. There were no people—not even any animals or birds. Yet, there was ample evidence of former residents, which made the sad story of Easter Island, now all but dead, all the more tragic.

"Heads up," Mr. Coy announced.

He was right—literally. Up ahead, as the company trekked deeper inland, sat a row of fifteen giant statues. They were the most bizarre objects Ret had ever seen. Instead of being the sculpted representation of some famous person or iconic creature, each of these behemoth busts simply featured a huge head on an even bigger torso. The shadow of each figure's overhanging forehead created the illusion of eyeballs in sunken sockets. A well-defined nose protruded above small but visible lips. Then, the unusually large and rectangular head gave way to the equally square body. A pair of skinny, handless arms flanked each side, the bare chest ending in a slightly rounded belly. Stopping at the waist, the stone effigies stood in a line atop a raised pedestal, a couple feet high and long enough to accommodate a family of fifteen. Some measuring nearly three dozen feet in height, the monstrous monoliths loomed ominously above the gawking spectators they dwarfed below.

"What are *those?*" Ret wondered with awe.

"They're called moai," answered Lionel.

"Relatives of yours?" Coy jabbed.

"No," Lionel returned definitively, "they're the *chief's* relatives. Weren't you listening at the lake?" Mr Coy stuck out his tongue at Lionel's omniscience. "Actually, the chief's lore is spot-on with modern theory. These statues," Lionel explained, "are thought to be the deified ancestors of the people who once lived here. They believed in a sort of symbiotic relationship with their dead, which is why most of the moai stand with their backs to the sea, as the chief pointed out. They're made out of tuff—carved right out of the hardened ash and cinders of the island's volcanic rock. But no one really knows why they built them or how they transported them."

"Except for the chief," Ret astutely observed, not a whit behind.

"Except for the chief," Lionel confirmed with a pleased grin.

"So why, then, is this place called *Easter* Island?" Ishmael asked.

"Because it was discovered by explorers on Easter Sunday," Lionel educated.

"Actually," theorized Mr. Coy, who had been derisively flapping his mouth to imitate Lionel, the know-it-all, "it's because those statues are really giant chocolate bunnies."

"That's it!" Ret exclaimed, as if decoding a grand mystery.

"Bunnies?" Coy questioned.

"The moai!" Ret clapped. "That's my scar!" He held out his hand for the others to confirm the scar.

"Just as we thought all along," Mr. Coy asserted.

Ret shot him a disbelieving glare and stated, reminding him, "Squatting gummy bear man?" Coy smiled broadly.

"I thought you said they were chocolate?" Ishmael asked, a little disappointed.

The band pushed onward, passing many more collections of moai as they hiked across the island. Upon reaching a hilltop, Ret swept the landscape with a panoramic gaze and spotted hundreds of moai statues, dotting the scenery like freckles. Some were erect, others had been toppled, and scores were strewn around the quarry where they had been chiseled but abandoned en route to their destinations. Whenever they passed a moai that had fallen, Ret utilized his power over its volcanic consistency to return it to an upright position.

It was with a common feeling of dread that the group reacted to a sudden shaking of the ground.

Though the quaking lasted but a few seconds, the guards faltered with fear while their hostages were forced to no longer ignore a menacing monster: the island's enormous volcano. It was truly a mammoth volcano, its magnitude perhaps compounded by the petite size of the island. Towering above the sea, it dominated the crown of the island's triangular shape. As tall as it was wide, its barren slopes bore evidence of frequent rockslides. From its mouth fumed wispy plumes of smoke, harbingers of impending pyroclastic flow. It seemed to seethe with energy and breathe with power.

But the volcano was every bit as foreboding as it was majestic. It had come to be a representation of pure terror—a symbol of certain death by compulsory means. To look into its swirling steam was to look into the shroud that befogged the eyes of the lake people. Yet, it was not the fountain of fire itself that those island dwellers feared, at whose base they had lived in peace for generations. No, their horror found its genesis in the flames of passion, lit and fanned by the men with flaming hair. It was the unflinching desires of these wicked men—their willingness to sacrifice anything (and any*one*) but their own will— that had cursed the volcano and plagued a society. Fire Island teemed not with the bones of dead men but with the mistakes of marked men, who, trembling at every tremor, seemed grimly aware that, in the last, their uncooled passion would erupt in their own doom.

"Would you mind giving me a hand?" Mr. Coy importuned Ret, holding out his bound wrists. By sheer mind power, Ret engaged Mr. Coy's stone cuffs in combustion until they completely disintegrated. "Thanks." Then, reaching into his pocket, Mr. Coy added, "You might need this."

Mr. Coy rolled the Oracle into Ret's promptly-cupped hands. It took him a bit by surprise, suddenly seeing an object that meant so much to him despite such minimal interaction with it. Just by holding it, the ethereal sphere filled Ret with joy—a mixture of peaceful assurance and energizing hope—a feeling that contrasted starkly against the gruesome backdrop of the volcano. Here was a thing, so small and unassuming, that nevertheless dictated others' destinies and fueled Ret's aspirations. And yet, it did not enforce its designs on anyone or anything; rather, it waited—it tarried—until the season and the setting and the souls were right. In his innocent vigor, Ret reflected, he had tried his mightiest to speed things up, racking his brain and exhausting his strength to find the elements and fill the Oracle. But, like an elusive butterfly, only when he had calmed his tenacious mind and stilled his overzealous heart, did the fluttering gem alight upon *him*.

"Good luck in there," said Coy supportively, motioning to the volcano. Ret looked at Mr. Coy's undaunted face. The braveness of his tempered smile transferred to Ret's bosom as the possibility of finding the next element inside the volcano's core became certain reality. For a moment, Ret wished Mr. Coy could accompany him on whatever lie ahead but knew that was out of the question.

Unbeknownst to the two of them, Lionel had not taken his eyes off the Oracle ever since it was unveiled by Mr. Coy. Given how stubbornly Mr. Coy had refused to show the artifact to Lionel when he and Ret visited the Manor (or the fence, at least) a few months ago, Lionel postulated that he might never see the most intriguing piece of the growing equation. No wonder his face now beamed with elation, his eyes wide and lit like a child in a toy store. Undoubtedly spurred by the inquisitive and scientific side of him, Lionel ogled the orb with full-blown envy, not unlike his appearance during the queasy climax of Ret's tour of the power plant on that same day.

Meanwhile, Ishmael was staring at Lionel as ardently as Lionel was the Oracle. Lionel's preoccupied, open-mouthed, and almost worshipful glaring caused Ishmael to feel very uncomfortable. As if personally threatened, Ishmael made a mental note to always view Lionel through a lens of suspicion.

In time, their route across the island merged with the volcano's trail, whose end would take them to the summit. After only a few hundred yards, the entire party was joined by perspiration and panting, so steep was the path that scaled the slopes. Onward and upward they climbed, pausing only to take cover during rumblings from the volcano's viscera.

"You don't look so hot," Mr. Coy commented, visually assessing Lionel's abnormal condition.

"Phew!" Lionel yelled during his brief pause between breaths, wiping his shirt sleeve across his sweat-laden forehead. "This adventure is aging me!" It was no lie: he looked tired and weak, his voice wheezy and steps wobbly. Skin pale and eyes flushed, his exhaustion seemed to bring out the gray in his otherwise dark hair. "I suppose all those days at the office are starting to catch up with me."

Lucky for Lionel, they reached the summit a few minutes later. Ret had just helped Lionel sit down to catch his breath when he heard someone shout his name.

"Ret!"

He knew the voice. He turned around to find Paige, next to Pauline and Ana, a little further along the rim of the volcano's crater. They were still tied up, but newfound hope seemed to rejuvenate Paige at the sight of Ret. He was relieved to see the girls, especially Paige, and any lingering feelings of prior misunderstanding melted away immediately.

Rather instinctively, Ret started to run to the girls but was impeded when a pair of swords lunged in front of him, crossing impassably with a sharp clang.

"Cool it, lover boy," Miss Carmen ridiculed, appearing on the other side of the swords. Then Bubba stepped next to her.

"Remember me?" he sneered. "We're glad you could join our little party so quickly." Apparently, Miss Carmen had placed her call to Ret via Ana's phone just moments earlier.

Not amused, Ret demanded, "What do you want with us?"

"We want *you*," Miss Carmen answered, as if speaking to a child, "to jump in *here*." She strode over to the edge of the volcano's rim and pointed into the smoking crater.

"Jump?" Ret gulped. "In *there?*"

"Jump, dive, cannonball—whatever you want to do," Bubba sighed impatiently, "just as long as you get in there."

"And, once I'm down there," said Ret, "then what do I do?"

"Well, if you don't die instantly from the searing heat," said Bubba casually, "feel free to swim around— you know, do a couple laps, practice your backstroke, whatever floats your boat."

"So you need me to...*die?*" Ret wanted to clarify.

"This island's only big enough for one man with bright-colored hair," Miss Carmen hissed poisonously, giving Bubba a kiss, "and I prefer redheads."

As if mulling over the proposition put forth by his enemies, Ret became enveloped in thought. He cast his eyes about the setting: the girls held hostage in front of him, with the men held prisoner behind him; his antagonistic couple beguiling him, surrounded by the listless guards waiting to be told what to do; the volatile volcano at his side. Amid such disorder, Ret enjoyed a brief moment of clarity. Besides the stifling heat, Ret could feel the immense power of the raging fire within the volcano's core. With swelling confidence and inflamed resolve, he could feel the element near. He sensed the volcano wanted *him* to retrieve it and would provide a way to that end. Although unsure how, he at least knew what he needed to do.

"Okay," Ret said brightly, complying with the terms.

"Really?" asked Bubba incredulously.

Then Ret stipulated, "Under one condition: you free my friends—all of them—," he added with emphasis, "as soon as I jump in."

"Done!" Miss Carmen gloried. "Prepare the sacrifice!"

"No, Ret!" Paige screamed.

"They can't be trusted!" yelled Pauline.

Guards began to escort Ret to the plank-like platform, which extended beyond the rim in the fashion of a short pier. With the guards preoccupied, Mr. Coy and Ishmael hurried over to the girls to comfort them.

"It's okay," Mr. Coy reassured them.

"Okay? *Okay?*" Pauline balked. "Ret's about to jump inside an active volcano, and it's *okay?*"

"He knows what he's doing," Mr. Coy persisted. "Trust him."

Ret could hear his kin's frantic conversation as the guards hauled him ever closer to the edge of the rim. Glancing over his shoulder, with his hands behind his back, he flashed his gleaming scar in their direction, hoping it would quiet their fears.

Registering the scar, Pauline observed cynically, "So my boy's fate now depends on this Oracle stuff, does it?"

"Then it's a good thing I trust it," Paige responded, leaning lovingly into the arm of the frenzied mother.

Despite her whimpering, Pauline remained quiet for several moments, calmed by Paige's confidence as they watched Ret prepare for his plunge. Then, noticing how Mr. Coy was the only one not enchained, Pauline asked, "Why aren't *you* tied up?"

The beans spilled, a nearby guard promptly came and secured a fresh clamp over Mr. Coy's hands once again.

"Thanks," said Coy sarcastically, further straining an already stressed relationship.

The scene was like a marriage ceremony. Two parallel rows of guards stood facing each other like the ends of pews, the gap between them creating a sort of aisle. At one end lurked Bubba and Miss Carmen, with Ret's loved ones huddled beyond them, straining to see the proceedings. At the other end was nothing but a perilous precipice—the diving board of death.

Ret started down the aisle. Besides the occasional gurgling from the volcano, the only noise was the sound of his slow footsteps on the dirt. The sentinels stood as still as stone. Bubba and Miss Carmen exulted silently. Mr. Coy and Ishmael steadied the girls' trepidation. Ret walked with his head high.

"Wait!"

An urgent plea interrupted the ritual. Hastening to the site was Lionel, only somewhat recovered from their strenuous hike. Clearly in pain, he hurriedly hobbled to the gathering and stopped in front of Bubba and Miss Carmen.

"Take me instead," Lionel begged.

"Lionel, no!" Ret refused.

"Please," Lionel persisted, falling to his knees, "let the boy go."

"Who is this?" Miss Carmen asked with disgust.

"I am a true friend of Ret," answered Lionel. "Please, take me in his place."

A few steps away from the groveling, Mr. Coy glared at Ishmael with a face that was approaching panic. "Ishmael," he hummed through his teeth, trying to conceal his alarm, "what's going on with Lionel?"

Ishmael shrugged vehemently, ignorant of any wrongdoing.

"Why is he acting so noble?" Mr. Coy interrogated with the same singsong voice.

"Because he's a good friend," said Pauline, almost willing to support Lionel's offer.

Bubba lightly kicked Lionel's leg and said, a bit humiliated, "Get up."

Lionel obeyed, then grabbed Bubba by the collar and pled, "Please, please! I'll do anything. Just let him go—let him live!"

Flustered by Lionel's forwardness, Bubba ordered, "Guards! Seize this man!" A pair of guards fell on the scene. With great difficulty, they pried Lionel from Bubba.

"Take him away," Bubba instructed.

"No! Please!" Lionel persevered, all the more emphatically. "Ret, save yourself. No one can survive this—it's suicide." With unexpected strength, Lionel escaped the guards' hold and lunged for Bubba, who was saved when a second pair of guards restrained the unruly protestor.

"Gag him!" barked Bubba. "Lock him up!"

"Coy! Pauline!" Lionel entreated. "Don't let them—"

A guard shoved the butt of his dagger in Lionel's mouth as they carried him down the volcano and out of sight.

Back at the ceremony, the atmosphere was one of shock. Among those in attendance who knew him, Lionel was a man of high repute whose opinion carried a fair bit of weight. In direct response to Lionel's claims, Mr. Coy, to say nothing of the livid girls, was beginning to doubt the idea of Ret's voluntary plunge. He couldn't help but feel at least partly responsible for Lionel's radically honorable behavior, a sentiment that sent Ishmael into a fearful flurry, wondering if he had administered too much extract to Lionel.

Back at the aisle, even Ret was getting cold feet. He trusted Lionel; he was a true friend indeed. But was he right? Was there, perhaps, a better, less dangerous way? He consulted his scar, which shone ever brighter, rekindling his confidence.

Scared but assured, Ret crept the last few, vertiginous steps until he reached the edge of the launch pad. He peered down into the treacherous throat of the volcano. Like a salivating tongue, a sea of lava lapped the sides of the narrow funnel. He swallowed, his own throat slightly clogged by his lingering second thoughts.

"Wait!"

Ret spun around in a flash to learn who had cried. Paige had burst between Bubba and Miss Carmen, sprinting toward Ret.

"Oh, for Pete's sake," moaned Bubba at the presence of yet another protestor. He signaled for the guards to restrain Paige, but before they could do so, the entire scene erupted in waves of dirt. Ret buried both rows of guards in two tsunami-like waves of earth. As the soil was settling, Ret ran towards Paige, not slowing until their lips met. Despite the flying dirt and ash and smoke, they professed their love with an honest kiss. For all to see and with no one to interfere, they prolonged their treasured moment out of fear for the unknown future.

Then, withdrawing, Ret turned around, broke into a sprint, and dove off the edge.

CHAPTER 13

ALL IN ASHES

Paige's heart leapt with Ret. Her lips still moist and longing, she stood motionless, incapable of exhaling the breath they had just shared. Her fondest wish and worst fear had both come to pass in the selfsame moment. Even though her heart had faith in Ret's survival, her mind mocked such irrational ruminations. As if in spite of her agony, a great calm came over the volcano. Its hunger at bay, the shaking and smoking ceased now that it had something to chew on.

Paige ran to the edge and fell to her knees. Peering into the unforgiving throat of the volcano, she yelled, "Ret!" There was no response but the echoes of her own plea.

"Now let us go, flame boy," Mr. Coy demanded of Bubba, holding out his still-bound hands.

"Sorry," said Bubba unapologetically, "but I don't think I will."

"Untie us this instant," Pauline ordered.

"I'm afraid that wasn't part of the deal," Miss Carmen smirked.

"But you agreed to free us!" Mr. Coy reminded angrily.

"Precisely," said Miss Carmen. "And so, you're free to go." She daintily fluttered her fingers as if shooing a meddlesome pet.

"Ciao!" Bubba smiled as he and Miss Carmen began to walk away, snickering devilishly.

"Why you—" Infuriated, Mr. Coy charged towards them. A pair of guards planted themselves in his path, their weapons extended. Like a giant fist, Mr. Coy wielded the volcanic rock clasped around his hands, snapping the guards' spears like twigs and delivering powerful blows to each. With a shriek, Miss Carmen fled Bubba's side as Mr. Coy pinned him up against a wall of rocks.

"Let us go right now," Mr. Coy threatened through clenched teeth, "or I'll—"

Mr. Coy paused at the sound of a curious noise. Coming up the trail were the reverberations of a rhythmic sort of tapping, something being struck, again and again, against the hard ground. All eyes slowly turned to face the landing, anxious to learn the cause of the eerie ticking.

"Lord Lye," Bubba breathed with deference when the culprit of the clicking finally emerged.

Having never seen the age-old nemesis for themselves, all the Coys and Coopers knew about Lye was what Ret had told them. From a distance, he seemed to them but a frail beggar, hunched and harmless, relying more on his cane than his own two legs. As he slithered nearer, however, the details of his hideous features became, unfortunately, clearer. Like a character from the early days of television, everything about his person was either the darkest of black or the palest of white. The train of his dark robes was laden with dust from his ascent of the volcano, while his long hair from head and beard shone vibrantly. The only color to besmirch his visage was the yellowing of his pointed fingernails and the yolk-like whites of his eyes. Like the talons of a vulture, he clutched the top of an ivory-colored, spirally-twisted cane, eternally glued to his hand.

"Ret wasn't kidding," Paige whispered to Pauline, both petrified with fright at the sight of such a gruesome individual.

Less discernible and, therefore, perhaps more alarming was the subtle shroud that had fallen upon the scene. Like a freak storm driven by the wind, a cold and creepy air heralded Lye's arrival, swallowing the sun and swirling the clouds. It was as if nature hid her face and shut her doors at the presence of such a vile creature.

Lye waved his cane at Mr. Coy, who still had Bubba propped up against the wall. Overcome by some strong force, Mr. Coy was repelled and forced to abandon his chokehold. Released, Bubba flocked to Lye and knelt at his feet with obeisance.

"Ret has been terminated in the volcano, my lord," Bubba informed his superior.

"Excellent," Lye hissed. "Return at once to the excavation site and resume operations. I suspect lava levels are already receding, exposing tunnels and tubes that haven't been uncovered in centuries."

"It shall be done, my lord," Bubba vowed. "And the prisoners?"

"I will tend to them now," said Lye, "as well as the misfit I passed along the way."

"Lionel," Pauline whispered, worried.

"I left instructions with your men to take him onboard my ship," Lye explained to Bubba. "He's an old friend, and we have a lot of...*catching up* to do." He smiled, exposing his sharp and yellow teeth in remembrance of his feigned friendship with Lionel, which spoiled in Sunken Earth.

"Very well, my lord," Bubba submitted.

"Now, back to work!" Lye growled. "All haste! The prize is in sight."

Linking arms, Bubba and Miss Carmen scurried down the volcano, their gaggle of guards following.

Lye hobbled over to where the only remaining people on the summit were gathered. There stood Pauline and Ana, Mr. Coy and Paige, and Ishmael. The women naturally huddled close to the men, though all were in suspense of what Lye had in store for them.

Lye stopped in front of them and began to search for something within his robes. "I believe I owe you my thanks," he said with unsettling pleasantness. Then, upon retrieving Ishmael's pack, outrage ensued.

"Where did you get that?" Mr. Coy bellowed, lunging at Lye. "None of that belongs to you—you thief, you good-for-nothing—"

"Now, now," Lye said playfully. With another wave of his cane, an invisible hand squeezed Mr. Coy's neck, depriving him of the ability to breathe or speak. Falling to all fours, Mr. Coy strained painfully for several seconds, choking for want of air, before Lye finally relinquished.

"Does anyone else have something to say?" Lye queried rhetorically. The others held their tongues.

"Now then," Lye resumed, "as I was saying..." He pulled Ret's stone shoes from Ishmael's bag and slipped his own feet into them. "...Please accept my deepest gratitude for locating this second pair." Then, removing a bottle of ointment from the pack, he added, "And this fire retardant will be most useful. Coy cream, is it?" The more Mr. Coy frowned, the more Lye smiled.

Lye uncorked the bottle of cream and emptied it, using his cane to suspend it midair in a single glob in front of him. Then, with a flick of his wrist, he vaporized the cream and covered himself in it.

"Many thanks," Lye mocked Mr. Coy. Enraged but purposely speechless, Mr. Coy spat at Lye's feet, at which gesture Lye promptly sent the spit back into Mr. Coy's mouth.

Turning to Ishmael, Lye said, "A promise is a promise." With his cane, he tapped Ishmael's clasps, which incinerated in an instant. Ishmael caressed his aching wrists.

Mr. Coy glared at his assistant, this time truly without words at such perceived treachery.

"Now, if you'll excuse me," said Lye, "I have an element to collect." Given the wobbly nature of the shoes, he made his way over to the rim of the volcano with caution. The crater was like a funnel, with sloping sides that drained to the volcano's throat. Instead of diving headfirst as Ret had done, Lye chose instead to gradually descend by walking around the periphery in a swirling, whirling manner. Like a cross-country skier, he trudged through thick layers of ash, greatly aided by the long, thick spikes of the shoes. When he finally disappeared from view, his onlookers found their voices.

"Traitor!" Mr. Coy roared, stomping towards Ishmael. "Liar!"

"But, sir—" Ishmael cowered.

"How could you?" Coy asked heatedly, adding a pinch of sorrow to his anger. "After all I've done for you and your family..."

"I would never—" Ishmael quivered in the face of Mr. Coy's indignation.

"I should've known better than to trust you," Coy regretted, rife with resentment, "you and that conniving sister of yours—once a criminal, always a criminal!"

"It wasn't me," Ishmael swore sincerely. "I promise—"

"Oh? Then who tipped off the old geezer, hmm?" Coy interrogated, getting in Ishmael's face all the more. "It wasn't me; it wasn't Ret; and you and I *both* know it sure wasn't Lionel."

A perplexed look came over Pauline. "Since when are you vouching for Lionel?" she wondered of Mr. Coy.

Coy winced, regretting the words he had just uttered. "Great," he muttered to Ishmael, "now I have to explain the extract to the shrew!" He turned around with a pretended face of untroubled lightheartedness. "All it took was one trip abroad together," he fibbed, "and now Lionel and I are just peachy." Pauline wasn't buying it. "BFF's," Coy added with a desperate smile, almost questioning his own words.

"Do I look stupid to you?" Pauline asked.

Coy considered it for a moment, but before Pauline could snap back, he confessed flatly, "We've been drugging Lionel."

"You've been *what?*"

"It was merely integritas extract," Coy explained to soften the situation. "It ennobles a person; makes him trustworthy. Perfectly harmless, I assure you."

"Humph!" Pauline snorted disbelievingly. "It sounds like *you* need a dose of your own medicine."

"I *am* trustworthy," Coy asserted, offended. Then, pointing at Ishmael and again railing on him with raised voice, *"He's* the one who betrayed us!"

"Ben, if you would just listen to me—" Ishmael pled desperately.

"Get out of here!" Mr. Coy hollered, his eyes filling with tears. "Just—just go away!" Mr. Coy motioned to the trail down the volcano. "And n-never come back!"

With sad countenance, Ishmael picked up his picked-over pack and slogged away, mournfully looking back more than once.

Down in the volcano, one step away from fully entering the throat, Lye paused to overhear the irate conversation. Then, smiling with self-satisfaction, he continued.

Fuming, Mr. Coy returned to the three girls, avoiding eye contact, and sat down heavily. For a moment, it seemed as though everything that *could* go wrong *had* gone wrong: Ret's existence was unknown, Lionel was likely slated for torturous questioning, Ishmael had proved to be confederate, and Lye was winning his own game; to say nothing of themselves, still enchained and stranded on a remote island. Claiming responsibility for it all, Mr. Coy was teetering with depression just as Ana was tottering out of it.

"You didn't listen to him," Ana said numbly, her face still in pain. She earned all of their stares. It was the first time she had spoken since they landed on Fire Island.

"You didn't even let him explain," she added, obviously addressing Coy's interaction with Ishmael. "You were so fired up that you abandoned all reason, and now you've done something that you'll regret." She spoke not out of condemnation but, oddly enough, introspection. "I know," she admitted, "because that's exactly what I did."

"Oh, Ana," Pauline mollified, swooping in to soothe her daughter.

"No, Mom, it's true," Ana countered with maturity. "You told me not to go with Miss Carmen. You warned me that it wasn't a good idea. But did I listen? No." Pauline said nothing, confirming the truth of Ana's words. "I was so wooed by Miss Carmen — so blinded by my own desires — that I couldn't see the danger. And *now* look at us. This is all my fault." Her ducts were too depleted to emit any more tears.

In this moment, Pauline wished for nothing else than to put her arms around her grieving daughter, but her bounds dictated otherwise. She simply nestled into her shoulder as tenderly as she could, a gesture that Paige mimicked on Ana's other side. Meanwhile, Mr. Coy, alone and cooling, pensively digested Ana's valuable reflections, acquired at a high price.

O   O   O

"Framed!" Ishmael cursed as he trudged along the trail from the volcano's summit. "I was framed!" He was moving rapidly down the steep path, his pack bouncing on his back. "I'm innocent!" he maintained, mind racing. "I'll prove it!" He harbored no animosity toward Mr. Coy, directing it instead at his phantom accuser.

Returning to the island's lowlands, he set out in search of the excavation site that Lye had mentioned in his instructions to Bubba. Rounding the base of the volcano, he discovered a small settlement on its east side, a little ways from one of the only beaches on the island. Resembling a long-term campsite more than a legitimate establishment, the settlement surrounded what was obviously the excavation site: a deep hole in the volcano's side. The sounds of picks striking rocks and shovels scooping dirt filled the air, with a never-ending stream of guards filing out of the quarry to dump countless loads of excised dirt and ash.

Ishmael tiptoed toward the camp's only enclosure, which was little more than a weathered tarp wrapped around stakes like a teepee, hoping it housed Bubba. It was perched atop a mound of moved dirt so as to overlook the operation. Ishmael snuck into the compound. As the ground was littered with fallen moai, he scurried from statue to statue, not drawing an ounce of attention to himself, for all guards were aiding in the archeological effort.

And what a curious effort it was! The team seemed bent on reaching the volcano's core not from its top but rather through its side. Undoubtedly the accumulated product of centuries' worth of toil, they had carved a considerable gorge out of sheer rock. Their path bore evidence that they had struck lava on several occasions over the years, as large pools of once-molten rock had oozed out of the mine. With every inch, their endeavor grew in precariousness, a danger felt most by the excavators along the frontline. Like termites, they chipped away at the volcano's belly, and though their armor absorbed much of the heat, a special unit had the charge of dousing sizzling rocks and seeping magma with seawater. It was a complex operation of monstrous proportion, performed by provincial people by primitive means.

Ishmael crept behind the crude hut, crouched near the ground, and laid his ear against its side.

"I wonder what Lye intends to do with them?" he heard Miss Carmen say.

"Probably throw them in the volcano after he gets enough information out of them," Bubba replied without remorse, "if he hasn't already."

"You don't think they'll try to escape?" Miss Carmen asked. "They're a pretty stubborn lot, you know, especially Ana."

"Where're they gonna go?" Bubba put forth, matter-of-factly. "This place is an island, remember? Plus, Lye ordered our jet onboard his fleet, and the last rowboat must have taken Lionel to Lye's ship."

"What about *us?*" said Miss Carmen, skeptical of her own escape.

"Relax," Bubba reassured, striding next to her. "There's always the Navel Rock if we ever need to...disappear for a while."

Ishmael heard the conversation segue to a passionate kiss. He rose to his feet, about to interrupt the romance, when Bubba said urgently, "What's that noise?"

Ishmael froze, not aware that Bubba was referring to a strange sound coming from the excavation grounds.

"Sounds like the boys are fighting again," Miss

Carmen sighed, displeased with the disruption.

"Would you take care of them?" Bubba petitioned. "They take orders so much better when they come from you."

"They're not the only ones," she said with a flirtatious smile as she slipped out of the tent.

Brandishing her beauty, Miss Carmen erupted in a flurry of sharp commands as she stalked off to restore order. Capitalizing on her absence, Ishmael snuck to the front of the tent and peeked inside to learn Bubba's location. Without a sound, Ishmael inserted a narrow straw between the flaps of the tent door and blew into it like a spit wad.

Bubba was leaning back in a chair, with legs stretched and feet crossed on a table, when a small, needled dart came flying at him from the tent door and stuck in his neck. With sudden alertness, he yanked it out and visually inspected the vicinity, searching frantically.

Slipping a bottle of extract into his pocket, Ishmael counted off three seconds before striding through the door.

"Why, Ishmael!" Bubba greeted bubbly, the extract already doing its job. "How do you do, sir? Come, come! Sit down, sit down!" With unusual jovialness, he bid Ishmael take the seat across from him. "To what do I owe the pleasure?"

"How did Lye know about my pack?' Ishmael

questioned, getting down to business immediately.

"Pack?" Bubba asked innocently. "Pack of what? Pack of wolves? Pack of gum? Pachyderm?"

"*This* pack," Ishmael clarified, holding up his bag.

"I can't say it rings any bells," Bubba told truthfully, "but a fine bag it is. What is the brand, I wonder? Louis Vuitton, perchance?"

"Never mind," Ishmael muttered, rubbing his forehead with frustration at the naiveté he had caused to come upon Bubba. Moving on, he asked, "What is this fleet that Lye has?"

"Sixty-four, top-of-the-line battle cruisers," said Bubba cheerfully. "Counted them myself. It's Lye's personal armada, completely surrounding this island as we speak, poised and ready for attack should anything go awry with the prisoners, which is odd since they seem like such nice people."

Ishmael remained silent for several seconds, digesting this frightful information. Breaking the quiet, Bubba said, his eyes glazed with gaiety, "Would you like a foot massage?"

"Maybe later," dismissed Ishmael. "I need you to take me to the Navel Rock."

"Hi-ho cheerio! A fieldtrip?" Bubba celebrated. "How exciting!"

"Quietly," hushed Ishmael.

"Oh, a *quiet* fieldtrip," Bubba whispered.

"Yes," Ishmael agreed. "And let's make it snappy."

"Got it," said Bubba. "A quiet, *snappy* fieldtrip." As they slipped out the back of the tent, Bubba began to snap his fingers with each of his quiet steps on the grass.

"Wait a minute!" Bubba cried softly.

Adrenaline surged through Ishmael, fearing the extract had already worn off. Scrambling to prepare another dose, his heart found relief when Bubba simply asked, "Should I bring the cleats?"

From that question, Bubba confirmed what Ishmael had supposed, namely that the Navel Rock was the location of Easter Island's time-warp.

"Yes, of course!" Ishmael breathed.

They dashed back to the tent, where, to Ishmael's dismay, they saw Miss Carmen entering. Bubba was about to bodaciously waltz right inside, but Ishmael restrained him.

"I'll get them," Ishmael volunteered.

"But you don't know where they are," Bubba pointed out.

"Then tell me."

"Okay," Bubba submitted. "They're inside a nesting doll, which is standing in a clay pot, which is sitting under my cot. You'll find the pot underneath where I lay my head. Then hatch the first four layers of dolls. Inside the fifth doll, that's where you'll find the cleats." Then, with a serious face, Bubba added, "Be very careful with them."

"The cleats?" Ishmael wondered, knowing they weren't exceptionally fragile.

"No, the dolls!" Bubba corrected. "They're a twelfth-generation heirloom, formed from the mortared marrow of an ancient breed of alpaca, that a dying widow bequeathed to me on the cliffs of Cusco." Ishmael shot him a troubled stare. "Although," Bubba continued, distraught, "I distinctly remember *stealing* the doll from that woman, but that doesn't sound like me at all, now, does it?"

"Not a bit," Ishmael concurred. "Wait here."

"Hold on," said Bubba. Then, holding out his fist, he requested, "Fist bump." Ishmael obliged. "Go get 'em!" Bubba rooted.

Ishmael gently lifted the bottom of the tent flap and peeked inside to survey the room. Miss Carmen sat on the side opposite the cot, patiently waiting for her lover to return from wherever he had gone. Ishmael rolled a small device into the center of the room. Without a sound, it released a colorless, odorless gas, but it did not spread to fill the room. Instead, it confined itself to a single layer, creating a vertical wall within the small shelter. When the wall had stretched from ceiling to floor and from side to side, it stabilized into a vaporous solid. Like a camera, Ishmael's mirror gas had taken a photograph of the scene behind it and now was reflecting it.

Free to move around half of the room without being

seen, Ishmael crawled inside and located the nesting doll inside the pot. The doll was in the shape of a woman with an unusually large bodice, which, by the fifth shell, was the perfect size in which to fit the shoes. The chore of unnesting all the dolls proved to be quite time-consuming, given the situation, and Ishmael broke into a sweat as he rushed to reassemble the doll as the mirror gas was beginning to dissipate. With jittery hands, he hastily put the doll back in the pot, which wobbled like a bowling pin when brushed by the ball. At the sound, Miss Carmen arose suspiciously and slowly stepped toward the cot. Ishmael returned to steady the pot, then hurried out of the tent just as the gas expired and Miss Carmen approached the scene, where she found all to be well.

"That was close," Ishmael said as they galloped away, Bubba snapping his fingers rhythmically to their quick pace.

About a stone's throw away from the camp rested the Navel Rock. Like the Intihuatana Stone and the Sacred Rocks, this time-warp on Easter Island was also peculiarly designed. There was a circular wall of jagged rocks, only a few feet in height but perhaps a dozen feet in diameter. Enclosed within this wall were five very round and smooth stones, four of which were about the size of a small watermelon and had been placed around the fifth, which was many times larger, like the cardinal directions on a weather vane. The entire ensemble stood very near an exceptionally rocky shoreline.

"Here we are," Bubba announced, "the Navel Rock."

"Great," said Ishmael. "Now just put on the cleats, and we'll be on our way."

"I can't do *that*," Bubba disagreed pleasantly. "Lye specifically told me that no one is to leave the island."

"Well, *I* am telling you differently," Ishmael retorted, losing his patience.

"If you're not willing to obey orders," Bubba harped, "then I'm afraid I'm going to have to report you."

"I thought it might come to this," Ishmael mumbled calmly. He retrieved a large syringe from his pack and promptly jammed it into Bubba's arm.

"That feels most unpleasant," Bubba complained. Then, when the serum had been exhausted, Bubba said, "I suddenly feel very tired. I think I will take a nap." And he slumped onto the ground.

"Finally," Ishmael sighed, pleased by the silence. "That ought to keep him quiet for a while."

Ishmael picked up the cleats and slipped them onto Bubba's limp feet. Then he stepped within the stone wall of the Navel Rock and heaved Bubba inside, standing him erect so that both of his feet made contact with the ground of the time-warp. In a rapturous instant, they both disappeared.

CHAPTER 14

THE GUARDIAN'S GIFT

Although Ret dove into the volcano with confidence, he hardly knew what he was going to do next. Manipulating the ashy dirt to cushion his fall, Ret fell onto the sloping sides of the crater and slid downward on his chest like a human snowboard. Despite his ever-increasing speed, he cast mounds of earth in front of him to slow his glide as he approached the throat of the volcano, where, coming to a stop, he peered over the edge.

The scene before his eyes was one of raw power. It was a lake of lava, a viciously viscous sea of living liquid. Like a stomach, it chewed and churned its red and glowing contents, crashing against the inside of the volcano and sending geysers up its walls. Mucky bubbles, large and small, swelled and then burst, spraying globs in all directions and sounding like a witch's brew. The steamy air was stifling, almost suffocating, even worse than Tybee's most humid, summer days. A bright orange color bathed the entire view, resembling the innermost coals of a fire. It was a staggering sight to take in, one truly beyond description.

Yet, Ret was puzzled by the volcano's misleading character. On the outside, this smoking heap of earth was not much more than an ordinary hill; but, despite such lack of external evidence, on the inside raged a phenomenal storm of unpredictable behavior. Ret wondered how anything could keep such vast and uncontainable power so bottled up. Of course, he knew it was in a volcano's nature to erupt from time to time, but why? And why so spontaneously, so impulsively, so destructively? Such was not a pleasant way of life, Ret reasoned, and he was grateful that no traits of volcanism coincided with humanism.

Most intense of all, however, was the immense heat. It seemed as though every particle had been supercharged by the pervasive warmth, glowing and pulsating. Ret could feel the heat as it boiled his blood and broiled his skin, but there was no pain; on the contrary, it energized and empowered him. He marveled at how hot it had to be in order for rock to exist in a fluid state. In fact, the molten material reminded him of Sunken Earth, when the grains of salt melted from exposure to the energy that was harvested from the soil.

For several minutes, Ret lay at the rim of the throat, contemplating such a miraculous creation. Unlike a skyscraper or a suspension bridge, as impressive as those modern marvels can be, *this* wonder of the natural world had not been forged by any human hands. It was purely a product of the earth—an ocean of magma that had leaked from the planet's pressurized core and exploded to the surface. But *why* did it ever think to do that? Does Mother Nature squeeze some volcano-making into her schedule whenever there's a lull between meetings? Better yet, *where* does such power come from? Like the nuclear reactor at the power plant or the electric generator at Coy Manor or even the solar-powered battery of Coy's hot-air balloon, from what source do the planets find their energy? Ret wanted to know because he could feel it in every fiber of his body.

And so, with only one thing to do, Ret jumped in the lava. It did not feel hot to him, and neither his skin nor his hair—not even his clothes—got singed in the least degree. In fact, the lava washed away from him like oil amid water, clean and hydrophobic. At times, it seemed as though he was swimming in paint, sinking only slowly, as if caught in quicksand. He swished his hand across the surface, creating waves and swells according to his own will and pleasure.

Not long after his dive, in fact, the level of the lava began to go down. Ret's very presence, it seemed, had a profoundly calming effect on the volcano. The lava stopped spewing and spitting and, instead, started draining, slowly exposing more and more of the charred walls. It was by no means a fast withdrawal, but the volcanic liquid was lowering nonetheless.

Ret paddled to the side of the core and rotated his hand in a swirling motion. He transformed the lake into a stationary whirlpool, with a tornado-like funnel growing in the center. Since there were no obvious paths to continue his journey, Ret hoped to uncover the way he should go by learning what avenues the volcano's long throat had to offer. With the vortex growing ever deeper, he swam to its edge and looked down to see a bottom-less shaft, which actually grew wider the further it plunged into the earth. All along the sides of this vertical chamber were gaping holes, as you might expect to see after drilling through a sponge. Upon closer examina-tion, these cavities were actually cavernous tunnels, each beginning at the volcano's throat. Like the cilia that line the respiratory tract, the lava tubes projected into the shaft and whisked away any lava that happened to pass through them.

Suddenly finding himself with innumerable pathways, Ret didn't waste any time. He stretched himself out and started swimming down the side of the swirling lava. As he passed by the first few rows of lava tubes, he glanced inside but found each of them to be dark and empty, insofar as he could observe. For many strokes, he encountered more of the same; in fact, no matter how deep he descended, the prospects never brightened, and neither did the lighting, for things had grown darker and dimmer until all that lit Ret's path was a faint gleam not unlike that of dying embers.

At this point, Ret extended his left hand and used the glow of his scar to light the way. Though perhaps on account of his ever-darkening surroundings, Ret's moai man scar seemed to shine more brightly with every passing moment. Although he had initially made his descent in a spiraled trail, he now felt a familiar, magnetic pull attracting his scar and altering his route. He had little idea where it intended to take him, and whenever he apparently veered off course, he could feel the unseen connection drawing him back on track. He passed scores of tubes before his scar led him into a certain one whose mouth was smaller than all the others. Climbing inside the cave's entrance, Ret turned and shined his scar down into the apparently never-ending shaft. He could see neither the bottom nor any other tubes.

Ret set to walking. At first, the lava tube was scarcely taller than he was, but it became roomier with every step. Aided solely by the vibrant illumination of his scar, he made his way through the mostly straight corridor. The rounded walls bore evidence of the varying heights and lengths of former lava flows, telling a geological story like the layered sides of a canyon. His footsteps echoed against the hard rock, although there were puddles of fresh and cooling lava strewn along the floor. At times, it seemed to Ret as though he was passing through the abandoned track of an underground subway, while at other times, given the dark and warm atmosphere, he felt more like a piece of excrement passing through an intestine.

In time, Ret arrived at what appeared to be a dead end. Shining his scar along the edges of the impassable wall, however, he came to the conclusion that it was, in fact, a giant boulder. Although it plugged the tube with cork-like perfection, the stone's aggregate makeup was totally different from that of the surrounding rock; it did not look volcanic at all. While entertaining the idea of turning back and trying a different tube, Ret glanced at the base of the boulder and noticed that the residual lava was dripping into a sort of drain underneath it.

Undeterred by the impasse, Ret placed his hands on the boulder and prepared for it to combust. But it neither sparked nor fumed; in fact, it didn't do anything. It apparently was not volcanic after all. With a shrug of his shoulders, he reached to the back burner and summoned his power over earth, pushing the giant rock forward until he had uncovered the drain in the floor enough for him to slip inside.

The lava tube had become a waterslide of sorts, with Ret gliding down a curvy pipeline, made slick by years of lava flow. It was a suspenseful ride, whose thrill was enhanced by its unknown destination. Though moving along at a fair clip, the chute quickly ended, flush with the ground, causing Ret to briefly hydroplane on puddles of lava like a cat hurtling on its belly across a waxed floor.

Rising to his feet, Ret took one sweeping look around and stood in awe at the ceaseless wonders of Fire Island. He now found himself in an enormous cavern of cosmic proportions. Simply stated, it was a continuation of the volcano; indeed, it was the rest of it. If what he had descended earlier was the throat, then this was the belly. It was in the shape of a trapezoidal beaker, the kind Ret had used in science class, with a very broad bottom and an exceptionally narrow neck. Far below him was a boundless ocean of lava. It was so expansive that what he had seen before in the upper reaches of the volcano now seemed but a mere raindrop. Since he could not see the end of it in any direction, Ret considered its vastness akin to that of Sunken Earth.

Ret was standing quite close to what must have been the ceiling of this gargantuan, underground cavity, perched on a rocky ledge that hung from the top, without support from anything below it, like the chunks of frost that accumulate on the inside roof of a freezer. With a plain as long as a football field, it connected with a similar and equally large and stalactitical structure hanging not far away. But it was the center of this runway that intrigued Ret the most.

From the moment he saw it, Ret knew he had finally found the hiding place of the fire element. It was but a small, single flame, flickering like a pilot light. At least, that's what it looked like, for Ret stood a considerable distance away from the coveted element. It was located in the center of this prairie-like plain on an earthen island that was surrounded by a moat of air. Indeed, it was floating in mid air! But unlike their reed-made counterparts on the waters of Lake Titicaca, this suspended island was totally unreachable: there was no bridge; no convenient zip line; and to jump was totally out of the question, even for Ret.

The island was of a unique shape. Well did it resemble a sort of flattened candlesnuffer, complete with a hollow foundation. In the middle of the island was a hole, directly over which hovered the element. A subtle conduit seemed to enclose the element, stretching infinitely both downwards, getting lost in the steam arising from the lava, and also upwards, eventually colliding with the ceiling.

Enveloped by the vast quantity of astounding things to behold, Ret was startled by an unexpected, though gentle, voice from behind him.

"I thought you'd never come," the voice rasped, sounding as if it hadn't been used in centuries.

Ret spun around to find an elderly man slowly walking towards him. Whereas most people would have been scared out of their wits in such a situation, Ret was actually quite relieved, for he knew, based on his present location and the tenderness of the stranger's voice, that he was in the company of one of the Guardians of the Elements.

"Are you, sir, the Guardian of the Fire Element?" Ret asked, rather instinctively bowing his head in reverence.

"Please, please," the Guardian pled graciously, as if Ret's gesture of respect did not bode well with his humble character, "call me Argo. It's my real name, after all."

"But you *are* the Guardian, right?" Ret iterated, wanting to be sure.

"Oh, I suppose," responded Argo nonchalantly, smiling. He waved his hand at a pile of volcanic rocks, which made them molten just long enough for him to mold them into a place to sit. Then, without any sign of haste, he sat down with a heavy sigh. It was proof enough for Ret.

Argo looked much the same as the Guardian of the Earth Element. He was old, yet nimble, with a well-groomed appearance. His hair, short and gray with a distinct part down one side, looked so immaculate that Ret wondered if it naturally grew that way. A plain robe covered all but his extremities, and his eyes conveyed a soul of perfect mildness. His skin was tanned and supple, as if charred by fire but moisturized by steam for years. In his very presence, Ret felt safe and protected.

"So you've already collected the earth element, have you?" Argo stated more than he questioned.

Suspicious, Ret replied, "How do you know I've—"

"Because you got passed my barrier," answered Argo with a sense of pride.

"You mean the rock in the lava tube?"

"Precisely," said the Guardian. "Granted, it's probably not the most difficult obstacle to overcome, but all your First Father told me was what element would be collected before mine and that I ought to do something that required you to have it before you could get this one." Ret had wondered before if there was a prescribed order to the procurement of the elements, and he was glad that at least the Oracle knew what it was doing. "By the way, who was the Guardian of the Earth Element?"

"Uh…" Ret stuttered, trying to recall any distinguishing features of the Guardian at Sunken Earth. "Well, he was a lot like you, except he was bald, and, uh…"

"Do you recall his name?"

"No," Ret thought, "I don't think he ever told me his name."

"Must have been Heliu," was Argo's deduction. "He was always a little spacey. Lye called him the airhead. How did he look?"

"Fine," Ret guessed. To be honest, what Ret remembered best about the Guardian of the Earth Element—or "Heliu"—was the smile on his face when he passed away, so he added, "He died smiling."

Argo couldn't suppress a smile of his own at the remembrance of what must have been an endearing friend. Ret paused to let Argo savor the moment before beginning his interrogation.

"Sir," said Ret, "where exactly are we?"

"We're in the magma chamber," the Guardian taught. "It's the pocket under the earth's crust that feeds this great volcano. In an eruption, magma fills the chamber and shoots through its only outlet." He pointed to the large, circular area in the ceiling above the element. "That's the conduit, which leads to the throat, which is where you came in." Then, noticing Ret's awe-struck face, Argo observed, "Pretty impressive, huh? It goes to show how smart that little flame is," pointing to the element, "picking a place like this to conceal itself. I won't even tell you how long it took me to find it."

Knowing his time with the Guardian was painfully precious and probably short, Ret kept rattling off the many questions that were on his mind: "Argo, sir, how is that island floating?" Ret pointed to the scrap of land above which the element hovered.

"Since it's sort of shaped like a parachute," Argo explained, "the gases and convection currents rising from the magma keep it aloft."

"And, if you don't mind me asking," said Ret, "how am I supposed to, you know, get to it?"

The Guardian shrugged, "I was hoping *you* would know the answer to that one, son." Ret was stunned by Argo's lack of information on such a crucial matter, to say nothing of his vexation regarding the chore of figuring out how to access the element on his own. Still, it was one of those topics that seemed so daunting that Ret shoved it aside, not even wanting to attempt to tackle it at the moment.

"You must have more questions?" Argo probed like a patient school teacher.

"Yes!" Ret blurted out, anxious to ask his most burning question of all. "Do you know anything about the other four elements? *What* they are? *Where* they are? Anything at all?"

As if searching his brain, the Guardian thought hard for a moment and then said, "Not a thing." Ret was afraid he would say that. "But that reminds me," Argo rejoined. "Your First Father *did* instruct me to give you *this.*"

After digging in one of his deep pockets, Argo reached out and extended a curious object to Ret, who accepted it methodically. It appeared to be some kind of hour glass: two hollow chambers connected narrowly at each of their funneled ends. Made of blown glass, it measured quite small: no larger than Ret's little finger. One end was filled halfway with shiny flecks, but when Ret stood the device upright to watch the flecks fall through to the bottom, they stayed put. Perhaps it was plugged.

"What is this?" Ret queried.

"You know, after all these years, I can't recall," Argo admitted, much to Ret's chagrin. "The glass doesn't look familiar to me, but I know for a fact that those little flecks of gold came from the Great River. That's where all our precious metals came from, though it likely doesn't exist anymore, as a result of all the physical upheaval when the Oracle's elements were scattered." The Guardian was more or less rambling now, saying everything he knew since he realized he wasn't being of much help to Ret. Then, scratching his head and creating a ruffle in his flawless hairdo, he reasoned, "Still, its purpose escapes me. Just before he embarked to scatter the elements, your First Father gave each of us a little trinket like that, then said we were to give it to the one with the scars."

"Wait a minute," Ret verbally stepped back, "he gave one to *each* of you?"

"If my memory serves me right," Argo asserted sheepishly, now doubting the validity of his own words, noticing how important this was to Ret.

"The other Guard—I mean, *Heliu*," Ret corrected himself, "didn't give me anything like this."

With a grin, Argo looked down and, shaking his head, chuckled, "First his own name and now this— forgetful to the end!" Ret didn't find the situation so amusing.

Suddenly, the sound of a loud blast abruptly killed the conversation. It would have seemed but another one of the many explosions constantly taking place throughout the magma chamber if it had not come from the wall of rock where Ret's chute had slid him out. Scrutinizing this ledge for the first time, Ret noticed that there were dozens of holes all over the wall, just like the one he had exited. It seemed many, if not all, of the lava tubes led to this central location.

Only a few seconds after the echoes of the blast died down, another noise greeted their ears, this time the sound of a great many particles cascading down the chute. Soon, the noisemakers manifested them- selves as an avalanche of small stones and pebbles came rushing out one of the other lava tubes. It was then when Ret realized that the rolling rubble had once been a giant boulder that, like his own, was blocking the path of someone—someone who obviously didn't bear his scars and, thus, didn't possess his powers.

While the dust was still settling, the two poised men next heard the sound of a body sliding down the chute. Although Ret had no clue what friend or foe was approaching, Argo apparently did. Skin flushed and eyes aflame, the Guardian lowered his arms and ignited a fire in each of his hands, ready to spurn his unwanted guest.

CHAPTER 15

FIRE ISLAND

The unidentified newcomer's feet had scarcely slid into view when the entire scene erupted in fiery explosion. Without hesitation, the Guardian produced a constant stream of flames that engulfed the opening of the lava tube. Relentlessly, Argo pummeled the unknown visitor, who certainly would die of asphyxiation if not incineration. After several moments of idle observation, Ret's sympathy intervened.

"Stop!" Ret ordered, tugging at the drooping sleeves of Argo's extended arms. "We don't even know who it is!"

The Guardian obliged, although Ret wasn't sure if the sudden cessation was due to Ret's remonstration or the cremation's completion. In silence, they waited as the smoke cleared, Argo's palms still steaming. The entire backdrop surrounding the lava tube had been charred, so much so that the rock had begun to melt. The mysterious person stood barely inside the chute, crouched behind a protective wall of water. When the excitement had subsided, he abandoned his shield and stepped out of the tube. Ret couldn't believe his eyes.

"Lye?" Ret asked, utterly stupefied. "But how...how did you...," Ret stuttered, groping for words to convey his astonishment. Then, stating with wondrous dread, "You're alive!"

"No thanks to *you*," Lye snarled, dusting off his robes and leaning on his spiraled cane, "leaving me to die atop that dreadful mountain."

"But how...how did you—*escape?*" Ret was completely beside himself to find that Lye, let alone anyone, had survived the cataclysmic collapse of Sunken Earth. "It was Bubba, wasn't it? *He* helped you escape."

"That hothead?" Lye balked. "He and that woman of his don't know anything about my *real* motives. They still believe they're going to strike oil or find buried treasure or something! Do you really think I would tell them about the element—about the Oracle?"

"So you lied to them?" Ret stated, putting things together. "You—you *used* them?"

"Oh, Ret!" the shriveled hunchback cackled with pleasure. "Your innocence never ceases to amaze me! So naïve! So gullible!" Lye's menacing laughter seemed to shroud the air in darkness. "You should never have left me alive. You should have killed me when you had the chance. But you couldn't, could you? You were too noble, too compassionate. You see, Ret, to be merciful is to be weak!"

"That *will* do!" Argo interjected. He was still standing next to Ret, stone-faced, looking as though it was all he could do to restrain himself from resuming his assault on Lye.

"Why, if it isn't Argo," Lye hissed, turning to face the Guardian for the first time. "My apologies, old friend: I hardly saw you standing there. You never were one to draw much attention to yourself."

"Unlike *you*," Argo retorted.

"Let this be a lesson to you, Ret," Lye taught. "The so-called 'Guardians of the Elements' are no more than a pathetic group of weaklings and simpletons—experts in nothing but mediocrity. Haven't you ever wondered why *they* were the ones 'chosen' to protect the elements?" Then, answering his own question, Lye barked, "Because they're pawns! So submissive and obedient to foolish traditions—ignorant of the Oracle's *real* power and too foolish to wield it themselves." His voice was growing ever louder. "But *I* am different; *I*, and *I* alone, understand the grand secret of the whole matter: rather than let the Oracle control *me*, *I* will control the Oracle!"

"LIAR!" Argo bellowed. In his hot displeasure, the Guardian recommenced his role as a human flamethrower, though with much greater ferocity than before. Not a whit behind him, Lye blocked his attacker with a horizontal geyser of water, collected from the humid air. Like a fire-breathing dragon versus an uncapped fire hydrant, the two forces collided head-on, erupting in a dazzling display of steam.

Ret looked on, unsure of what to do.

"Help me!" Argo supplicated through clenched teeth, obviously exerting great effort. "Let's take Lye down once and for all!"

Ret heeded the Guardian's call to arms. Through pure brainpower, Ret started to heat the ground underneath Lye's feet. Then, glowing like a burner on a stove, the stone floor melted away, prompting Lye to quickly jump to safety, though his pilfered cleats fell far below into the lava of the magma chamber.

Utilizing Lye's brief distractedness, Argo laid both arms at his sides and gradually raised them like a maestro conducting an orchestra's dramatic crescendo. As his hands extended above his head, two massive waves of lava rose from the depths of the chamber, one on each side of the platform affixed to the ceiling. Then, letting his hands fall downward together, the torrents of lava came crashing down on Lye, who enclosed himself in a bubble of water just prior to being consumed.

Neither Ret nor the Guardian moved, not even flinching as the lava licked their legs as it drained off the platform back to where it came. When it had come in contact with the water of Lye's enclosure, it had hardened, leaving a spherical shell of rock surrounding the villain. Ret called upon his power over earth and rolled the solid bubble, containing Lye, over the edge.

As the casing approached the churning sea of lava, a brilliant flash of light shot through its base. The protective cage cracked open like an egg, and Lye came hurtling out of it, straddling his cane as it propelled him upward. Argo commanded the waves of lava to heave themselves mightily in an attempt to swallow Lye, but, like a nimble witch on her broom, Lye evaded the danger and flew to the other platform, on the other side of the fire element.

There was another radiant flash of light, and an electrical current like lightning shot out of Lye's cane. It crashed into the narrow neck that connected the ceiling to the body of the platform where Ret and Argo were standing. A growing crack zigzagged through the stone, accompanied by the deep sounds of buckling rock. Just as the platform threatened to break off and plummet, Ret held it in place long enough for Argo to melt the rock and weld it back together.

Now with a sizeable space between them, Argo engaged Lye in a more long-distance battle. The

Guardian turned each puddle of residual lava into a sort of missile turret, launching liquid bullets at his rival. Argo fired dozens of rounds simultaneously from all directions, but Lye met each one with a simple squirt of water that turned it to rock, which abruptly fell toward the lava below. Seizing the opportunity, Ret then caught each falling bullet of volcanic rock and aimed them at Lye. Still, Lye proved to be impressively dexterous as he not only addressed each of Argo's projectiles but also blocked each of Ret's pellets with his cane.

"I'll cover you," Argo said to Ret, realizing they were not making any progress. "You collect the element. Go!"

Though Ret understood the command, he still had little idea how we was expected to fulfill it. The floating island had not become any more accessible than it had been moments earlier. Yet, Ret was determined. As Lye continued to harden Argo's lava bullets, Ret gathered some of the rocks and laid them before him to form a sort of levitating walkway. He stepped onto the first one and found it challenging to maintain his balance on such a meager support while standing on but one foot. Then he jumped onto the next stepping stone, almost falling. As he leapt, however, he noticed the island immediately counteract his motion: it began to float even higher, though cockeyed, as if something was pushing up on the side farthest from him. With each arduous jump toward it, the element floated further away.

Completely perplexed, Ret's languishing logic was interrupted when Lye began pulverizing his stepping stones. Each bolt of electricity reduced a stone to dust. Abandoning his first attempt, Ret left his current step just as Lye destroyed it, then launched himself back to the ledge where he had begun.

"Did you see that?" Ret asked the Guardian, referring to how the island evaded him.

"It seems as though anything that enters the moat around the island," Argo stipulated, now flinging discs of lava at Lye, "disrupts the equilibrium achieved by the rising currents and gases. Can't you control the island— you know, bring it to *you?*"

"No, it's resisting," Ret answered. "Besides, even if I could control the island, I can't move the element."

"Well, I hope you figure it out soon," Argo wished. "I can't keep this madman at bay much longer."

Ret had the sudden idea to try to simply walk out to the island. If there was enough thrust keeping it afloat, he reasoned, perhaps it would do the same for him. Warily, he stopped mid-step and let his foot hang over the edge. The island seemed to quiver at the disturbance. He felt nothing buoyant about the situation, but he lifted up his other foot to finish his first step anyway, since he had no other ideas.

Not surprisingly, he could not walk on air at all but, instead, began falling towards the endless belly of lava. Dropping feet-first, however, he was shocked to discover a form of combustion occurring underneath his feet. It was like each of his shoes had been transformed into a rocket. It took him a few moments to get the hang of it, but in very little time, Ret was zooming upwards to the island like a rocketeer.

To his great dismay, however, he *still* could not reach the island. No matter what angle he approached from or what speed he flew in with, Ret was unable to obtain the element that he so desperately wanted.

"I can't do it," Ret said in defeat as he returned to the Guardian's side. Argo had just enclosed Lye in a flaming box of fire. Like a caged animal, Lye stomped inside the box, trying to devise a way to escape without getting singed. Finally, he rolled through the flames, some of his hair and garb burning until he commanded the water in the air to his advantage.

Lye looked thoroughly angry, miffed at being toyed with by someone he deemed exceptionally inferior.

"Enough!" he roared with hatred in his eyes. He lifted his cane and stamped it on the ground directly in front of him, sending a narrow shockwave that blasted Argo and flung him into the rock wall that was bespeckled with lava tubes. Ret watched in horror as the Guardian fell to the earth, barely alive. Then Ret turned back around to face Lye, wondering what havoc he had in store for him.

Lye approached the edge of the other platform, mimicking Ret's location on the other and purposely positioning himself so that the fire element flickered directly in their line of sight.

"This is the last time I will make you this offer, Ret," said Lye with sudden patience. "Join me. Join me like old times. We used to be friends, you and I. We worked together; we helped one another." His tone had almost become fatherly now. "I can teach you the real purpose of the Oracle; I can help you unlock its full potential. I can tell you about your past." The offer suddenly seemed very tempting. "You need me; you need my wisdom and experience. Join me, and I will give you the upper hand."

Those last few words rang in Ret's ears like a fire alarm. He had heard those words before. In an instant, a flurry of images flashed within his mind as his brain reviewed the past. Those words were familiar, he knew it. They were from something recent, he recalled. And then the connection was made: Lionel had said that same phrase when they were at the Intihuatana Stone at Machu Picchu—when Lionel had taught Ret that he couldn't have something unless he was first willing to not have it. Suddenly, it was all beginning to make perfect sense.

"That's it!" Ret beamed, still facing Lye but focusing his eyes on the element.

"It is?" Lye questioned, slightly confused. "So you'll join me?"

"No!" Ret shouted joyfully at the absurdity. He looked over his shoulder at the failing Guardian, lying near the lava tube that Ret had taken. Then he glanced above him at the chamber's roof directly above where the element hovered. With newfound purpose, Ret turned around and darted for the lava tube.

"Wait!" Lye cried out. "Where are you going? You don't want the element?"

"Exactly!" Ret agreed, remembering Lionel's lesson. He dove into the tube, initiated the piston-like combustion at his feet, and took off. In no time at all, he had slithered up the chute, slipped past the boulder, and flew through the rest of the tube. Reaching the volcano's throat, Ret bent his course downward into the darkness. Then, blasting through the artificial bottom of the volcano, he descended into the lava chamber directly above the island, where he alighted gracefully within arm's reach of the element.

"How did you think to do that?" Lye queried with concealed awe, still standing on the edge of his platform.

"A good friend once taught me that you can't have anything unless you're willing to walk away from it," Ret smiled. "Which explains why you still don't have *this."* Ret retrieved the Oracle from his pocket. Lye gawked at the Oracle in worshipful admiration. Though far from his grasp, he instinctively reached for it, his mouth open, like a child at the window of a confectionary.

For a brief moment, the Oracle seemed to command the attention of every living thing. The small sphere of transparent glass glowed like a red ruby, reflecting the bubbling lava all around. Ret held it, in cupped hands, under the fire element. As it had done before, the Oracle aligned its scars with those on Ret's palms, then lifted itself above his hands and gracefully opened. With a hinge at the base, it parted into six separate wedges, one of which already housed the earth element and another about to be filled with the fire element.

"Fool!" Lye derided, coming to his senses. "You can't have anything unless you take it by force!" From his cane, he shot an electric bolt at the Oracle, sending it soaring out of Ret's possession and onto the platform behind him. It landed right-side-up and slid, like a spider on its back, until stopped by the wall of lava tubes, not far from where Argo lay lifelessly.

As Lye exultantly hastened over to where the Oracle had come to rest, Ret made eye-contact with Argo. With one eye half-opened, the Guardian had faithfully observed the goings-on. He winked at Ret, then dragged himself over to where the Oracle sat.

Feeling reassured, Ret made it his objective to obstruct Lye as much as possible. He rolled rocks in his path and splashed lava on his robes. He tripped Lye with divots in the ground and obscured his view with sporadic fireballs. In the end, the agile antagonist arrived at the side of Argo, who was curled up and clutching something earnestly.

"Give it up, old man," Lye demanded coldly. Having been ignored, Lye bent down, insensitively rolled the Guardian onto his back, and pried open his hands. Argo, now smiling contentedly, was holding a rock.

Incensed, Lye spun around to face Ret. During his prematurely triumphant trek to fetch the Oracle, Lye hadn't noticed a subtle move made by the Guardian. As his life's final gesture to protect the element he had been entrusted to guard, Argo had slid the Oracle off the platform and into the lava below. Then, he positioned it directly underneath the island where Ret was standing and created a sort of growing lava fountain to elevate it up to the floating island and through the hole at its center.

Just as Lye's incredulous eyes fell upon Ret, the Oracle closed around the fire element.

CHAPTER 16

OUT OF THE
FRYING PAN

It had been exactly forty-seven minutes since Ret leapt into the volcano; Paige had tallied every one of them. She sat between Pauline and Ana, all huddled together near the crater's edge, while Mr. Coy paced ponderously behind them. When the volcano had calmed shortly after consuming Ret, they weren't sure whether they should repose or repine. The longer they waited, the more their resolve waned.

Forty-eight minutes.

Truth be told, the female trio still had their doubts about the strange curio called the Oracle. Despite all the supporting evidence, it was still hard for them to believe that something so reticent would exert such a pretentious agenda. How could an object, virtually unknown to the world, expect to change it? Such self-proclaimed preeminence seemed illogical because it was beyond their finite comprehension, for, in this moment, all they wished was for Ret's safety.

Forty-nine.

"We can't stay up here any longer," Mr. Coy advised with expired patience. "Any minute now, Ret's going to collect the fire element, and this volcano's going to blow." With grief-stricken eyes, the girls glanced at each other, knowing Mr. Coy was right but not willing to abandon their vigil just yet. "If this is anything like Sunken Earth," Coy recalled with gravity, "we'll want to be as far away as possible."

"Just how far away can we get on an island?" Ana muttered to her mother as they rose to their feet and followed Mr. Coy. When they failed to find Paige with them, they stopped and looked back.

Paige was standing at the rim of the volcano, morose and melancholy. An unseen foe weighed on her sunken shoulders and pulled on her bowed head, like the last mourner at a fresh gravesite. Though motionless, the light breeze blew through her blonde curls, now speckled with ash.

Leaving Pauline's side, Ana advanced to comfort her friend.

"You're a lot stronger than I am," Ana said tenderly, referring to the recent lesson she had gleaned from their turbulent trip. "That's for sure."

"Am I a fool to think Ret's still alive?" Paige questioned dismally.

"What does your heart tell you?"

Paige gently placed her hand to her chest, as if she wanted to touch the feeling that suddenly warmed her heart. A hopeful smile forced itself to her lips, which was answer enough for Ana.

"I thought so," Ana cheered as they turned to join Pauline, their spirits brightening. "Still, you have to be careful about those warm, fuzzy feelings," Ana cautioned as they started down the volcano. "They could just be from heartburn, you know. Like, remember the time in middle school when..." Though listening, Paige grinned and rolled her eyes, glad to have the real Ana back.

In fact, Ana didn't stop talking during the entire hike down the volcano's trail, as if it was her chance to finally unleash all the things she had wanted to say while corked by her speechless introspection. While her mother and friend nodded with the occasional "uh-huh," Mr. Coy maintained a considerable distance in front of them, safely out of earshot of Ana's babbling.

On account of their elevated vista, they had scarcely commenced their descent when Mr. Coy scanned the horizon and caught sight of a ship sailing towards Fire Island. Although initially perplexed, it was with quick dread that he remembered Lye mentioning something about a ship in his conversation with Bubba relative to Lionel. Then, expanding his view, he was filled with dismay when he saw dozens of other boats anchored in the outlying waters all around the island. It was a full-blown fleet, consisting not of harmless trading vessels but of ill-intentioned battleships.

Rounding the final corner of their downward trek, Ana, still blabbing, abruptly swallowed her voice upon encountering an armed receiving party waiting for them at the bottom of the volcano.

"Where is he?!" Miss Carmen shouted as Paige and the Coopers stopped at Mr. Coy's side. "I said," she repeated, fuming with fury, "where *is* he?!"

"Where is *who?*" Coy asked.

"Don't play stupid with me," Miss Carmen snarled. "You know very well who 'who' is!"

"Who who?" Ana comically mumbled to Paige, deriding her former role model.

"Where is Bubba?" Miss Carmen screamed.

Then, learning that Bubba was the one who was missing, Paige added to Ana, "I think you mean *woo*hoo!"

"Where is my darling Bubba?" Miss Carmen continued to rave. "Where is he?"

"Join the club, toots," remarked Ana, referring to how they themselves didn't know the exact whereabouts of Ret either.

"What did you say, girl?" Miss Carmen interrogated, rushing close to Ana's face.

"We don't know where your precious lover boy is," Mr. Coy confessed irritably. "Now get out of our way and let us through."

"Humph!" Miss Carmen snorted like a spoiled pooch. "You're not going anywhere until you tell us what you've done with Bubba."

"But we don't—" Pauline tried to insert.

"Then it looks like we'll have to do it the hard way," Miss Carmen sneered. Then, pointing at Ana, she ordered, "Seize her!" The guards immediately grabbed Ana and brought her before Miss Carmen. "I'd love to add a few scars to your pretty face," she hissed. Amid shrieks of protest from Pauline, Miss Carmen snatched a hand knife from her pocket and prepared to deface her former volleyball player.

Just as the blade was about to mar Ana's cheek, a curious object in the sky caught Miss Carmen's eye. Distracted, she postponed Ana's facial to study the unidentified flyer. It was moving rather quickly, bobbing in the air above the ocean as it approached the island, headed straight for the confrontation at the foot of the volcano.

"Is that a bird?" Miss Carmen wondered aloud, squinting quizzically at the sky. "Or—a plane?"

"No, doofus," Ana ridiculed, "it's a floating

basket." Then, realizing the absurdity of what she had just said, Ana did a double take. "It's a floating basket!?" she reasserted, though with much confusion.

"My balloon!" Mr. Coy rejoiced. "It must be Ishmael!"

To everyone's surprise, it certainly was Ishmael. With all but its wicker basket hidden from view, the balloon swooped down on the scene like a fowl. Ishmael stood at the controls, a look of heroic confidence washing over his countenance upon realizing he had come to the rescue in the nick of time. He maneuvered the balloon over the guards' heads and landed near Mr. Coy and the girls.

"Balloon?" Miss Carmen queried distastefully. "I don't see any balloon. And—you!" She finally recognized Ishmael. "You're with *them!* Here to save the day, are you?"

"That," Ishmael concurred, "and to drop off some extra baggage." He disappeared from view briefly as he bent down inside the basket to pick up something heavy. Then, reappearing, he rolled Bubba over the side and onto the grass with a thud.

"Bubba!" Miss Carmen gasped, rushing to his side.

As if awaking from a deep sleep, Bubba staggered to his feet, blinking repeatedly and massaging his head.

"Are you alright, my sweet?" Miss Carmen crooned, trying to smooth his disheveled hair, which looked all the more flaming.

"I've just had the most horrible dream," Bubba explained, dazed and confused. "I was on an island, in the middle of a lake, surrounded by a bunch of people who wanted to—to kill me."

Just then, several more stowaways revealed themselves from within the basket. Standing shoulder to shoulder all around Ishmael was a legion of natives from Lake Titicaca, armed and ready for battle.

Catching sight of these additional passengers, the faces of Miss Carmen and Bubba surged with fear.

"It's a dream come true," Ishmael said brightly.

With a sudden cry, the island people rushed forward, pouring out of the basket. Bubba and Miss Carmen let out terrified screams in unison as they stumbled backwards into their guards' serried ranks, seeking refuge from the herd of wild banshees now charging towards them at full speed.

With their antagonists preoccupied, Mr. Coy and the girls looked to Ishmael for a safe getaway.

"Quick!" Ishmael called out to them from inside the balloon. "Get in!" Mr. Coy hastened to the foot of the balloon and prepared to help the girls climb aboard first.

Ishmael had almost grabbed the first, desperate, still-bound pair of hands when a set of invisible but powerful shockwaves burst upon the scene. Although both claimed the volcano as their epicenter, each jolt was opposite in nature. The first, like the suction of a vacuum cleaner, seemed to pull everything inward, toward the volcano, as if it was threatening to implode. Brief but strong, it brought everyone to the ground and even swallowed all sound for a moment. Then, as if switched into reverse, the secondary wave detonated, pushing everything outward, away from the volcano, with far greater force than its forerunner. Like the thunderclaps of a thousand lightning bolts, the previously muted volume exploded with a deafening blast. The wave sent every mobile body rolling before extending out to sea in all directions, creating monstrous ripples.

"That's a good sign," Mr. Coy announced over the dying noise. He and the others had been scattered by the tremor and were stumbling to their feet.

"Good news for Ret," said Ana, "bad news for us."

"Ishmael!" Coy yelled. "Get over here before this whole place erupts!"

The sudden gust in the airwaves had caught the balloon and carried it away from the stranded party and back into the sky. As Ishmael reapproached the ground, he threw the ladder over the side of the basket, hoping to expedite the boarding process.

As the helpless quartet sprinted toward the dangling ladder, they could feel the ground rumbling beneath their feet. The tall grass seemed to transform into a sea of snakes as a result of the constant agitation. Even the seawater along the rocky shoreline was as frothy as a bubble bath.

Breathless, Mr. Coy was preparing to latch onto the first rung of their lifeline when it suddenly skyrocketed out of reach. With a booming roar, the volcano exploded with terrible glory. A humongous plume of pyroclastic flow launched from the throat as if headed into orbit, filling the air with all manner of hot gases and a sooty mixture of gray smoke and ivory ash. Following closely behind was the first of many loads of lava—so large, in fact, that it destroyed the upper fringe of the volcano's peak. It burst free like a once-caged animal, squirting into the sky like a paint sprayer. Bright red and glowing, the endless lava bubbled over the rim and cascaded down the slopes, creating wave after wave of unstoppable avalanches that melted everything in their path.

The volcano's eruption was a truly magnificent display of raw power that commanded everyone's attention. Even the guards and the natives paused their warfare to admire the apocalyptic event. But the stunning vantage point came at a startling price as awe faded to fear—fear for life.

The eruption brought instant and intense heat to the landscape. As soon as the volcano began to

discharge, Mr. Coy and the girls could feel the unre-
lenting heat against their bodies, as if they were sitting
next to a bonfire at the beach. An earthquake occurred in
conjunction with the eruption, and the land continued to
tremble unceasingly, making it all the more difficult for
Mr. Coy and the girls to reunite.

"Ishmael!" Mr. Coy hollered. "Ishmael!"

The servant could scarcely hear his master, so high
had the balloon been forced into the sky.

"I'm trying, sir!" Ishmael replied, flustered.
"There's too much heat—too much gas—in the air. I
can't descend any lower." Indeed, the conditions
rendered the hot-air balloon powerless.

"Do something—anything!" Mr. Coy pled,
keeping a constant watch on the ever-flowing lava. "The
guy-lines—throw the guy-lines!"

Ishmael obeyed. He heaved the long ropes over the
side of the basket. After unraveling, they stopped just
feet from the ground.

Mr. Coy darted for the line. As soon as he flung his
bound hands over the hook at the end of the guy-line,
however, another eruption dislodged the connection, and
Mr. Coy flopped to the ground. This second eruption
exploded through the side of the volcano, creating a
gaping hole through which lava was pouring profusely.

Its volcano hemorrhaging, Fire Island was in a
state of total and irreparable chaos. Lava had dribbled

onto the mainland now, slithering unpredictably across the ground. In very little time, it reached its nearest shore, where it gushed over the coastline and into the ocean, adding torrents of blinding steam to the bedlam. What's more, the earth refused to be comforted, now plagued by giant fissures that cracked and opened in random order. The island was fragmenting — splintering into yet smaller pieces, through which still more lava began to bubble like miniature volcanoes. Fanned by the wind, the clouds of smoke stretched across the heavens, veiling the sun and turning it blood red.

Meanwhile, the ongoing battle between both kinds of islanders — floating and fire — had waxed exceedingly sore. Every minute, the dwindling combatants on both sides yielded up yet another casualty, each of which was quickly consumed by the advancing lava. The natives fought with impressive strength, partly to defend themselves against the guards but mostly to prevent themselves from being overtaken by the approaching lava. At the rear of their troops cowered Bubba and Miss Carmen, barking orders and hoping they wouldn't run out of men before they ran out of land.

The Coys and the Coopers found themselves in a similar plight — a race against time and space. The balloon was unreachable now: each eruption funneled still more gaseous material into the air. The dire problem was only compounded by the excessive heat rising from the lava, which was covering more surface area every second. Panic-stricken, Ishmael buzzed about the basket, exhausting all resources but inventing nothing useful. Eventually, all he could do was lean over the side of the basket and stare grimly at his trapped comrades.

The fissuring ground had separated all four of the Coys and Coopers, each marooned alone on his or her own isle, their retreats growing smaller every second by the irrepressible lava.

"Help!" Paige screamed. "Help us, Ret!" But her plea was without hope, for, in this moment, even Paige was convinced that Ret had already suffered the fate that now lapped at her feet.

With the seething lava closing in around her, Paige teetered on one foot as another powerful eruption shot from the crumbling volcano's side. Unlike the other blasts, however, Paige noticed a familiar figure mixed in with all the flying debris. It was Ret!

"He's alive!" Paige rejoiced, nearly falling over with joy. She enthusiastically pointed at Ret within the cloud of rock and ash so that the others could spot him and join in her celebration.

"It's about time," Ana complained with relief.

Aided by the vast amount of heat and gas in the air, Ret initiated combustive reactions at his feet to remain airborne, thus preventing himself from plunging to the ground far below. Given the chaotic condition of things, Ret's aerial scan of Fire Island was overwhelming. In fact, it was the desperate cries of his endangered friends that quickly grabbed his attention.

"Since when can Ret fly?" Ana asked, very impressed though slightly envious.

"He must have collected the element," Mr. Coy replied, hollering to her from his own isolated island, which was growing ever smaller.

"HELP!" Paige screamed, now tiptoeing on one foot.

Noticing her fatal circumstance, Ret soared to Paige's rescue, fervently hoping to beat the lava. With no other alternative, Paige shut her eyes and jumped straight up as the lava finally overtook the last patch of untouched earth. Relief flooded her racing heart when, instead of landing in deadly molten rock, she felt Ret's embrace.

"Oh, Ret!" Paige cheered upon opening her eyes. With both hands, she grabbed his ashen face and pressed her lips to his. For a brief moment, osculating amid the pandemonium, all was bliss.

"Hey, lovebirds!" the couple heard a familiar voice say. "Sorry to interrupt," yelled Ana, "but don't forget about the rest of us!"

The reminder was well deserved. The lava was oozing dangerously close to Ana, mimicking Paige's plight, while Mr. Coy stood helplessly and Pauline did all she could not to faint. Knowing he couldn't carry all four of them simultaneously, Ret anxiously searched for a solution.

"The statues!" Paige pointed out. "Ret, use the statues!"

Ret's gaze immediately fell upon the dozens of giant moai statues that littered the island. Towering unharmed above the creeping sea of liquid rock, they were obviously the only things capable of withstanding the lava. At Paige's insistence, Ret waved his hand to command one of the moai. He lifted it out of the ground and into the air, the lava quickly rushing in to fill the imprint left behind. Then he effortlessly carried the statue across the island and set it down next to Ana, who immediately climbed to the top of the protective volcanic rock.

"This doesn't mean you can forget about me," Ana called out, sitting safely atop the monolith as the lava lapped at its base. Ret smiled, knowing the purpose of the tactic was to buy some time. He repeated the same procedure with two other moai, setting one by both Pauline and Mr. Coy, who promptly climbed to safety.

"Good thinking," Ret remarked to Paige. Now that the others were no longer in immediate danger, Ret flew to a nearby part of the island whose elevation had postponed it from being overrun by the rampant lava. Alighting gracefully upon the unscathed ground, he gently released Paige before heading back to retrieve the others.

"So, Superman," said Ana playfully upon Ret's return. "What took you so long?" With haste, he brought her down to join Paige before launching off again.

While Ret was away, Ana and Paige witnessed a curious occurrence. Their elevated viewpoint allowed them to overlook a large portion of the island, including the excavation site. The fragile settlement of tents and teepees had been washed away by the large outpourings of lava that continued to burst through the gnarly gash that Bubba and his guards had carved in the side of the volcano. There was nothing intriguing about this until Ana saw a large, steaming boulder roll out of the cavern. With her interest piqued, she turned her attention to the unusual sight and silently bade Paige to do likewise.

The giant boulder rolled through the excavation site, gliding along the lava in a path so unnatural that Ana wondered if it was being controlled remotely. When it neared the island's sole beach, the girls noticed a motorboat that had snuck ashore, waiting in the shallow waves.

As soon as the boulder reached the sea, a brilliant light flashed, and the rock split open like a coconut. Instead of milk, however, water came pouring out, as well as a wretched old man.

"Lye," Paige whispered to Ana, alarm in their eyes.

Looking pitiful, Lye staggered toward the motorboat, from which two men promptly emerged.

Like servants, they hastened to Lye's side and aided him in boarding the craft.

Meanwhile, Ret had retrieved Pauline. Too exhausted and frazzled for words, she showed her gratitude by planting a simple kiss on Ret's cheek. He swiftly but softly unloaded her at the site with the other two girls before setting off to fetch Mr. Coy.

Paige and Ana hardly noticed Ret's drop-off, so enthralled were they by the hushed event taking place on the beach. Ana was especially intrigued because one of Lye's two helpers looked very familiar to her. With borderline obsession, she watched this recognizable figure, studying his movements and mannerisms. Though crouched a considerable distance away, she noted his distinguishing features, though careful not to jump to any conclusions.

Mr. Coy was last to be rescued. "Don't expect any kisses from *me*," he stated upfront, though feeling rather humbled as Ret scooped him up. "But," Coy added soberly, "thank you." Ret smiled as he headed to the site where he had deposited the others.

"So I take it you collected the element?" Coy wondered.

"Fire element procured," Ret stated with pride.

"Did Lye put up much of a fight?" asked Coy, vividly remembering the grief he felt when Lye followed Ret into the volcano wearing the stolen cleats and cream.

"Yeah," Ret recalled, "a much stronger fight than last time, at least. I was so surprised when he showed up—alive. I mean, I always kind of felt he survived Sunken Earth, somehow, but still." Ret shrugged. "If it hadn't been for Argo, I doubt things would have worked out so well."

"Argo?"

"The Guardian," Ret explained.

"So did Lye survive—again?" Coy questioned.

"I don't know," Ret admitted, having learned not to underestimate his enemy. "Possibly—probably. Right before the volcano blew, I saw him hovering over Argo, searching his pockets frantically, though I'm not sure why."

Rejoining the others, Ret noticed the captivation that had befallen Paige and Ana. "What are you looking at?" he inquired, curious to know what was so enchanting.

"It's Lye," Paige whispered, pointing at the motorboat that was now speeding away from Fire Island.

"Unbelievable," Ret sighed as he looked on, though not too terribly surprised.

"And he was with two others," Paige informed.

"Who?" Ret asked eagerly. "Was one of them Lionel?" He seemed ready to charge forward to rescue his dear friend.

"I don't think so," Paige replied with uncertainty. Naturally, she turned to Ana, who looked like she had just seen a ghost.

"Mom," she said in all seriousness, "did you just see that?"

"Not now, dear," Pauline dismissed. "I'm still trying to collect myself."

"But, Mom—" Ana pressed.

Pauline was saved from her daughter's petitions by a sudden bang. Sharp and quick, it was a stark contrast from the long groans and deep blasts that they had come to recognize as volcanic eruptions. Like deer under fire, the Coys and Coopers searched sea, land, and sky to find the genesis of the outburst. Seconds later, they saw a fireball flare up on a nearby part of the island.

"That was a bomb," Mr. Coy deduced in disbelief. He traced a faint stream of exhaust from the flames of the explosion to a battleship floating a ways off shore. "That's the ship I saw earlier," he recognized.

"And look!" Ret chimed in, pointing at the speeding motorboat. "That's where Lye is headed."

"But what are they firing at?" Mr. Coy asked.

As each of them stared in the direction of the artillery strike, Coy's question was answered when a group of runaways emerged from a concealing valley. Bubba and Miss Carmen were sprinting along the unburned coastline, trying to escape the relentless natives of Lake Titicaca. Every last one of the guards had fallen, and the few surviving natives were overtaking their final two foes when Lye's ship opened fire.

Suddenly, another spark appeared from the deck of the battleship, followed by a deadly blast at the island's coast. A few of the natives at the back of the pack were consumed while the residual ones ran for their lives.

"We've got to help them!" Ret pled in earnest.

"Don't look at me," Coy replied. *"You're* the only one with enough fire power to contend with something like *that."* He motioned at the imposing battleship.

Despite Ret's good intentions, the remaining natives were wiped out by a final round of fire from the overpowering guns of the battleship. Noticing the direct hit, Bubba and Miss Carmen ceased fleeing and turned around to exult over the devastation. Amid their victorious embrace, however, they failed to notice the massive moai statue standing on a ledge beside them. The force of the blast had shaken the earth enough to dislodge the moai. When Bubba and Miss Carmen finally realized the statue's impending fall, it was too late. In one grand collapse, the massive moai crashed to the ground, crushing them. Pauline gasped.

During all of their activity, Ishmael did not sit in idle stupor. Observing Ret's rescue efforts, buzzing back and forth across the island like a bee from flower to hive, Ishmael set off to see if he could bring the balloon to their place of retreat. He maneuvered the balloon out to sea, venturing as far away as necessary so as to not be affected by the meddlesome heat and gas being discharged by the volcano. Then, when he was able to descend low enough, he made his way back to Fire Island, flying as low as possible, hoping to stay beneath the heat. After several failed attempts, it worked, and Ishmael successfully approached his weary comrades.

"Hurry before that death ship notices the basket and turns on *us!*" Mr. Coy warned.

Not another word of instruction was needed. Ishmael heaved the ladder over the side of the basket while Ret burned away the lingering bands around the girls' wrists, as well as the stone handcuffs clasped around Mr. Coy's hands. One by one, they climbed toward the balloon.

Ret was the last living soul to ever set foot on Fire Island. After helping everyone else mount the ladder, he brought up the rear, though he did not copy his associates' hurried climb. Instead, Ret paused after ascending each rung, his mind too engrossed in the scene of carnage all around him.

It was doomsday on Fire Island, which looked much like a bleeding heart in the belly of the sea. There was not one square inch of ground that had not been overtaken by the inexhaustible lava, including their elevated retreat. The island, which had previously been one contiguous landmass, had now splintered into an inordinate archipelago. Even the volcano, which was continuously caving in on itself, had proven incapable of enduring such widespread upheaval.

Ret had done it again. Scenes of the destruction of Sunken Earth flashed in his mind, serving as an unsolicited reminder of the cosmic consequences wrought by the procurement of each element. Why, for each of these two civilizations so far, had life itself depended upon its respective element? Was there no other way? Perhaps one with less death and desolation?

As the balloon pulled away with Ret still a few rungs from the safety of the basket, the distant scene took on a new look: the suppressive lava now came to resemble blood—some of it from the veins of guilty men, yes, but most of it from the pure hearts of centuries' worth of innocent martyrs. Ret bowed his head in reverence and sorrow.

Suddenly, as if finally giving up the ghost, the volcano totally collapsed. Then, as if its plug had been pulled, the whole island began to pour into the throat of the defunct volcano. Large chunks of lava-covered land, riding waves of steamy ocean water, plummeted into the shaft. The hundreds of moai statues, which once dotted the landscape as striking emblems of mystery and grandeur, were seen tumbling into the chute with no regard to antiquity or craftsmanship. Their purpose served, these elephantine structures rolled and bounced like weightless insects, evidence of the mighty forces of nature at work. Ret's thoughts turned to Argo's lifeless body down in the magma chamber, which was now filling up like a great septic tank. The sky, dressed in black from the abundant smoke, lit up with brilliant lightning as the heat and gas reacted with the atmosphere, as if the heavens mourned the death of Fire Island.

When he reached the top of the ladder, Ret's attention shifted to the battleship that had fired on the natives. Now that it had collected Lye, it was sailing away with great haste.

"Look!" Ret said, pointing at the speeding vessel as he finally hopped into the basket. They all glanced at the craft, which was heading west and would soon slip from view.

To everyone's surprise, Mr. Coy ordered, "Follow that ship!"

CHAPTER 18

HOT ON THE TRAIL

"Really?" Ret wondered, shocked by Mr. Coy's announcement to pursue Lye's battle cruiser.

"Of course," Coy replied. "We've got to get your buddy Lionel back, don't we?"

The floating basket fell silent. Although everyone wanted to retrieve Lionel, no one ever expected Mr. Coy to be the one to initiate such a rescue.

"Wait a minute," said Ret suspiciously, *"you* want to get Lionel back?"

With a face full of dread as if rehashing old wounds, Mr. Coy unwillingly explained, "It's not so much that I *want* to but that I *ought* to. You see, it's just that...well," he stalled, "it might be, kind of, more or less, my — my fault."

Meanwhile, Ana was tugging on Pauline's arm, trying to get her mother's attention.

"Mom," she whispered urgently, "did you see that man back there, helping Lye?"

"Not now, dear," Pauline hushed her, gleefully entrapped by the other conversation. "Mr. Coy's about to admit he was wrong!"

"But Mom—"

"—Shush!"

Feeling put upon, Ana stomped off and slouched in one of the corners of the basket.

Still glaring at Mr. Coy with confusion, Ret asked, "How is it your fault?"

"Well," Coy began, looking very uncomfortable, "you know how I don't trust Lionel. To make sure he didn't do anything sneaky on this trip, I administered a daily extract to him without his knowledge."

"You did what?" Ret questioned, provoked.

"Don't worry; it didn't hurt him or anything," Coy tried to pacify. "It just ennobled him—made him more trustworthy. It's what caused him to stand up to Bubba and stick up for you back at the volcano. That's all." Ret's consternation seemed to abate a bit. "And, since it was technically *my* doing, I figured I ought to correct *my* mistake. Although," he added, as if finding a loophole to excuse himself, "Ishmael was the one who *actually* administered it." Ishmael rolled his eyes.

Just then, Pauline, beaming with satisfaction and brimming with triumph, put her hand on Mr.

Coy's shoulder and said, "It's called being responsible, Ben."

"Call it what you want, lady," responded Coy, who
cringed to hear Pauline call him by his first name, "just
as long as it gets you off my back." As if it was an
unwanted rodent, he picked up Pauline's hand and lifted
it from his shoulder. "Now, as I said before," bellowed
Coy, "westward ho!"

Ishmael jumped to the controls and steered the
balloon into the setting sun. For being such a large
vessel, Lye's boat maintained a quick pace, leaving a
long stream of frothy waters in its wake. Mr. Coy
advised Ishmael to fly the airship just underneath the
sparse layer of clouds so as to conceal their location as
much as possible without reducing their vision. Eying
the compass, the two pilots maintained a direction that
was both westerly and southerly, though more so the
former than the latter.

"I apologize for the way I mistreated you," spoke
Mr. Coy to Ishmael in sober tones, "back there, at the top
of the volcano." His speech was low, almost inaudible
over the hum of the engine, and he frequently glanced
over at Pauline to make sure she couldn't hear his
confession. "I jumped to conclusions and overreacted,
and I'm sorry."

"Apology accepted," Ishmael smiled with frank
forgiveness.

"I have to admit," Coy continued in lighter spirits, as if a weight had been removed from his shoulders, "I wasn't expecting you to come back so soon, let alone with the balloon—and full of lake people, too!" Ishmael chuckled. "Very impressive; very—*coy.*"

"I learned from the best," Ishmael said tenderly.

"How did you woo Bubba?" Coy queried.

"With the extract," Ishmael described. "It was easy, really. And as soon as the natives at Lake Titicaca saw Bubba—or, I should say, the 'man with flaming hair'—they wanted to put an end to him right then and there. It was all I could do to hold them off until we got back to Easter Island."

"And his shoes?"

"I thought we'd keep them—as a souvenir, of course," Ishmael smirked. "And who knows? They might come in handy someday. There *were* a few additional stops on my way back to the lake."

"So you're not the one who tipped off Lye then, hmm?" Coy asked.

"Definitely not, sir," Ishmael answered truthfully.

"Curious," Coy mumbled pensively, "very curious, indeed." His gaze naturally fell on Ret.

But Ret's mind was elsewhere. With his back toward the interior of the basket, he was leaning over its side, staring back at what used to be Fire Island. It was now a gaping void—a black hole—bent on swallowing everything around it. The land had long since been sucked in, leaving not so much as a hint that solid ground had once existed there. Under such unsupported weight, the ceiling of the colossal magma chamber had given way, with gravity pushing a huge swath of the Pacific Ocean to rush in and fill the empty space. With agonizing familiarity, Ret looked on.

His only comfort came when Paige silently strode to his side and passed her arm around his back. Their eyes met, and Ret smiled briefly. Paige rested her head on his shoulder and joined Ret's gaze. For several moments, not a word was exchanged, for something greater than speech was at work. It was a silent conversation between his soul and hers. Spurred by Paige's concerted effort to think what Ret was thinking and feel what he was feeling, their hearts harmonized in a profound way. She ached at his pain; she mourned for his loss. And so, with psyches in sync and auras in alignment, more of their differences disappeared while more of their natures became one—all without speaking a single word.

"So let's see this element," Mr. Coy interrupted with a clap, trying to spread some cheer amid the dreary mood in the basket.

Ret reached in his pocket and pulled out the Oracle. He held it up for all to see. The radiant beauty of the Oracle stood in striking contrast to the dismal scene of destruction behind them. Like a chandelier with a thousand jewels, it caught and reflected the waning sunlight with perfect beauty. The red flame of the fire element danced in its compartment, happy to be home, while its neighbor, the shining earth element, seemed overjoyed at the return of a friend. In a manner that almost seemed to mock the great sacrifices rendered on their behalf, the blissful elements in the pristine Oracle exuded emotions of peace, security, and contentment. In the face of such pervasive havoc and hardship, the Oracle seemed to promise that, in the end, everything would be okay.

"Two down," Ret summarized, his stricken voice void of any celebration, "four to go."

"We're on fire!" Mr. Coy applauded, pleased by his pun.

No one moved to respond. The conversation died as its members dispersed, preferring instead to rest their weary hearts and exhausted frames. Ret and Paige retreated to one of the basket's unoccupied corners, where they hunkered down amid the cooling air of the approaching evening. Mr. Coy returned to Ishmael's side to oversee the steering.

Finding a lull in things, Pauline approached her daughter, who was still moping in her chosen corner.

"Now, dear" she addressed Ana, whose lingering frustration was finally lessening now that she had at last gained her mother's attention, "what was it you were trying to tell me? Something about a man helping Lye back there?"

"Mom," Ana stated with unrivaled soberness, "I think it was Dad."

Made in the USA
San Bernardino, CA
21 May 2019